SLEIGHED!

LOSERS CLUB BOOK FOUR

YVONNE VINCENT

Copyright © 2022 Yvonne Vincent
All rights reserved.

By Yvonne Vincent:

The Big Blue Jobbie
The Big Blue Jobbie #2
The Wee Hairy Anthology

Frock In Hell

Losers Club (Losers Club Book 1)
The Laird's Ladle (Losers Club Book 2)
The Angels' Share (Losers Club Book 3)
Sleighed! (Losers Club Book 4)
The Juniper Key (Losers Club Book 5)
Beacon Brodie (Losers Club Book 6)

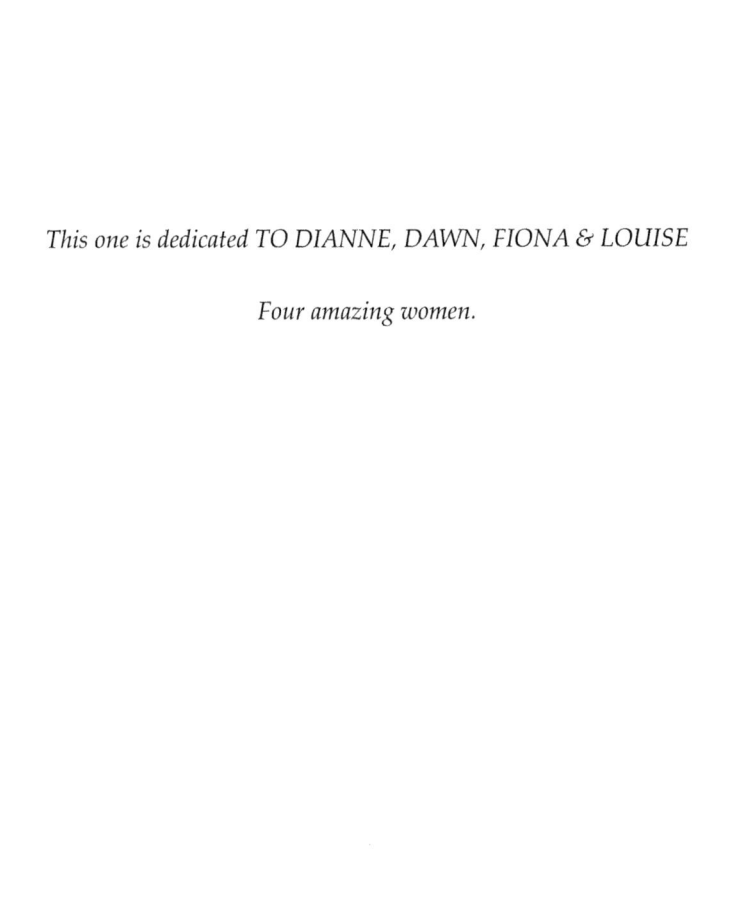

This one is dedicated TO DIANNE, DAWN, FIONA & LOUISE

Four amazing women.

A WEE WORD BEFORE WE BEGIN

The Losers Club books are set on an island in the North East of Scotland. I try not to throw in too many words from the local Scots dialect (language?), Doric, yet it wouldn't be right to use none at all. You will understand them from the context, but here's a wee guide:

- Fit like (how are you?)
- Dwam (a daydream)
- Gadgie (man – not unique to Doric)
- Fechtin (fighting)
- Keek (look)
- Bampot (an obnoxious, disruptive person – not unique to Doric)
- Blin drift (blizzard)
- Scunner (a nuisance – not unique to Doric)
- Thochtie (a small amount)
- Puckle (a fair amount)
- Quine (girl)
- Loon (boy)
- Nyaff (stupid, irritating person – not unique to Doric)

If you would like to know more about Doric, this article is affa guid: https://www.bbc.com/travel/article/20210321-scotlands-little-known-fourth-language

PROLOGUE

IK GAZETTE 23rd December

DIAMONDS ARE A LAIRD'S BEST FRIEND

Record numbers of tourists have visited Vik this winter, attracted by the island's festive offerings, chief among them the largest diamond in Scotland, currently on display at Vik Castle. This boost in numbers is good news for Elsie's Book Club, with the charity set to receive half the profits from the display.

The Christmas Star diamond is said to have once belonged to Mary Queen of Scots and was gifted to William Deer, Earl of Marnoch, by King James himself, shortly before his ascension to the English throne in 1603.

Now the diamond's current owner, Laird

Hamish Deer, has pledged to donate half the money raised from the display to the fundraising efforts of children from Port Vik Primary School. The remainder will be used for urgent renovations on the castle and its gardens.

The Elsie's Book Club charity has so far distributed five thousand books to schools and libraries throughout Scotland in a drive to keep the nation reading. Set up following the death of Port Vik librarian Elsie Read, the charity restores old books, supports new authors and gives books to the next generation of readers. High profile supporters such as Hollywood legends Johnny Munroe and Al Cuppachino have helped raise the charity's profile.

Laird Hamish says, "It's a no-brainer. Elsie's Book Club keeps the past, present and future of Scotland alive. It's the real diamond here. The fundraising done by the local children over the past few months has been astounding and we are thanking them with a party at the castle on Christmas Eve."

Local shop owner, Mrs Hubbard, who was instrumental in expanding the charity following her friend's death, told the Gazette, "I can't believe it, dearie. We gave the Twitter a virus. It's so good of wee Hamish to chip in."

Indeed, the charity's video, Read for Scotland, has gone viral, as has the number of visitors making the trip to see the Christmas Star, making this a very merry season for all.

CHAPTER 1

'I'll look ridiculous,' wailed Penny, eyeing the candy stripe tights and green shorts suspiciously. 'My thighs will look huge. I don't have a thigh gap. I have thigh muffins!'

'Stop stressing, woman,' said Jim. 'It's the school party. A bunch of ten-year-olds aren't going to be interested in your thighs. Anyway, I like your thigh muffins.'

'Are you trying to say my thighs are fat?' asked Penny, her voice dangerously low.

'Mmm...no?' said Jim, his expression taking on a slightly hunted look. 'I was just saying that you will be the sexiest and most beautiful elf a Santa has ever had.'

'Nice save, Santa, but why couldn't I be Mrs Santa instead? Red is more my colour, don't you think?'

'We've been through this,' Jim sighed. 'Mrs Hay has already hired the costume. Since she started cooking for Ernie On The Other Side, well, let's just say that there's an extra false teeth glass by her bedside now. I think she's planning on giving him the Christmas of his life. I suppose at ninety-six, you have to make it count.'

Jim clipped his belt below the pillow beneath his red suit and held his arms out.

'Maybe you and I could…you know? Have a merry Christmas?'

Penny looked at the six-foot beacon of obesity before her and decided that if he asked her to sit on his knee, she'd have to punch him. There really was no other choice.

'Do you need a hand with your beard?' she asked, changing the subject.

'How come when I ask you the same thing, you get all offended?'

Penny briefly wondered if she should bring the timing of that punch forward but decided to ignore him and tackle the dreaded tights instead. She hated tights. They were always either concertinaed around her ankles or the gusset was so low that her knees sprung together after every step. She'd never found a pair that fit. Including this pair, she thought, as she pulled the waist up to under her bra. Lordy, the makers of tights have a very strange idea of women. Is there a Mr Denier out there somewhere, proudly walking around with a seven-foot tall, size zero woman on his arm?

And pockets, she silently ranted. Don't even get me started on why they don't make women's clothes with pockets. Like some sort of conspiracy between the makers of handbags and clothes. A weird symbiosis where the sales of one depend upon the deficiencies of the other. And we just accept it! Ooh, and fake pockets. Yes. Ridiculous, loathsome things. Never mind human rights and political outrage. Perhaps womankind should rise up and march on parliament demanding pockets and a good pair of tights.

Jim regarded Penny anxiously. She looked quite annoyed. Maybe this wasn't the best moment to ask if she'd sit on his knee. Come to think of it, maybe this wasn't the best moment to mention that she'd put the tights on outside in and back to front. He could see the little label on the seam that ran up her belly and under her bra.

By the time they were both dressed and ready to set off, Penny had worked herself up to planning a petition to make bra underwire illegal. She regarded herself in the mirror, scowling at her reflection, before jamming on the green elf hat with such fury that it slid over her eyes, the fur trim tickling her nose.

'And another thing,' she declared, pulling off the hat and glaring at Jim. 'Why do men get trousers in a variety of lengths, and we don't?'

Jim had no real answer for this. He just assumed that whatever was going on here must be his fault, so he decided that telling her she was right about everything was the safest course of action.

'It's a scandal,' he agreed. 'And I'll tell you what else you're right about. Your thighs look huge in those tights.'

The bickering continued all the way outside to the car, faltering only when their words were carried away on the blasts of frigid air whipping in from the sea. Jim looked doubtfully at the slate sky, where clouds pregnant with snow hung ominously over the island.

'We should take Phil,' he said, referring to the ancient Land Rover that had stood the test of potholed farm roads across the island.

'But I've loaded everything into my car,' Penny protested. 'All the presents for the children and the food that Mrs Goggins asked me to pick up.'

'Okay, fine, but don't blame me if we get stuck in snow on the way back. Although, if we get stranded, at least we have a couple of thigh muffins to keep us going 'til morning.'

Jim clocked Penny's pursed lips and held up his hands.

'Just joking. Anyway, where are Eileen and Ricky? They should have been here by now.'

'Get yourself into the car and I'll call her.'

Penny left Jim trying to squeeze his pillowed belly into the front passenger seat while she called her friend.

Eileen picked up on the first ring.

'Hello, national elf service. Rudelf speaking.'

'If you're Rudelf, who am I?' asked Penny.

The line went silent as Eileen thought for a moment.

'Gandelf,' she eventually declared.

'Gandelf? Couldn't it be something a bit less beardy? I've had enough of Jim going on about my chin hair.'

'Nope. It's definitely Gandelf because you're very wise and totally magic. Not like real magic, because that would be spooky, unless...you don't do spells, do you?'

'No, but if I did, I'd be casting a hurry up spell on you.'

'Hint taken, and on my way, Gandelf. Did you get chocolate fingers?'

For a split second, Penny thought that Eileen was still talking about spells, then her brain caught up and she remembered the phone call from the castle cook yesterday. Apparently, the chocolate fingers were a key component of Mrs Goggins' Christmas tree centrepiece.

'Bugger, I forgot,' said Penny. 'We'll have to stop on the way.'

Ten minutes later, Penny pulled into the supermarket car park. Beside her, Jim was wedged into the passenger seat, the seatbelt straining against his belly.

'I'm not going in for the chocolate fingers,' he said. 'It took me ten minutes to get this seatbelt on.'

'You could have removed the pillow and put it back on when we got to the castle,' Penny pointed out. She looked in the rearview mirror at her passenger. Eileen was suddenly very fascinated by the view of the recycling bins.

'Oh, for goodness' sake, I'll go,' Penny huffed.

She got out of the car and stomped towards the supermarket entrance, the bells on her hat and shoes heralding her arrival.

No wonder I'm in a bad mood today, she thought. I'm surrounded by inconsiderate gits. What a bloody kerfuffle for a Christmas party for ten-year-olds. When I was ten, we were happy with a game of musical chairs in the church hall, but no, this lot had to go and get themselves on the local news for raising loads of money for charity, and Laird Hamish bloody

Deer, the biggest inconsiderate git of them all, has to throw a bloody party for them at the castle. Gits, gits, gits.

Penny threw a filthy look at the startled security guard who, unused to seeing elves in his shop, had stopped picking his nose for long enough to gawp. He discreetly fingered the hem of his blazer, trying to dislodge a bogie from under his fingernail, then gave Penny a cheeky wink and crooned, 'Have your elf a merry little Christmas.'

Ignoring him, she stalked into the shop, intent on locating the chocolate fingers and getting out of there as soon as possible. She was well aware that she looked ridiculous. When she'd agreed to help out, she'd thought that Hamish meant her to chaperone the kids or give Mrs Goggins a hand with the food. It was only when Jim had turned up with the costumes that she realised she and Eileen would be his little helpers. Little. Harumph. More like Santa's solid little helper. She'd put on half a stone in the past week from comfort eating her way through the tin of Quality Street that she'd ostensibly bought for Christmas Day.

She knew she was being entirely unreasonable in grumping about the party and her costume. What she was really angry about was the fact that Alex Moon, aka the ex-husband, aka Chief Wankpuffin of the clan MacTwatdoodle, had insisted on having the twins with him in London for Christmas. And her little cherubs had gone without a backward glance!

She'd dropped them off at Aberdeen Airport a few days before, trying to look happy as she waved goodbye, while all the time seething inside and wondering if it was bad parenting to dial in an anonymous tip to the airport police that Hector and Edith Moon were carrying drugs. They weren't, of course, but by the time the police had completed a full cavity search the plane would be long gone, and they'd have to come home to mummy. Fortunately, common sense had kicked in and she'd made do with adding Hector and

Edith to her list of gits. Even though she loved them very much indeed. Most of the time.

Penny took a few deep breaths and tried to push the reset button on her mood. Focus on the here and now, she told herself. Think of the positives. First Christmas with Jim, the twins would have a great time in London and, best of all, her mother wasn't cooking Christmas dinner this year. Instead, along with Eileen's family, they were all going to Jim's dad's house. Ivor Space was a dab hand in the kitchen and, unlike her mother, didn't insist on tartare sauce with the turkey.

Righty-ho ho ho. Mood restored. Now, where do they keep the chocolate fingers?

Penny jingled her way through the shop, only dimly aware of the astonished looks from other shoppers. She was on the biscuit aisle, debating whether buying and eating an entire box of Family Circle on your own could be excused on the grounds that it was Christmas, when she heard the tannoy spring to life.

"Bing bong. This is an elf and safety announcement for customers. There's a little Sprite on the floor in aisle four, so please watch your mistle-toes."

Penny moved along a few feet. Perhaps she'd resist the Family Circle…ooh, what about a box of Deans…mmm, she really liked–

"Bing bong. Another alert for aisle four. We apologise to customers wishing to purchase Deans *short*bread. A very elfish customer has taken the last box."

Penny looked around her. She was beginning to suspect that something was amiss. Carefully, she put the box of Deans back and continued scanning the biscuits for chocolate fingers.

Ah! There they were! Right at the top. If she stood on tiptoe, she might just be able to reach. Streeeetch, Penny. Nope, it was no use. She'd have to stand on something.

"Bing bong. Manager to aisle four please. There's an elf on the shelf."

Penny swiped two boxes of chocolate fingers neatly into her basket and headed to the checkout. Even at the ten items or less till there was a large queue. She stood, impatiently tapping a belled foot, while baskets were unloaded onto the belt and the little plastic "next customer" baton at the front was passed back down the line in an ultra-polite supermarket relay.

The woman behind the till was rendered sallow by the harsh strip-lighting and her eyes bore dark circles that spoke of a day spent dealing with an unrelenting flow of shoppers. Even the tinsel, hung from a pole behind her, sagged miserably from a single piece of sticky tape, its once jaunty loops now slumped between two checkouts, like a shiny garotte poised to catch the unwary shopper. All around was hustle and bustle as the islanders stocked up for Christmas like Seventh Day Adventists facing a month of Saturdays. What is it about the human race, Penny wondered, that we can abstain from visiting a supermarket for a week, surviving on out-of-date tins of soup because we're too lazy to do the big shop, yet when the supermarket is closed for one day, we are driven to buy twenty pints of milk, five loaves and enough toilet roll to wipe the bums of Belgium?

She finally shuffled to the front of the queue and glanced towards the customer service desk where Eileen's brother-in-law, Robbie Bates, was leaning over a microphone.

'Bing bong. Security to checkout number one, please. A customer is trying to pay with jingle bills.'

Robbie flashed her a cheeky grin and winked. In response, Penny discreetly raised a middle finger and scratched her eyebrow.

'Fit like?' Robbie asked, catching up with her once she'd paid. 'Are you off to Laird Hamish's shindig at the castle?'

'Aye. We have about twenty ten-year-olds to entertain. Eileen and I are helping Santa. Mrs Hubbard's telling them a Christmas story in honour of Elsie, which is a nice touch, and Sandra Next Door is in charge of discipline.'

'Are Fiona and Gordon not going? Fiona helped organise the fundraising, didn't she?'

'They've bowed out. The baby's due soon and I think Fiona's using every spare minute to clean the cottage.'

Robbie grimaced. 'They may as well make the most of it. It'll be the last time the place is clean and tidy for the next eighteen years. Hey, I hope Hamish is giving you a wee look at the Christmas Star. I haven't been up to see it myself yet, but I was going to take the wife in the New Year, once the fuss has died down.'

'Yeah, I haven't seen it yet either,' said Penny. 'I'm really looking forward to a private viewing.'

'Enjoy the party. If Eileen's away, I might take a bottle of whisky and a permanent marker round to Kenny and see if we can beat Ricky and Gervais' high scores on the PlayStation.'

'I don't think the whisky will help with the scores,' said Penny doubtfully.

'Maybe no. But it sends Kenny straight to sleep, and me and the kids are dab hands at drawing handlebar moustaches. Eileen will think she's married Poirot by the time we're done.'

Penny wondered whether to warn her friend that the family photos would be a little different this Christmas but decided to let Robbie have his fun. She returned to the car, clipped on her seatbelt and turned to smile at Jim and Eileen.

'Sorry for being an old grumpy pants. I actually have a good feeling about this party. Great food, dancing and Santa. What more could you want? It's going to be perfect.'

CHAPTER 2

Penny parked by what would once have been the servants' entrance to Vik Castle but was now merely Laird Hamish and Lady Cara's back door. The gravel drive narrowed into a path which led to Hamish's pride and joy; his gardens. In the spring and summer months, the neat beds were a burgeoning riot of glorious colour. Now, however, they were iced with a fine frosting of the snow which, if it continued to fall, would soon form an undulating shroud, turning the plants and low bushes into mysterious lumps in the dimming late afternoon light.

Jim once more looked to the heavens.

'I think we're in for a fair bit of snow. I'll ring Randy Mair and ask him if he can plough the castle road with his tractor before the end of the party.'

'Surely it can't get that bad in the space of a couple of hours,' said Penny, unloading a box of goodies from the boot.

'Oh, it can,' Eileen assured her. 'Kenny and I took the boys to Santa's grotto at the loch a few years ago. It started snowing as we left, and by the time we drove home a couple of hours later, you could see the flashes of the power lines coming down under the weight of the snow. We barely made it back before the town got cut off.'

Penny smiled wistfully and gazed across the gardens, thinking back to the winters of her childhood, where numb fingers were soon warmed by a mug of her mum's hot chocolate.

'I suppose you forget what it's like when you've been living in London,' she mused. 'Half a centimetre of snow down south and the whole place grinds to a halt. Plus, it was different when we were kids. Do you remember sledging down Randy's field on an old car bonnet? About ten of us piled one atop the other, taking it in turns to be on the bottom.'

'Aye,' said Jim sourly. 'The school was closed for a week and my dad made me stay in and do homework.'

Eileen sighed, her eyes following Penny's gaze past the lawn to the snow-tipped hedges.

'That was the year Kenny wrote "I love you" in the snow. It was so romantic.'

'It was yellow snow,' Penny reminded her.

'Still, it was quite a long sentence and he even put a wee love heart on the end.'

'Wee being the operative word,' Penny laughed.

It was Jim's turn to look wistful, as he chuckled and said, 'That laddie could pee the whole alphabet. What a legend.'

The sound of a throat being cleared behind them made them turn. Mrs Goggins, dressed in a fresh apron and Ugg boots, was helping herself to two bulging carrier bags from the boot.

'You can stand out here in a dwam and freeze all day, or you can help me in with these and put the kettle on,' she said by way of greeting.

'And happy Christmas to you, too, Mrs Goggins,' said Penny.

Jim and Eileen grabbed the remainder of the bags, and they followed Mrs Goggins into the enormous castle kitchen.

The first thing that hit them was the smell of fresh baking; clean, warm and floury, with just a hint of nutmeg. If I had a granny, thought Penny, this is what her hugs would smell like.

She and Jim had been frequent visitors to the castle since solving the mystery of the Laird's Ladle. Of course, Jim was already friendly with Hamish, but she had found an unexpected ally in Cara, who had joined Penny's weight loss group, Losers Club, claiming that she needed to shift a couple of pounds, even though she was impossibly slim and glamorous. Penny suspected that Cara was simply lonely, so had taken her under her wing.

Over the past few months, the two women had helped Mrs Hubbard administer the book restoration charity set up by the older woman's best friend, Elsie, shortly before her death. Thanks to a combination of Cara's contacts, Penny's determination and Mrs Hubbard's ability to blackmail almost anyone into submission, important historical documents were rescued from mouldering oblivion and now took pride of place in both the museum and the castle, where they enriched the story of the island.

As someone with no past beyond her own parents, the older Penny became, the more she valued her connection to Vik. Despite her adolescent drive to escape the place and carve out her future in the world across the water, she now realised that the island was in her very bones.

'If you want to daydream, shift your lazy bum out of my kitchen. Or you can make yourself useful and help me with these volley vents,' said Mrs Goggins, handing Penny an apron.

'Right, volley vents,' said Penny, eyeing the tray of tiny pastry cases. 'What do you need me to do?'

The next hour was spent stuffing and icing and slicing and screeching, as fingers were burnt and hundreds of tiny pastries and cakes were transferred from ovens to the plates which soon covered every available surface. Sandra Next Door and Mrs Hubbard arrived, and Mrs Goggins put them straight to work on what she called "things on sticks." Under her watchful eye, they soon had a banquet fit for any discerning ten-year-old with an aversion to vegetables and an eye for carbs.

Disco Bob passed through, lugging the huge case which contained his DJ equipment. His attempt to swipe a sandwich on the way by was quickly thwarted by Mrs Goggins, who delivered a sharp rap to the knuckles with the fish slice she'd just used to decant a pizza from the oven. He yelped and put his hand to his mouth, sucking the sting and glaring defiantly at the stern cook.

'Who knows where your mucky fingers have been,' she told him. 'Probably all over other people's belongings. I don't know what Laird Hamish was thinking of, letting you within a hundred feet of the castle, especially with the Christmas Star here. Well, you better keep your fingers to yourself. And I'll be keeping *my* eye on *you*.'

Disco Bob ran a nervous hand through his thinning dark hair and said, 'That was then, and this is now. Laird Hamish, may God bless him, believes in giving people second chances.'

Mrs Goggins snorted disbelievingly.

'Aye, and I believe a leotard doesn't change its spots.'

'A leopard. It's a leopard that doesn't change its spots.'

Mrs Goggins drew herself up to her full five-foot-two and angrily shook the fish slice at him.

'I thought you'd found God in prison, yet here you are, being rude about the afflicted. For centuries, those poor people were thrown out of their communities and–'

'Leopard. Big spotty cat!' said Disco Bob, raising his voice to cut off Mrs Goggins' rant just as she reached full flow.

'Nonsense. Why would we be comparing people to leopards? Leotards make far more sense. Now, go and get your disco set up in the big hall. The children will be here any minute.'

Disco Bob shuffled off with his giant case, muttering darkly about how leotards made absolutely no sense. A moment later, they heard him swearing loudly as his case became stuck on the narrow, winding, stone staircase. Jim decided to spare the poor man another telling off by rushing to help unwedge the thing and manoeuvre it the rest of the way.

Mrs Goggins turned to Penny, Eileen, Sandra Next Door and Mrs Hubbard.

'If you help me take these plates upstairs, there should be time for a wee look at the Christmas Star before the children arrive.'

Within half an hour, the four women were slumped in chairs, looking on in astonishment as the tiny figure of Mrs Goggins dashed upstairs with what must be her twentieth load of plates.

'I don't think I can take another step, dearie,' panted Mrs Hubbard. 'How on earth Imelda Goggins manages all these stairs at her age, I'll never know.'

'How old is she?' asked Sandra Next Door. 'She's one of those people who seem timeless.'

'Five hundred and one,' said Eileen with a wry grin. 'She's probably been here since the castle was built in 1521.'

'That school trip all those moons ago wasn't wasted, then,' said Penny.

'Nah. She's been using up the…what's the French for napkins? The…the…oubliettes they bought for the fifth centenary celebrations last year.'

Hearing footsteps on the stairs, the women sat up straight, fully anticipating a lecture on slackers and scoundrels from the rather stern cook. Instead, a pair of shiny brogues appeared, followed by the man himself, Lord Hamish Deer, Laird of Vik.

His face was red and shiny, and his eyes sparkled with excitement. He was wearing a kilt in the Black Watch tartan and a green t-shirt which proclaimed him to be "The World's Sexiest Laird."

'An early Christmas present from Cara,' he said, following

Penny's gaze towards his chest. 'I'll change before the kids get here, but it was a bit of fun while we put up the Christmas decorations in the big hall.'

'I thought you already had decorations in there,' said Penny.

'Aye, the posh visitors decorations. These are the family ones. We always put them up on Christmas Eve once the staff and tourists are gone. You can't beat a good paper chain and the wonky angel that Raine made in primary school. We were going to wait until after the party, but I thought it would make the kids feel at home if it was all a bit more personal.'

'That was very thoughtful. Have you met Eileen, Mrs Hubbard and Sandra Next Door before?' said Penny, gesturing to her friends, who had somehow staggered to their exhausted feet to greet their host.

'Ah, Minty,' said Hamish, pulling the older woman into an embrace. 'I need to talk to your Douglas about the posters for the Craft Fair in the village hall.'

'He's a genius with a slogan,' wheezed Mrs Hubbard, her eyes bulging as Hamish squeezed a little too tightly.

'I was Hamish's nanny before we bought the shop,' she explained to the others once he'd released her. 'I bet he still doesn't clean his teeth properly.'

Hamish flashed her a wide smile and said, 'No fillings, Mrs H. You taught me well. Now, who is this gorgeous creature with the big hair?'

Sandra Next Door patted her lacquered, blonde bob, then giggled in a most unsandralike fashion as he gallantly kissed her hand before moving on to Eileen.

'I believe you're the elf who dived into my septic tank to rescue your coat about thirty years ago,' he said, raising an eyebrow.

Eileen sank into a deep curtsy and peered up at him through her thick lashes.

'Pleased to meet you, your Majesty. And sorry about that, your Majesty. My sandwiches were in the pocket.'

Hamish's lips twitched, and Penny could see him struggling to maintain his composure as he helped Eileen up and said, 'Never has my septic tank been graced with such perfumed beauty.'

'Thank you very much, your Majesty. People do say that.'

'What? About you jumping into their septic tanks?'

Eileen reddened. 'No, I mean they like my perfume.'

'Ah, right,' said Hamish. 'Glad to hear you don't make a habit of...never mind. What about a private viewing of the Christmas Star before the sprogs show up, eh?'

He led them upstairs, explaining, 'It's said that if the Christmas Star leaves the Deer family, then the heir will suffer a painful death. Each laird leaves a will forbidding the next from selling it, so no matter how skint we are, the bugger has to stay in a vault in Edinburgh, otherwise the heir dies a painful death, and the diamond reverts to the Crown.

'I was going to display it for the quincentenary, but the insurance was too high. I've managed to hire a couple of security guards to do night shifts this time, though, which has brought the cost down. Ridiculous, really. The thing's in an alarmed case that hooks up to the mainland and the local police. I mean, we're on an island, for God's sake. Who's going to steal it? The minute the alarm goes off, they shut down any transport links and the thief's trapped!'

'Good to know,' said a voice at the top of the stairs. 'Nothing's safe around Penny. She's a master burglar.'

'Ha bloody ha, Jim,' said Penny. 'Where have you been?'

'I was helping Disco Bob set up. That's some piece of kit he's got there. Mind you, complete overkill for a kids' party. By the way, Hamish, Cara wants you to help her hang a disco ball from the chandelier. I offered, but she said she couldn't be bothered with the paperwork if I had an accident. Whereas you, my friend, are worth a fortune to her dead.'

'Then let us beat a hasty retreat through to the display room,' said Hamish, pulling aside a tapestry to reveal a hidden door. 'We'll take the exciting route. Secret passageway shortcut. Castle's riddled with them.'

Frowning, Mrs Hubbard said, 'I hope you told the security company about them, dearie. Although this explains why I could never find you when it came to bedtime.'

'Don't worry. We gave everyone a map of the castle with all the passageways and tunnels clearly marked. Well, the ones that we know about.'

Insulated by thick walls from the fireplaces and radiators that kept the main areas of the castle warm, the narrow passageway was chilly and, Eileen whispered, 'Proper ghostie territory.'

Eileen was endlessly fascinated by the occult, the spiritual, conspiracy theories and aliens. In fact, thought Penny, if Jeanie Campbell was anything like her daughter in her younger days, it's little wonder she got caught up in a cult. It's a pity she turned into a fierce old bag, albeit one with a heart of slightly tarnished silver. Penny hoped that Eileen wouldn't follow in her mother's footsteps, although with her friend's air of innocent happiness enduring well into her forties, there was little chance of that happening.

Hamish suddenly stopped at a door with a keypad, and everyone crowded in behind him as he tapped in a code. The keypad gave an ominous single bleep. He tried again, with the same result.

'Bugger,' he said. 'Only one more try and we're locked out. I was sure it was Cara's birthday.'

'What have you been putting in?' asked Penny, peering at her phone.

'Two, five, eight, three.'

'Try three, five, eight, two.'

Hamish input the digits and they heard a click.

'How on earth did you know that?' he asked, pushing the door open.

'Because I have her details from when she joined Losers Club.'

'Aren't there laws about sharing personal details?' asked Hamish.

'How about a deal? If you don't tell on me, I won't tell your wife that you forgot her birthday.'

'Fair enough.'

'Can we move along?' said Sandra Next Door from the back of the line. 'I'm stuck behind Jim and I'm getting claustrophobic.'

'Good one, Sandra Next Door, *claus*trophobic,' said Jim. 'Don't worry. We have private elf care.'

Sandra Next Door looked at him like he'd just asked her to roller-skate naked down Main Street.

'I'm actually claustrophobic, you fool. I'm feeling quite faint.'

'Ah. Hamish, hurry up. Sandra's not feeling like herelf.'

The line of people shuffled forward, and Sandra Next Door breathed a sigh of relief as she walked through the door into a large, wood-panelled room, at the centre of which stood a glass case on a plinth.

The group fanned out and her sigh of relief turned to a gasp of awe. There, sparkling on a purple cushion, was the largest diamond in Scotland.

'It's the most beautiful thing I've ever seen,' Sandra Next Door whispered, her tone devoid of its usual bitter sarcasm.

'Well, bugger me with a ball of tinsel, my flabber is gasted,' said Jim.

'The glass could do with a wee polish,' said Mrs Hubbard, reaching into her cavernous handbag and pulling out a bottle of something blue and a cloth.

She stepped forward, aiming the bottle at the glass, and was just about to spray when Hamish shouted, 'No!'

'It just needs a bit of elbow grease, dearie,' said Mrs Hubbard.

'No!' exclaimed Hamish, his voice an octave higher than its normal deep baritone. 'It's alarmed. You'll have the whole island shut down and the place swarming with police. So, no grease please, and no elbows.'

'Can I help you, sir?' said a voice from the main doorway.

'It's okay,' said Hamish, sounding harassed. 'Mrs Hubbard was just...never mind. Everyone, this is Noel Bowes, one of the security guards I was telling you about.'

Beside her, Penny could hear Jim snickering. She gave him a sharp poke in the pillow, ignoring his whispered, 'No elbows. That's pure class.'

Noel sidled into the room, followed by another man. Both were as tall as basketball players, had identical buzzcuts and wore the blue uniforms of security guards. Under normal circumstances they were probably quite intimidating, but in the presence of the man who paid their wages, they removed their caps and adopted an obsequious air.

Hamish introduced the slightly shorter giant as Jack Hughes, a former soldier from Buckie. His slow, broad, North East accent contrasted with Noel's nasal Glaswegian whine, and Penny was relieved that there was a way to tell them apart. Not that she'd probably need to, but not getting people mixed up was surely a common courtesy. After all, look what happened when her mother sexted Len Harper, the chairman of the golf club, instead of Len Hopper, her husband. Penny's father had had to disable Mary's phone camera and write a letter of apology. Mr Harper had, of course, demanded that Mary write the letter, but she'd learned the emojis by that stage and simply responded by texting him all the rude ones she knew.

That was Mary all over; unashamed and unapologetic unless she deemed it truly warranted. Sometimes Penny wished she could be more like her mother. Mary Hopper would have told Alex where to go when he asked to have the twins for Christmas, and to hell with the consequences. Instead, the upright streak of decency that Penny had inherited from her father triumphed, and she gave in without a fight. Nevertheless, a tiny, defiant spark of the Mary in her hoped that they all had a rotten time and the twins decided that never again would they spend Christmas with their dad. Ooh Penny, she told herself, you're definitely on the naughty list.

'Whatcha thinking about, Gandelf,' Eileen whispered. 'It'd better be making Jim get something the size of that thing set into an engagement ring.'

Penny rolled her eyes. 'Could I please be have a name that's a bit more classy? What about Elvish Presley?'

'Nope. Rudelf and Gandelf are more Christmassy.'

'How is Gandelf Christmassy?'

'He's magic!' Eileen hissed, as if it were obvious. 'And he has a beard. Beards are Christmassy. Sorry, Gandelf, but you're Gandelf and that's the end of it.'

'It's not the end of it. I'm Elvish Presley.'

'Gandelf.'

'Are you Gandelf?' whispered Jim.

'No, I'm Elvish Presley!'

'Aye well, you don't have the hips for Elvish, but you've definitely got the Gandalf thing going on.'

Jim rubbed his chin and winked at her.

Before Penny could respond, Hamish announced that they should leave because the children would be arriving soon. With a last backward glance at the diamond, the party obligingly followed him through the main door and down to the big hall, where Cara was waiting with mulled wine and chocolates.

'I just have one last thing to do,' he told his wife, giving Penny a knowing wink before wandering off, muttering about changing that damn door code.

CHAPTER 3

Gordon watched Fiona, wondering whether he could start a petition to end this household dictatorship. Everything had been cleaned and organised, with rules put in place as to its future use. Gordon couldn't remember all the rules, but he knew from bitter experience that leaving crumbs on the worktop was punishable by forced labour – or, as she called it, "changing the duvet cover." Gordon didn't do duvet covers. He was secretly hoping that if Fiona died before him, she'd leave a diagram in her will, otherwise he'd simply moulder.

It was like being married to an exceptionally rotund tyrant who came armed with a toilet brush and a bottle of white vinegar. That morning, he'd found her scrubbing the shoe rack and now, having emptied the toaster crumb catcher and descaled the kettle, she was rearranging their bags for life by putting them into other bags for life according to the likely amount of life left.

Gordon observed his wife's progress with a growing sense of trepidation. To his dismay, his favourite bag out of the approximately five thousand they owned had been consigned to the "plenty of life" bag, which was nestled at the bottom of the "quite a bit of life" bag, which itself was tucked inside the "might do a few more turns" bag. She'd watched a YouTube video on how to fold the darn things and now he was faced with navigating the bag equivalent of a Russian doll every time he wanted to go to the supermarket. Not that he ever *wanted* to go to the supermarket, but this was apparently what had to happen when one left one's dirty socks on the bedroom floor.

'Pass me a bag,' he sighed. 'I'll go to the supermarket now. The snow's starting to lie, and I wouldn't be surprised if the farm road is blocked in a few hours. Do you need more strawberry jam for your tuna sandwiches?'

Fiona rubbed her swollen belly and said, 'No, Mrs Hubbard came by with some the other day, but we could do with bin bags. I'm planning a clear-out of the loft.'

'You can't go in the loft. You'll never fit through the hatch, for a start!'

'I didn't say I'd be the one going in.'

Gordon's shoulders slumped. He was looking forward to the arrival of their baby, if only for some peace and quiet.

'Help me into my dungarees and I'll come with you,' said Fiona. 'We need quite a few things, and I fancy getting out of the house for an hour.'

Gordon's shoulders slumped some more. He'd been hoping that if he took ages to make the trip and came back without the bin bags, she'd abandon her plans for the loft.

'Are you sure?' he asked. 'The supermarket will be heaving.'

'I'm sure,' Fiona confirmed, wincing as she felt a tightening somewhere deep inside.

Gordon looked at her anxiously. 'Are you okay?'

'Yes, I'm fine. Probably just the baby moving or something. Make haste with the dungarees, please. The sooner we get the bin bags, the sooner you can start on the loft.'

Gordon's shoulders refused to slump any further, so he went to fetch the dungarees and spend a little quiet time in the toilet on the way.

By the time Fiona was dungareed and strapped into the van and Gordon had dutifully scrubbed away any trace of his quality Gordon-time in the loo, it was becoming dark. He peered through the windscreen and again asked Fiona if she was sure about making this trip.

'Because if this snow keeps up, we might have to leave the van in the field and walk the last bit home,' he warned.

'Is the sledge in the back?' Fiona asked.

Gordon nodded miserably, knowing what was coming next.

'Then you'll be in charge of pulling. Come on, Prancer. Whoo-tchhhh.' She mimed cracking a whip. 'Giddy-up.'

The supermarket was indeed more crowded than would make for their usual tootle round with the trolley. Instead of a straight run, the aisles had become a veritable obstacle course of groups of gossiping grannies and dawdling parents, locked into life-or-death decisions about whether they really had bought enough sweets and biscuits to sustain wee Jimmy or Morag through the next two days. Were they making Christmas *special* enough for their little darling? Wee Jimmy-Morag meanwhile, rendered corybantic by the big chocolate from door number twenty-four of his advent calendar, was scaling the shelves in search of mince pies and howling at the injustice of being made to come to the supermarket on Christmas Eve. Gordon felt a twinge of sympathy for the little git and, for a brief nanosecond, wondered what Fiona would do if he joined Jimmy-Morag on the top shelf.

'Do we need mince pies?' he asked.

'No,' said Fiona firmly. 'We mainly need the basics - milk, bread, bin bags, that sort of thing. And whatever we're having for pudding tomorrow.'

Neither of them had ventured out recently, preferring to remain holed up in the nest of their cottage, waiting for the first signs that the baby was on its way. There had been the odd trip to Mrs Hubbard's Cupboard, but Fiona had sent the village shop into uproar when she'd turned too quickly and knocked Douglas Hubbard's carefully constructed Christmas tree crashing to the ground. Well, Christmas tree was perhaps a misnomer. It was a stack of tuna tins, with breadstick branches, sweets for baubles and a "star" fashioned from a stuffed, yellow rubber glove. Douglas was going through a creative phase.

Despite his horror at the destruction of his masterpiece, Douglas had kindly banned them both from the premises until the baby arrived and had offered to deliver their shopping instead. However, with Mrs Hubbard up at the castle today, Douglas had shut the shop at lunchtime and gone off to the Bowling Club committee Christmas bash. Hence the supermarket run if Fiona and Gordon were to avoid surviving on water and selection boxes.

Gordon noticed Fiona rubbing her belly again.

'Are you sure you're okay? Do you want to sit in the van, and I'll finish up here?'

Fiona looked him straight in the eye.

'If I told you to get Bio-Oil, where would you go?'

Gordon's brow furrowed in puzzlement. He knew this was a trick question but for the life of him, he didn't know the answer.

'I don't understand why you'd need the stuff,' he said eventually. 'The van's working fine. Anyway, the garage is closed until the twenty-seventh.'

'Wrong answer,' said Fiona, barging her way towards the lotions and potions section. 'It's stuff for stretchmarks.'

'I thought you were doing traditional home remedies for that.'

'I am. But a few drops of modern won't do any harm once the wee one's here. Ooh!' Fiona puffed and bent over.

'Oh God, it's not happening, is it?' asked Gordon, rushing to support her.

'Of course not,' snapped Fiona. 'It's a month too early and I haven't even cleaned everything yet.'

'I don't care if you ask me to get brioche and I come back with a brush, I'm taking you to the van. It's all this bloody cleaning. You're doing far too much.'

'I know,' said Fiona, her eyes sparkling with tears. 'But I just want everything to be perfect for the baby.'

Gordon drew her towards him and, right there in Aisle Nine, Toothpaste and Deodorant, he wrapped his arms around her and whispered, 'Everything *will* be perfect for the baby because you're its mum, and you're perfect. We will love the wee thing so fierce, you and me.'

The tears threatened to spill over as Fiona drew her head back and gazed up at the man who had uncomplainingly tolerated all her pregnancy whims and nonsense.

'Aye, we will that,' she murmured, then sighed. 'You're right. I'll sit in the van while you finish the shopping. Oh, and bugger the bin bags. Clearing out the loft can wait until the baby's–'

'Eighteen?' said Gordon hopefully.

Fiona chuckled. 'I was going to say, "here and settled," but whatever, we'll get to it someday.'

She returned to the van and turned the engine on, fiddling with the blower to get some heat. The snow was blanketing the car park faster than the wheels of the cars could churn it into a salty, grey mush. It was unusual for the snow to lie this close to the sea. Further inland, however, the countryside would soon sit beneath an eerie shroud, glistening and still in the moonlight. A perfect Christmas Eve, she mused. Unless you were a couple of big eejits who decided to go to the bloody supermarket, of course.

The rear door opened and Gordon all but threw the shopping bags into the van. The short walk from the supermarket entrance had turned his beard from a ginger fluff to a snow-encrusted face mask, and Fiona couldn't help thinking of an old photograph she had once seen of a Himalayan climbing expedition. She really ought to cut his hair. He was one small step away from becoming a yeti.

'How's the bump?' asked Gordon, settling behind the wheel and putting his hands over the blower. Already, his beard was dripping, and clods of melting snow clung precariously to its straggly locks.

'Still…odd. Uncomfortable but not painful,' said Fiona.

'Are you sure it's not the beginnings of…'

'My waters haven't broken, and I thought it would hurt more than this.'

'We could swing past the hospital,' Gordon suggested.

'If we do that, we'll never get home. We'll spend Christmas on a ward. I'm not in labour, so let's get back to the cottage and enjoy this last one as a couple.'

'If you're sure?'

Fiona snapped that she was sure. Gordon was not very sure at all, but he knew that there was no point in arguing about anything with Fiona at the moment. His normally laid-back wife was a giant ball of hormones and high dudgeon, and all he could do was his very best to keep things as calm as possible for her. But, good Lord, she was enormous. He pulled on his seatbelt and let the car roll forward, praying that they'd make it up the farm road without the sledge being involved.

CHAPTER 4

The sound of excited chatter grew louder as the children approached the big hall. Twenty minutes ago, Penny, Mrs Hubbard and Sandra Next Door had been joined by Hamish's daughter, Raine, who had finally deigned to come downstairs, ostensibly to marshal the little darlings through the usual party games. She looked impossibly glamorous in a long, red, figure-hugging dress, brilliant tiara and a white faux fur stole. Beside her, Penny felt faintly ridiculous, dressed as she was in an ill-fitting elf costume with her candy-cane thunder-thighs on full display.

Penny admitted to herself that she was possibly being a little bitchy when she whispered to Mrs Hubbard that Raine would ace Musical Statues. As the Losers Club stalwarts had raced around, putting the finishing touches on the food and decorations, the young woman had barely stirred to help. While Penny and Sandra Next Door had struggled to light a fire in the grand fireplace, Raine had looked on, a faint trace of amusement curling the corners of her lips. It didn't help that Sandra Next Door had nearly set light to her head. The stiff, heavily sprayed helmet had come perilously close to a drifting piece of the newspaper that they'd used beneath the kindling, and it was only a quick shove from Penny that had saved her from a surprise Yuletide skinhead.

Raine had none of Hamish's bonhomie. A tall, thin woman in her early twenties, she was the product of a brief fling with an Irish pop star, whose thick auburn hair and sense of entitlement she had inherited. Raine's mother had taken little interest in her daughter, with the result that the girl had spent most of her childhood being shuttled back and forth between the island and her grandmother in Dublin. Penny felt a little sorry for her. She suspected that underneath the hauteur was a girl desperately wishing to belong.

Penny's sympathy lasted all of thirty seconds. Eileen, who had been stashing Santa Jim and the enormous sacks of presents in an antechamber, returned to declare, 'Jim says can he have some of them funny bushes because he's fu–' She put her hands over her own ears and whispered, '–king starving.'

'You know that only works on the kids,' laughed Penny, loading a plate with a selection of Mrs Goggins' amuse-bouches. 'If you're the one doing the swearing, you can still hear yourself.'

'Good to see that Dad's still keeping the island half-wits gainfully employed,' sneered Raine.

Eileen immediately reddened and snatched the plate from Penny before hurrying from the room. Looking startled, Mrs Hubbard hurried after her.

'That remark says more about you than it does about Eileen,' snapped Penny.

Any further comment, however, was silenced by Sandra Next Door, who stepped in front of Penny and roared, 'You go and apologise now. Or I'll…I'll…'

'You'll what?' sneered Raine. 'You'll nothing. So shut your mouth, old lady and go back to the kitchen or whatever it is you're here to do.'

Raine calmly took her phone from the mantelpiece and snapped a photograph. She typed something then turned the screen so that they could see what she'd written. It was an

Instagram post with the words "Met the Grinch today" underneath a picture of a scowling Sandra Next Door.

'You have picked on the wrong woman,' said Sandra, her voice dangerously low. 'Now, if you'll excuse me, I'm going to check on Eileen.'

Penny smiled gleefully at Raine.

'You should be afraid. Very afraid. Nobody messes with Sandra Next Door.'

Raine opened her mouth to issue what was no doubt going to be a smart retort, but she was interrupted by a burst of high-pitched squeals as twenty ten-year-olds burst through the doors and headed straight for her.

'Are you a real princess?' one little boy wanted to know.

'Are you Mrs Santa?' asked a little girl.

'Does the elf belong to you?'

'Yes, to all of those things!' exclaimed Raine. 'Now, who would like to be in a selfie with Princess Mrs Santa so that the people of Instagram can send lots of lovely likes?'

Amidst the hubbub of excited voices and little boys skidding along the floorboards on their knees, Mrs Hubbard and Sandra Next Door quietly slid back into the hall and sidled up to Penny. Disco Bob had lifted the mood with some jolly Christmas pop songs, but Sandra stood stiffly, glaring at Raine like she wanted to burn a hole through the woman's soul.

'How's Eileen?' asked Penny above the chirpy strains of Mariah Carey.

'Eileen's alright, dearie,' Mrs Hubbard assured her. 'She was upset, but she's fine now. She's gone to the bathroom to wash her face.'

'Thanks, Mrs H. That Raine's a piece of work.'

'Don't you worry, dearie. Sandra Next Door has it all in hand.' Mrs Hubbard tapped the side of her nose. 'I won't give you the details because I know you and Jim are friendly with Hamish. What is it they call it in the movies? Paso doble ability? Och, sometimes my brain just goes off on its own tango and I can't remember a thing.'

'Tangent,' said Penny.

'No, it's nothing to do with tangents. It's definitely paso doble something or other.'

'Plausible deniability?'

'That's the one!' exclaimed Mrs Hubbard, delighted and relieved.

'By any chance, were you and Douglas watching the Strictly Come Dancing final again?' Penny asked.

'And last night's Ballroom Bliss. How did you guess?' said Mrs Hubbard, astonished. 'If Eileen was here, she'd say you're side kick. You know how she loves all that mambo jumbo.'

Penny suppressed a snort of laughter and said, 'I'll go and see her. Could you tell Disco Bob to turn the music down and get the party games going please?'

Making her way towards the door, she paused for a moment to take in the scene, then murmured, 'Where *is* Disco Bob? And where are Hamish and Cara? They're supposed to be in charge of everything.'

Mildly puzzled, she exited the hall, leaving behind her a cacophony of excited squeals as twenty small people spotted the new arrivals and surrounded them, shouting, 'Mrs Hubbard! Mrs Next Door!'

Penny couldn't help but smile. For the past few months, Sandra Next Door had been an emergency lollipop lady, swooping in to cover a mysterious spate of absences among the crossing patrol community. Penny felt that her parents' irascible neighbour may finally have found her niche. Unfailingly kind to the children and unflinching in the face of frustrated drivers, for a couple of hours each weekday morning and afternoon, Sandra Next Door ruled the streets of Vik with an iron fist. Her reputation was such that when a rumour flew around the island that the council had offered her a full-time job as a traffic warden, there was a sharp increase in car parking revenues.

Despite her tough, sarky exterior, the children clearly loved Sandra Next Door, and Penny was glad that her friend now had something to worry about other than nagging Geoff Next Door about using coasters and keeping his feet off the furniture. To be fair, Penny wouldn't be too pleased if Geoff put his feet on her furniture. The man had a penchant for stiletto shoes and was once thrown out of the house because he left heel marks in Sandra's new kitchen lino.

Penny stood in the grand entrance, trying to remember where she could find the nearest bathroom. The castle was like a rabbit warren and even if you thought you knew the way, one wrong turn could bring you somewhere quite unexpected. On one occasion when she'd stayed the night, she went to the loo in the small hours and ended up on the battlements instead of her bedroom.

'I think it's down here,' she muttered to herself. 'Hamish should put up signs. No wonder he finds tourists in his dressing room.'

She was about to head down the corridor to her left when she spotted a familiar figure emerging from behind a suit of armour.

'Jim!' she exclaimed. 'What are you doing here? Have you been sneaking around Hamish's secret passageways?'

Beneath his beard, Jim smiled and winked. Penny leaned over and planted a kiss on what she hoped, under all the fuzz, was his mouth. Then, for good measure, she reached down and gave his jingle bells a loving squeeze.

'You're supposed to be hiding with the presents,' she told him. 'You better get back before the kids see you.'

Jim shrugged amiably and wandered off in the direction of the antechamber, leaving Penny to fix her sights on what she was sure must be the bathroom.

She had taken no more than a few steps when she heard raised voices. Naturally, being the proud daughter of Mary

Hopper and inheritor of extreme nosiness, Penny stopped to listen.

The voices appeared to be coming from behind a door further down the corridor, so Penny tiptoed towards it and pressed an ear to the polished oak.

She could hear a man with an Irish accent yelling, 'Listen, will you? There's going to be serious trouble for you unless you get me the money straight away.'

A woman replied, 'There's only one way to lay my hands on that much cash, and I'm not doing it. It would break his heart.'

With a start, Penny straightened and looked at the door. That was Cara's voice. What on earth was going on? She had thought it odd that her friend hadn't been there to greet her when they arrived at the castle, but she'd assumed that Cara must be busy. Lordy, it sounded a lot worse than being busy. Penny was just about to press her ear once more to the door when it was flung open, and an enraged Cara strode out.

'Penny!' she squealed, taken aback to find someone lurking.

'Sorry,' said Penny. 'I was looking for the bathroom and heard shouting. Is everything okay?'

'It's fine,' said Cara, casting a glance over her shoulder before hastily closing the door. However, she wasn't quite fast enough to prevent Penny getting a glimpse of the man inside the room. Odd, she thought, I recognise him from somewhere.

'Who's that?' Penny asked, ignoring the fact that Cara clearly hadn't wanted her to stick her nose in.

'It's nobody,' said Cara sharply. 'I'll see you in the big hall in a minute. I need to nip upstairs for something first. The bathroom's just there.'

Cara pointed to the door opposite then stood watching, as if to guard the door behind her, while Penny knocked and Eileen let her in.

Hearing Cara's footsteps disappear down the corridor,

Penny immediately opened the bathroom door again and stuck her head through the gap.

'What are you doing, Gandelf?' said Eileen behind her.

'Shh!' whispered Penny. 'Did you hear the ding-dong across the hall?'

'Aye,' Eileen whispered back. 'Cara and some gadgie fechtin. Something about money, but I couldn't hear properly.'

'I only heard the tail end of it. She came out and caught me listening. I managed to see the man before she shut the door, though. I think I've seen him somewhere before, but lord knows where. Do you fancy a wee keek?'

'We can't go barging in,' Eileen hissed. 'What if he's a raging bampot?'

'Then those self-defence classes at the church hall will come in handy. I'm going in anyway.'

With Eileen clinging to the back of her elf costume, Penny stepped out of the bathroom and crossed to the door opposite. Far more confidently than she felt, she turned the handle, swung the door open and marched inside. Then she stopped.

Bringing up the rear, Eileen lurched into Penny, sending them both stumbling forwards. They quickly righted themselves and looked around the room. It was a pleasant, feminine drawing room. The wallpaper depicted sprays of small ochre flowers, and mauve curtains dropped to silken puddles on the floor either side of a tall window. On the far wall, a sideboard stood beneath a large mirror, while at the other side of the room a grey, velvet chaise longue languished opposite the fireplace, with high wingback chairs standing sentinel at either side. Above the fireplace, a rather insipid woman gazed calmly down from the confines of an ornate gilt portrait frame. Some long dead ancestor of Hamish's, Penny supposed. Yet it was not the beautiful décor or even the magnificent marble fireplace that drew her to a halt. It was the fact that there was no one there.

'Where did he go?' she asked, bewildered. 'He couldn't have left. There wasn't time. I'd have seen him.'

'Are you sure you saw him? Maybe it was the castle ghost,' Eileen suggested.

'Do castle ghosts wear wax jackets and wellies and shout at the living about money?'

'The spirit world manifests itself in many forms,' said Eileen, clearly spouting some nonsense she'd read on the internet.

'This one manifested as one of the huntin' shootin' types that Cara and Hamish are old school pals with. If he didn't leave through the door, there must be a hidden entrance somewhere. Hamish says the place is riddled with them. Come and help me look.'

Penny began to tap on the wall around the fireplace, and Eileen did the same at the opposite side of the room.

This went on for some time, until Eileen asked, 'Why are we tapping?'

Penny was glad she had her back to her friend because she would not otherwise have been able to hide her exasperation.

'You mean you…all this time…we're listening for anything that sounds hollow, of course. Anything that might indicate there's a door behind the wall.'

'Oh. Right. Would this count?'

Penny turned to find Eileen standing on the sideboard, peering into a dark hole where the mirror had once been. The mirror itself had slid to one side.

'Duh, yes!' she exclaimed, rushing over to take a closer look.

Penny and Eileen scrambled on top of the sideboard and stuck their heads through the hole. Inside, the air smelled damp and musty. Pulling her phone from her bra (because elf costumes didn't have pockets – yet another thing to add to the petition), Penny shone the torch up and then down what appeared to be a shaft. Ropes on some sort of pulley system disappeared into the darkness above and below them, and there was a small handle to their right.

'I know what this is,' Penny breathed, keeping her voice low lest it carry through the tunnel. 'This must have once been a dining room. It's a dumb waiter.'

'Oh, I've had one of them,' said Eileen. 'Me, Kenny and Robbie were in that posh French place in Aberdeen, and I asked the waiter if we could have une ménage à trôis. I mean, it doesn't take a genius to fetch three menus, does it? The man looked at me like I'd just asked him to shit in his hands and clap! I didn't leave a tip.'

'Rudelf, ma cherie, you do know that the French for menu is menu, don't you?'

'Is it? Wow, I wonder what I asked for, then?'

'Google it when you get home. For now, could you crank the handle please?'

Eileen obligingly wound the handle, puffing slightly with the effort, and they heard a faint rumble below. Slowly, the noise grew closer until a large, shelved wooden box appeared.

'Top shelf or bottom?' Penny asked.

'Top,' said Eileen, grinning. 'That way, if the ropes snap, you'll break my fall.'

'Okay, but we're going to have to be coordinated about this. We have to manoeuvre the ropes at the same time. And they'll be stiff.'

Eileen clambered onto the top shelf and Penny onto the bottom. Penny grabbed one of the ropes and pushed upwards, whispering to Eileen to do the same. Nothing happened. The rope wouldn't budge.

Penny was struck by a sudden thought.

'Rudelf, are you pushing up or pulling down?'

'Pulling down. We're going down, aren't we?'

'You need to push upwards.'

'That makes no sense, Gandelf.'

'Trust me, it does. Just push.'

Their weight seemed to have steadied the mechanism, and the dumb waiter now moved silently downwards. Slowly, they lowered the box until it came to a halt on what felt like a solid platform. Small shafts of light outlined the edge of a door in front of them and both women leaned forward to peer through the tiny gap.

It was immediately clear that they had landed in the kitchen and were inside what Penny had previously assumed was a cupboard. Penny could just make out the aproned figure of Mrs Goggins. She was sitting at the large pine table, a mug of tea in front of her. But she was not alone. Beside her, a hand reached for a second mug of tea.

'I feel sick inside,' said Mrs Goggins.

'Don't worry about it. We did what we had to do,' said the other person.

Above her, Penny heard Eileen give a gasp of recognition. She'd only managed to muffle her own gasp by keeping her lips firmly closed.

'We should have taken him down and buried him.'

'No,' said Mrs Hubbard firmly. 'Where would we have put him? Everything's frozen solid. We need to put him somewhere until the ground is soft. I'll come back tomorrow. I'll take Douglas to help.'

'But it's Christmas Day tomorrow. Are you sure?'

'Fewer prying eyes and the family will be too busy to notice.'

'As ever, Minty, you're right. Now, get yourself back to the party. You've been gone too long, and folk will start whispering.'

Mrs Hubbard and Mrs Goggins stood up and moved out of Penny's vision. Their footsteps became fainter as they climbed the stairs, and she risked a gentle push on the door.

The moment they emerged from the dumb waiter cupboard, Penny and Eileen breathed a sigh of relief, brushed the cobwebs from their costumes and turned to look at one another.

Her eyes wide with shock, Eileen said, 'Holy guacamole! It sounds like Mrs Goggins and Mrs Hubbard have murdered someone. Do you think it was the man you saw arguing with Cara?'

'I don't know,' said Penny. 'They were talking about taking him down, which suggests that whoever is dead, he's somewhere upstairs.'

'We should go and look for him.'

'We're on the lowest floor and the castle has about a hundred and sixty gazillion rooms. Where do you suggest we start?'

'As ever, Gandelf, you're right,' said Eileen in an unconscious parody of Mrs Goggins. 'We should start at room one hundred and sixty gazillion and work our way backwards.'

'Don't be daft,' Penny started to say, then she saw Eileen's face fall and rushed to reassure her. 'Sorry, I didn't mean that. I meant there are too many rooms to search, plus the place is full of nooks and crannies that we don't know about. Let's keep our eyes and ears open, and if all else fails, we'll phone Sergeant Wilson.'

'You can't hand Mrs H over to the cops!'

'It's Sergeant Wilson. She may be a scary old boot, but I trust her to get to the bottom of things and be decent to Mrs Hubbard. Unless you have any other ideas?'

'We could investigate,' Eileen suggested.

'Investigate what? How?'

Defeated, Eileen sighed and agreed, 'Eyes and ears open, then.'

They headed back upstairs to the big hall and slipped unnoticed into the throng. The children were enthusiastically dancing to a frothy pop song and, much to Penny's delight, Sandra Next Door was teaching a group of boys how to do the robot. She was remarkably good at it, too. Goodness, I wonder where she learned to do that, Penny thought. And there's Mrs H, hovering around the edges like a sneaky bugger, trying to pretend that she's been here all the time.

The music transitioned to a thumping techno number, and Penny turned to ask Disco Bob to change it back to pop. However, Disco Bob still wasn't there. She looked around to check whether he was by the buffet, no doubt helping himself to more than his fair share of mince pies. Yet he wasn't there either. He wasn't anywhere. The only adults here were Eileen, Mrs Hubbard, Sandra Next Door and the two teachers who had arrived with the children.

The teachers were dressed for work, not play, she noted. The woman was a little dowdy in a long beige cardigan and a skirt which looked too large for her narrow frame, and the man wore ill-fitting black trousers and a white shirt, giving him the appearance of a slightly scruffy waiter. Perhaps they could tell her where Disco Bob had gone.

Penny ambled over to the teachers and shouted above the din, 'Hi. I'm Penny Moon, one of the helpers.'

'Mrs Snipples,' said the woman, pointing to herself, 'and this is Mr Black.'

'Pleased to meet you. Do you know where Disco Bob has gone?'

'I have no idea,' said Mrs Snipples. 'He seems to have set up a few tracks then disappeared. I must say, it's been a strange selection. We had Nicki Minaj followed by a Kylie classic.'

'This is absurd,' said Penny. 'A disappearing DJ, neither Hamish nor Cara have shown their faces yet, and where the heck is Raine?'

'Is she the one in the red dress?' asked Mr Black. 'She was doing party games, then she took a phone call and left. When you find Disco Bob, can you ask him to switch off the music please? I think it's time to feed the kids.'

He was eyeing a group of boys in the corner who were squaring up to a group of girls. Not fancying the boys' chances, Penny agreed that it was definitely feeding time. This lot were starting to get hangry.

She strode over to Disco Bob's set up and examined the

array of buttons and dials. Bloody hell, there were spaceships less complicated than this.

An experimental twiddle sent the children scurrying, their hands over their ears to block out the sudden high-pitched screech.

'Sorry,' said Penny over Disco Bob's microphone.

Staying away from the dials, she randomly pressed a few buttons. For a brief second, there was a burst of thrumming bass followed by a blast of Harry Styles, then a quick, garbled few seconds of Ed Sheeran before, oh blessed relief, silence.

'Line up, children,' said Mrs Snipples, ignoring the disappointed "aaawwww" from five girls who had been trying to synchronise an increasingly complicated series of dance moves. 'It's time to eat, and before we do, we should thank Mrs Goggins who made the lovely food.'

This resulted in a ragged chorus of "Thank you, Mrs Goggins," as some children began shouting before others, all topped off with a single roar of "Missus Goggins" from the tail end Charlie in the yellow shirt. Penny smiled. Eileen had once been that child. Never paying attention and always running that little bit behind everyone else. It was one of her many endearing qualities.

Mrs Goggins appeared at the door of the big hall, her arms full of fresh tea towels, and executed a deep bow.

'Dig in, my wee cherubs,' she said, her face beaming with pleasure.

The children lined up at the buffet, quickly decimating Mrs Goggins' volley vents, piles of sausage rolls, sandwiches and things on sticks. There was a run on the fairy cakes, but the miniature Christmas cakes, so carefully decorated by Mrs Hubbard, went largely untouched on the grounds of, ugh, marzipan.

The floor was soon teeming with little knots of children, sitting cross-legged as they slurped on orange squash and shoved as many treats down their throats as they could manage. Only one little boy sat alone, and Penny instantly felt a pang of sympathy for him. Among the boisterous lads, with their patterned shirts hanging untucked over new jeans, he was a solitary figure in a tweed waistcoat and bow tie.

Penny couldn't help herself. She sat down beside him and said, 'Are you enjoying the party?'

'Not really,' the boy replied. 'I don't like loud music, and I don't mix well with other children. They find me dull and annoying, you see.'

'Oh,' said Penny, taken aback by the matter-of-fact way in which the boy had delivered this statement. 'Erm, why's that?'

The boy sighed, as if it were obvious and Penny was being an idiot.

'I know a lot of things and I like to tell people about them. For instance, I'm very interested in maps and Romans. At my last school, I was bullied. It has been alright here so far, but time will tell. My mother says that it takes all kinds to make a world.'

'Do you not have any friends?' Penny asked, her heart breaking for this odd, strangely adult, child.

'I do, but Andy couldn't come today. He has epilepsy and sometimes he's unwell. That's why he's my friend. Nobody likes him either. But he's interested in Romans, so I like him. Then there's Pigsy. He's my guinea pig. So that's two friends. I'm Cameron, by the way.'

'Pleased to meet you. I'm Penny and my best friend is over there. She's called Eileen. If you need a break from the music, you can help Eileen and I with some jobs, like clearing away the food.'

'That's okay. I've brought a good book and I've found a quiet spot behind the Christmas tree.'

'Great. Okay, you enjoy what you can of the party. I have a little job of my own to do now. I'm one of Santa's helpers and I think I can hear reindeer bells in the distance.'

Cameron rolled his eyes. 'Santa. A social construct to manipulate the behaviour of children and enrich greedy corporations. Did you know that the real St Nicholas was born in what is now Turkey?'

'Hmm, right, I'll stick with my version, if you don't mind. Jolly fat man who gives presents. See you later, Cameron.'

Penny left Cameron picking the yellow bits out of a mince pie and caught up with Eileen, whose pink icing moustache belied her claim that she was definitely sticking to the healthy eating plan. No mince pies and fairy cakes for Eileen, no siree.

'The children are nearly finished their food,' said Penny. 'I think it's time we called for Santa. Is Jim ready?'

'I popped my head round the door a few minutes ago and he was sitting on the sofa reading his Kindle, so he's still awake, if that's what you're asking.'

'Brilliant. How are we going to do this?'

'Leave it with Rudelf, for she has small children and knows how to get their attention,' said Eileen, a glow of excitement staining her cheeks. 'You could give me a hand with the big Santa chair first.'

Together, Penny and Eileen lifted an enormous red chair and set it down beside the fireplace. Eileen moved a small side-table next to it and set down a plate of mince pies and a glass of milk.

'Ooh, this will be fun,' Penny whispered. 'Jim hates milk unless it's in tea or coffee.'

'One more thing,' said Eileen, positioning herself in front of the fireplace.

She beckoned Sandra Next Door over and handed her a small set of percussion bells.

'Could you go up to the gallery and when everyone shouts "Santa," ring these? Start faint and get louder. Like the reindeer are getting closer. Penny, can you dim the lights please?'

Eileen gave them both a thumbs up then, seemingly out of nowhere, she produced a large brass hand bell and began to ring it. Slowly, the chatter stopped, and the children turned to look at her. She signalled to them to come sit on the floor around the fireplace and they obediently shuffled forward.

'Boys and girls,' she cried, 'my name is Rudelf and over there is Gandelf. This is our happiest night of the year because we're Santa's helpers. But hush. I think I can hear Santa's sleigh, and I need you to help me guide him to the castle. On the count of three, I want you to shout his name as loudly as possible. Are you ready? One, two, three!'

There was an ear-splitting roar as twenty voices shouted, 'Santa!', followed by tail end Charlie in the yellow shirt, who bellowed so hard that his voice cracked.

Penny slowly dimmed the lights until the circle of children was lit by the orange glow from the fire.

Eileen cupped a hand over her ear and said, 'Now, listen very hard. Can you hear something?'

High above them there was a faint tinkle, and a ripple of excitement ran through the crowd.

'I think we need to be much louder. Three big shouts please.'

'SANTA, SANTA, SANTA!' the children yelled.

The sound of bells grew louder, and the tension became too much for one little girl, who began to wail, 'I don't want Santa. I need a pee.'

Mrs Snipples ran forward and quickly ushered her towards the door, where the girl could be heard howling, 'I don't want a pee. I want to stay for Santa.'

'Sorry,' said Mrs Snipples, pulling the girl away, 'she always does this when she gets overexcited. Come on, Olivia. You'll see Santa as soon as you get back.'

Penny dialled down the tension by turning up the lights and nodded to Eileen, who clapped her hands and announced, 'We need Santa here now, and it will help if we sing his special song. After me. One, two, three. Ohhhhhhh, jingle bells, jingle bells, jingle all the way…'

Penny's heart burst for the joy of her friend. Eileen was in her element, leading this ragged, roaring chorus. Yet even as she joined in, Penny couldn't help noticing something strange in the fireplace. Above the fire, there seemed to be an object hanging down. She sidled over to stand next to Eileen so that she could take a closer look. What on earth could it be? Still singing along, Penny leaned backwards, looking over her shoulder to inspect the item. It appeared to be a belt.

With her attention fully focused on the fire, Penny didn't realise that the singing had stopped and that she was now the only one Jingle Bellsing. The children had turned to face outwards towards the antechamber, through which Jim would appear at any moment. Penny had turned to face the fire.

Carefully poking a set of coal tongs into the flames, she grabbed the possible belt and tugged. There was a rumble, almost as though something was moving in the chimney. Penny tugged again. This time there came a longer, louder rumble. Penny tugged for a third time and sensed something shift. Beside her, Eileen too was now paying rapt attention to the fire. Penny put the tongs back into the flames, preparing for a fourth tug, when with a whoosh and a rush of soot, a large object came crashing into the fireplace.

For a few seconds, the world was held in suspended animation as Penny and Eileen beheld the red-suited figure smouldering on the fire. Then, as if in slow motion, small heads turned to see what was happening and the figure rolled onto the hearth, his beard and stomach ablaze.

Penny's cry was louder than the combined voices of twenty children. The pure animal wail came howling from her belly.

'Jim!'

And the lights went out.

CHAPTER 5

The polyester costume was rapidly melting, and flames leapt from the foam in the cushion beneath. Santa's face was charred and smoking, as the beard combusted then formed a thick, oily glaze over his nose and mouth. The air was thick with the smell of burning hair and the screams of children.

It was Sandra Next Door who saved the day. Where Penny and Eileen stood frozen in horror, held back from going to Jim's aid by the flames, Sandra quickly retrieved two large jugs of orange squash from the buffet and poured the contents over him. Then she roared, 'Mr Black, take the children out of here. Now! Mrs Hubbard, get everyone down to the kitchen and keep them there. Mrs Goggins, find as many candles as you can. Leave some in the kitchen and bring some here.'

Between them, Mr Black and Mrs Hubbard herded the children into a sniffling, sobbing crocodile and led them out of the hall. Mrs Goggins headed off to ferret out as many candles as possible, starting with the ornate candelabra in the grand dining room next door. Years of running up and down the castle stairs had given her the stamina of a much younger woman, and it was not long before there was enough light for

Penny, Eileen and Sandra Next Door to inspect the remains gently steaming in the hearth.

'Has anyone called the police?' asked Penny, coming out of her shocked daze.

'Of course,' snapped Sandra Next Door. 'But the phone signal here is useless. I can't get through.'

'What about broadband? Can we get a message through that way?'

'Don't be stupid. The power's out.'

'Oh. Right. Sorry, I'm not thinking straight.'

Penny was talking calmly, but tears were pouring unchecked down her cheeks and her limbs were trembling.

'I suppose we should move him,' she said. 'We can't leave him here. A single spark from the fire would…set him off again and the whole place could burn down. What's best, do you think?'

'Encase him in concrete and throw him in Loch Lannach,' said a voice from behind them.

Penny's heart leapt and this time her cry was a blend of relief, anger and joy.

'Jim!'

'Bugger me with a double A battery, what's going–'

The rest of the sentence was lost in an explosive "oof" as the wind was knocked out of him by a delirious Penny. She launched herself into him so forcefully that not even the pillow could protect his midriff and he staggered back under the impact.

Wrapping her arms around his chest, she sobbed, 'I thought you were dead. You're not allowed to die. We haven't had enough time yet.'

'Aye, well, I'll make sure I pop my clogs at a more suitable moment. When would be good for you?'

Penny said nothing. She merely tightened her grip and buried her head deeper into his pillow.

Jim rested his chin on her head and looked expectantly at

Sandra Next Door and Eileen, who were staring at him in disbelief.

'Well?' he asked. 'One minute I'm taking a power nap and the next I hear screaming. What's happened?'

'You came down the chimney and got burnt to a crisp,' said Eileen. 'Then you came back as a ghost, and now you're haunting us.'

'And the alternative explanation?' said Jim, inclining his head towards Sandra Next Door.

'Somebody murdered Santa,' she said, then qualified this with, 'Probably. It's not like folk accidentally fall down chimneys.'

'Although this *is* Santa we're talking about,' said Eileen, gesturing towards the fireplace. 'He's up and down chimneys all the time. If you think about it, it was an accident just waiting to happen.'

'So, what you're saying is that it's an–'

'If you say elf and safety matter,' came Penny's muffled voice from his chest, 'I'm going to roast your chestnuts on an open fire.'

'Aye, well,' said Jim, gently peeling Penny off him and turning her to face the others, 'first things first. We can't leave him here. We have to move him somewhere cool and dry, without disturbing any evidence he might have on him.'

'I doubt there's much evidence,' said Penny. 'It'll all be in the fire. How about we use the tablecloths from the buffet? Turn them over to the clean side and they should do the trick.'

'Good thinking, Gandelf,' said Eileen, making for the buffet table. 'By the way…and I may be out of line in assuming he's not the real Santa, but…does anyone know who he is?'

Sandra Next Door took a candelabra from the side-table and moved it closer to Santa's face.

'Hmm,' she said. 'Difficult to tell under all that muck.'

She plucked the napkin from the table, dipped it in the

glass of milk, then gently rubbed away some of the soot and melted beard from around the body's eyes and mouth.

'Evidence! I thought we were supposed to preserve the evidence,' said Jim.

'Too late for that,' said Sandra Next Door.

She pulled off what remained of his Santa hat, taking skin and hair with it. Between the raw patches of flesh, dark strands clung to the scalp.

'I'd say this is Disco Bob. Agreed?'

Penny nodded, not trusting herself to open her mouth. Her throat was currently in hot contention with her belly as to the location of her stomach contents, and she had no intention of the final destination being the floor.

'Aye, that's Disco Bob alright,' said Jim.

'Disco Bob,' muttered Eileen, laying a white tablecloth on the floor beside the hearth. Then she brightened. 'This is good news! It means the real Santa is still alive!'

'Unlikely. However, mythology is an important part of any culture, so I shall indulge your beliefs,' said a small voice in the darkness.

'Cameron!' exclaimed Penny. 'Why aren't you down in the kitchen with the other children?'

'I told you. I have a comfortable spot behind the Christmas tree. Can I suggest that before you wrap the body, you check inside its mouth and throat for signs of smoke inhalation? That will tell you whether or not the cause of death was fire.'

'I'm taking you to the kitchen,' said Penny.

'You can try,' Cameron shrugged, 'but I'll only come back. I'm quite annoying like that, you see. Of course, it's not conclusive, looking in the mouth and throat. A pathologist would have to check the lungs during autopsy.'

'You're ten. How do you even know this stuff?'

'I told you. I read. For goodness' sake woman, were you listening to *anything* I said?'

'The wee bugger's right,' said Jim. 'You never listen to

anything I say either. He's also right about smoke inhalation. Can I borrow your phone, Penny? I left mine back in the Santa room.'

Jim got down on his knees beside Disco Bob and, with a grunt of exertion, awkwardly rolled him onto the tablecloth, away from the heat of the fire. Shining the phone torch on Bob's face, Jim gently prised the jaw open and peered inside.

'It's no use,' he said. 'His tongue's in the way. I'll have to tilt his head back. Eileen, can you get me a teaspoon?'

Thanking the heavens that Mrs Goggins disapproved of ketchup bottles at the table, Eileen quickly retrieved a silver teaspoon from a pot of tomato sauce, wiped it on a napkin and handed it over. Jim put an arm under Bob's head to tilt it back and pressed the flat end of the teaspoon onto the tongue.

Realising that he needed a third hand, he said, 'Could one of you shine the phone torch down his throat please?'

Penny and Sandra Next Door started forward, but Cameron got there first. Jim frowned and Cameron rolled his eyes.

'I know you're an…unusual child, yet I don't think you should be doing this,' Jim told him.

'Let's get the child thing out of the way,' said Cameron. 'I have an IQ of a hundred and sixty, I speak three languages and I co-authored an academic paper on Roman farming methods. I think I can deal with looking down the mouth of a corpse without suffering undue trauma. In fact, it's quite interesting.'

'But your mother…' said Jim.

'Would in all likelihood freak out and ban me from advanced calculus for a week. However, she doesn't need to know.'

'Fair enough,' said Jim. 'Although you're only allowed to examine one dead body a day. Any more corpses, and I'll have to phone your mother. Is that understood?'

'Alright,' said Cameron reluctantly.

He shone the torch down Disco Bob's throat and nearly

clashed heads with Jim as they both leaned over to take a closer look.

After a few seconds, Jim straightened and declared, 'All pink. Nothing to show smoke damage, so he was probably dead before he hit the fire. Beyond that, it's hard to say whether getting stuck in the chimney killed him or if he was dead before he went in.'

'We could check his body for bruising,' Cameron suggested.

'What did I just say about corpses?'

'You said I was only allowed to examine one *dead body* a day, not do one *examination*.'

'Och, buggeration, I should have been more specific. Well, we're not taking his clothes off, and that's final. Right, oot the way, laddie. Penny, Eileen, let's get him wrapped up. It's a good job Mrs Goggins used the banqueting tablecloth for the buffet. We could get three Santas in there and still have room for sandwiches.'

By the time they were done, Disco Bob was a fat, white sausage on the floor of the big hall. Jim's initial suggestion of stashing him in Mrs Goggins' cold pantry was poo-pooed on the basis that they'd have to carry Bob through the kitchen, past the children. Surprisingly, it was Eileen who came up with the ideal solution.

'It has to be somewhere dry. Hamish has a collection of classic cars in a garage round the back of the castle. My Kenny comes up and fixes them for him. We could put Disco Bob in one of the cars.'

'Or leave him on the floor?' suggested Jim, knowing that he'd be the one to wrestle Disco Bob into a car.

'No, the floor will be filthy with oil and Kenny said the roof was leaking a few weeks ago. Ruined the leather of a 1953 something something.'

'Car it is, then,' Jim sighed. 'Everybody, grab an end.'

With Jim holding the head, Penny and Eileen at the feet and Sandra Next Door and Cameron supporting the middle, they manhandled Disco Bob out of the front entrance and down the stone steps.

The going was treacherous. The snow had fallen thickly while they had been indoors, and it was almost impossible to see where one step ended and another began. Their shoes were not made for snow and, working by the light of Penny's phone torch, they slipped and stumbled their way through the blizzard to the rear of the castle.

Jim's heart sank when they finally reached the garage only to find the door secured by a large padlock.

'Never fear, for Penny is here,' said Penny, her teeth chattering as an icy blast whipped round the corner.

She removed one of the pins securing her elf hat to her hair and, with fingers numbed by cold, began to manipulate the lock.

'Could you teach me how to do that?' asked Cameron.

'I will, when you're all grown up and need to break into places to hide dead bodies,' said Penny. 'Aha! That was easier than expected. I was worried the lock would be frozen.'

She pulled the padlock free of the hasp and relieved Jim at the head of Disco Bob so that he could pull the garage door open, which was no mean feat against a foot of snow.

The garage was a stone building with a corrugated roof, and as Jim pulled on the door, the vibration disturbed the snow above. There was little time to call out a warning. Before he could leap to one side, a small avalanche landed squarely on Jim's head, running down his body to bury him up to his hips.

'Oh, for f–' he started to say, but stopped himself when Eileen let go of Disco Bob's feet and clamped her hands over Cameron's ears. '–fffunky steak.'

He fished around in the pocket of his Santa suit. There was a short beep and lights shone through a snowdrift a few metres away.

'Get the snow shovel out of the boot, Penny. Actually,

don't. We'll just put Bob in the boot. I don't know why we didn't think of that in the first place.'

'Because we like to overcomplicate things?' said Penny.

'Because if we manage to get out of here at some point tonight, we'll have to either move him again or take him with us,' Sandra Next Door pointed out.

'Fffungal bell. Get the snow shovel, Penny.'

In the ten minutes it took Penny to dig Jim out and clear a path to open the garage door, Eileen, Cameron and Sandra Next Door dropped Disco Bob three times. Nobody was wearing coats, and only the exercise had prevented Penny from succumbing to the uncontrollable shivering which afflicted her friends. The moment that Jim was free, he helped her by furiously scooping mounds of snow behind him, like a dog scratching grass.

Finally, they were able to open the door wide enough to manoeuvre Disco Bob into the garage. Penny saw with some relief that Hamish had left a coat on a hook, and she rushed to wrap it around poor Cameron, who looked pale and shaky.

'Well done,' she told him. 'You've been a very brave boy.'

Cameron shot her a look which silently communicated all the eff words that Jim had tried to conceal.

'I prefer young man,' he said through chattering teeth. 'It's interesting to observe the effect of extreme cold on the body.'

'You shouldn't even be here,' said Penny. 'We should have put you down to the kitchen with the other children.'

'I wouldn't have gone. I don't feel like a child inside, so it's very difficult for me to do as I'm told. All I ask is that you set my age to one side and treat me with respect. Do that, and I'm sure we'll get along nicely.'

'You're a different one, that's for sure,' said Penny, vigorously rubbing some warmth into his arms.

'I am, but as my mother says–'

'It takes all kinds to make a world. Right, sit yourself on the bench while I help the others get Disco Bob into a car.'

They laid Disco Bob across the back seat of a 1936 Ford

something something. Eileen had wanted to put him in the driver's seat, but it was agreed that Bob should remain out of sight.

'Did you ever get through to Randy Mair to come and clear the road?' Penny asked Jim on their way back to the front entrance.

Jim was carrying Cameron piggy-back style and picking his way carefully across the drive, mindful of rocks and ornamental edging hidden by the snow.

'Aye,' he puffed, hitching Cameron a little higher. 'Mind you, I struggled to get a signal. I had to wander about the castle a bit. Don't worry. Nobody saw me.'

'Except me, of course,' Penny laughed.

Jim gave her a sideways glance, wondering if she was pulling his leg.

'You didn't see me,' he said, baffled.

'I did. Remember? I gave you a kiss, had a wee jingle of your bells and sent you on your way.'

'No, you didn't.'

'I did!'

'You really didn't. Are you sure it was my bells you were jingling.'

Penny was silent for a long time, then she whispered, 'Oh my god. Please tell me I didn't.'

'You did.'

'No. Please, no. I didn't.'

'You really did.'

'Just leave me here in the snow to die.'

Jim's laugh began as a small series of snorts, then progressed through the uproarious phase before finally peaking in a silent wheeze. Not even the slippery steps could put a dent in his hilarity, and it was with great difficulty that he bent to let Cameron slip to the floor in the entranceway.

By the time they reached the big hall, tears were streaming down his cheeks, and he was taking great, heaving breaths, all the while clutching his ribs and honking like a horny seal.

He eventually managed to calm down for long enough to strip off his wet trousers and hang them over the back of a chair in front of the fire. However, a fresh bubble of laughter welled up when he was eating a mince pie, and he sprayed pastry over Sandra Next Door. A promptly delivered kick in the shin rendered Jim instantly sober, yet he was unable to answer any queries as to what had provoked such mirth for fear of another episode. For her part, Penny remained tight-lipped and stoic throughout, refusing to further fuel his glee.

With their wet clothes gently steaming by the fire, the group dragged a sofa from the antechamber and slumped in exhausted quietude, transfixed by the dancing flames.

'How do you think Disco Bob got down the chimney?' said Penny after a while.

'Jumped, pushed, killed then stuffed down there. I dunno,' Jim yawned.

'No, I suppose I mean where did he come from that he ended up down the chimney. Did he have to come straight from the roof to the big hall, or could he have crawled down the chimney intending to go to another room?'

'Like is the chimney connected to other fireplaces?' asked Eileen. 'Hang on, it's not the same as Harry Potter, is it? Where you sneeze and end up in Knockturn Alley or something? Because that would totally mess up Santa's present delivery schedule.'

'You have a wonderful imagination, Eileen,' said Cameron.

'Thank you, Cameron. And you have a wonderful, erm, big coat.'

Cameron was still wearing Hamish's coat. It hung almost to his feet and his hands were lost up the sleeves, but with his smart black trousers being temporarily unavailable, it at least kept his legs warm.

'Stick to the point, Eileen,' said Sandra Next Door. 'I don't know whether the fireplaces share a chimney. If you go up to the battlements, you can see lots of chimneys.'

'How do you know?' asked Eileen.

'Geoff and I did the castle tour in the summertime.'

'I expect this fireplace is the only one connected to the chimney,' said Jim. 'For a start, it's bloody huge, and secondly, it's the oldest part of the castle; right in the middle. All the other rooms have been built around it later on. I think it's probably one ffflocking great big chimney.'

Penny stretched and yawned.

'I was wondering if Disco Bob was trying to use the chimney to get to where they're keeping the Christmas Star diamond, but there isn't a fireplace in the diamond room, and if the big hall chimney isn't connected to any other fireplaces, then that means there was no reason for Disco Bob to be coming down it.'

'Meaning he was *put* down it,' said Sandra Next Door.

'Precisely,' Penny agreed. 'Or pushed. Either way, he was murdered.'

'What did I tell you, Boy-genius?' said Jim, turning to Cameron. 'There was no need to take the man's clothes off to see if he was murdered.'

'You're very good at deductive reasoning, Penny,' said Cameron.

'Thanks, and you're very good at sucking up. What do you want?'

'I was thinking that as we're stuck here for a while, I might get my Santa present.'

Penny's heart softened. Somewhere, buried deep beneath the precociousness, there was still a ten-year-old boy.

'Of course you can. Jim?'

'Aye, wait there and I'll go and look for it.'

It was Christmas Eve, and in a snowbound castle on a small, Scottish island, a man in a Santa top and Rudolf the Red Nosed Reindeer underpants gave a small, lonely boy in an oversized coat his Christmas present.

CHAPTER 6

Gordon was struggling to see the road ahead. As the blizzard strengthened, the windscreen wipers became more ineffective, and the edges of the road were now almost impossible to see, obscured as they were beneath drifting snow.

He and Fiona had lived on Vik for long enough to be comfortable driving in most weathers, but driving in the dark, with the headlights performing no function other than to illuminate a swirling wall of icy crystals, was taking every ounce of concentration that Gordon possessed.

'Are we nearly there yet?' asked Fiona, shifting uncomfortably.

'To be honest, my darlin', I don't know where we are. I can barely see a thing, and what I can see, I don't recognise. We should have been at the farm road by now.'

'Why did we do something so stupid as to come out in this weather?'

'We were hungry, and it wasn't that bad when we left. I certainly didn't expect this! How's the tum?'

'The tum is sore. I thought it was Branston Pickles, but they shouldn't be sore like this.'

Gordon thought for a moment then checked, 'Braxton Hicks?'

'Aye, but Branston Pickles sounds friendlier. How near home are we?'

'I don't know. I wish we'd bought a van with satnav in it. Could you check the map on your phone? Maybe we can guide ourselves in using that, because I am not seeing any junctions or even roads in this blin drift. For all I know, we could be in a field right now.'

Gordon's heart sank when a moment later, Fiona said, 'There's no signal. I think the mast must have come down in the snow again.'

'Well, we're up the creek, then. We'll have to drive around until we see the lights of a house and get help.'

'We better be quick,' said Fiona, a note of alarm in her voice.

With trembling fingers, she switched on the interior light. Gordon glanced towards her, then followed her gaze downwards to her crotch and said a very ungordonlike word. A dark patch was creeping down the legs of Fiona's dungarees.

'Not the Branston Pickles,' he murmured.

'Not the Branston Pickles,' Fiona agreed.

'The real thing?'

'The Anglo Saxons.'

'The Anglo what now?'

'Jesus Christ, Gordon, contractions! I'm in labour. If I'm not allowed to make up my own rhyming slang now, then when the bleeping hell can I?'

In the blink of an eye, the reality hit Gordon that they were lost in the snow and about to have a baby. A real live baby! A proper one, with arms and legs and everything! Somewhere mid-blink, Gordon went from stoic calm to brainfartingly visceral panic. And that was the moment when things got an awful lot worse.

'The baby's coming,' Gordon squeaked. 'I don't even know how to breastfeed. Am I getting an epidural? What even is an epidural? Does it come with toast, Fiona? I like toast.'

'Breathe! In through the nose, and out through the mouth. That's it, you big bloody eejit. Slowly, in through the nose and out through the mouth. Gordon! I said breathe slowly. Gordon! Have you fainted? Well, that's just bloody inconven–'

Fiona lurched forward, the seatbelt cutting painfully into her shoulder, as the van veered to the left and hit a snowdrift. The soft thump followed by sudden silence was unnerving. For a few seconds, the only sounds were the short, shocked gasps of her own breathing, then a loud thunk sent Fiona's heart leaping into her throat, and she felt something give on the underside of the vehicle. They had been going so slowly that the airbags hadn't deployed. Which is a shame, thought Fiona, because Gordon really deserves a good whack in the face right now. He was currently leaning over the steering wheel, with his forehead on the horn, still out for the count. She pushed him upright, leaned over and turned the key in the ignition. Och, bums. Not so much as a polite cough.

She looked at the inert figure of her husband and said, 'Bugger. Do I stay here and hope to be rescued or do I get out and look for a farm? I don't know why I'm asking you. Jeeze, I hope you parent as well as you panic. Choices, choices, what to do. Fudgecakes, I'll have to look for a farm, and if I can't find one, then I'll bury all three of us in the snow to keep us warm until morning.'

Stepping out of the van, Fiona did a slight double-take as her foot sank unexpectedly deep into the snow. They must have gone into a ditch in front of the bank at the side of the road. Thank goodness for big wellies, she mused, walking round to the doors at the back. Now, how to get Gordon onto the sledge…

· · ·

Something smelled funny. A musty odour with a hint of... what was it? Fruity poo? And it was freezing! Maybe that was why his head was sore. Although it didn't feel like an inside sore head, more of an outside one.

Gordon slowly opened his eyes and raised a hand to his forehead, feeling the egg that had mysteriously sprouted there.

'Ouch!'

'You're awake, then.'

Fiona's voice came out of the darkness, somewhere to his right. There was a click and her face appeared, bathed in the soft glow of her phone screen. She set the phone down beside her, and he now saw that she was sitting on a hay bale, scoffing a multipack of Jaffa Cakes.

'Where are we? What happened?' he croaked.

'You had a panic attack, passed out and crashed the van,' she told him. 'We're at Gary and Lizzie Bield's farm. And no, you can't have a Jaffa Cake. You don't deserve one.'

'Bieldy's living room's a bit basic, like.'

'It's his barn. They're out and I couldn't get into the house to use the landline, so I've been waiting for you to wake up.'

'If I crashed the van, how did we get here?'

'I pulled you on the sledge. Tell you what, man, you need to lose some weight. Although, some of that was the shopping. I took a bag of shopping with us in case I got the munchies. Just as well! It took you so long to wake up, I'm on my third packet of Jaffa Cakes. I wouldn't be surprised if the baby comes out covered in chocolate, with a delicious orangey centre.'

'This is weird,' said Gordon. 'I've never fainted before.'

'To be fair, I think you also knocked yourself unconscious on the steering wheel when we crashed. A double whammy.'

Gordon rolled off the sledge onto the dirt floor and crawled over to Fiona. He levered himself onto the hay bale beside her and asked, 'Do you have any water in that shopping bag?'

Fiona produced a can of Irn Bru, telling him, 'This'll get your blood sugar up. I need you in peak condition, boyo. You have some housebreaking to do.'

'Why can't you do it?'

'Because the Anglo Saxons are coming every twenty minutes and I'll be damned if I'm having this baby in Bieldy's barn. On Christmas Eve, no less. This baby is not going to be a tired old cliché. The happy ending here is taking place in a hospital, with copious amounts of good drugs and a jolly midwife who'll cut the cord when you pass out again. Also, I tried and I'm too fat to get in the window.'

'Sorry,' said Gordon. 'I don't think my brain's working yet. Of course you can't do it. I'm amazed you got us this far. I should have insisted on taking you to see the doc when we were in town. I've made a right mess of things, haven't I?'

Fiona grimaced and clutched her stomach, saying in a strangled voice, 'Oof, we both have, and if you don't get us into that house, things are going to become a whole lot messier.'

Gordon scrambled to his feet and was surprised to find that his wellies were missing.

'Oh yes, I'd forgotten about that,' said Fiona between huffs and puffs. 'They fell off on the way here. I think there's some cling-film in the bag. Put it over your feet, and when you get in the house, borrow a pair of Bieldy's boots.'

'Can't I borrow yours?'

'I can't get them off. My feet have swollen. I've been sitting with them up, but no joy.'

Thus it was that a very anxious Gordon waded through the snow, cling-filmed to the thighs, and broke into Bieldy's farmhouse.

His first stop was the landline which, praise every deity that anyone had ever believed in, was working. Gordon's hand shook as he dialled the emergency services.

'Ambulance,' he roared in response to being asked what service he required. 'And make it quick. My wife's having a baby. It's definitely not Branston Pickles and the Anglo Saxons are coming every twenty minutes.'

That sorted, Gordon scoured the house for boots.

Fiona rolled off the sledge, through the front door and came to a halt next to Bieldy's slippers.

'I could have given you a hand, you know,' said Gordon, coming inside after her and shutting the door against the chill wind that was driving the snow into the front of the house.

Fiona lay on the floor looking up at him, grinning.

'My feet aren't working. I'll crawl the rest of the way.'

Gordon frowned. 'I'm a wee bit worried about your feet. I mentioned them to the emergency services wifie, and she sounded concerned too.'

He followed Fiona through to the living room and helped her onto the sofa, putting a cushion under her calves.

'Stay there and keep the feet up,' he ordered.

Fiona giggled. 'It's not *my* feet you should be worrying about. It's your own! Are they really the only boots you could find?'

Gordon looked down at Lizzie Bield's pink-sequinned, thigh-high disco boots and sighed.

'Aye. I think it might be karma.'

CHAPTER 7

'Colouring pens!' exclaimed Cameron. 'I asked for Black Holes by Professor Brian Cox!'

'Look, here, open this one. Embryo Richardson didn't come today, and I think she got a colouring-in book. It's got join-the-dots and everything.'

Cameron slumped back on the sofa, his arms crossed, and glared at Jim, who protested, 'How was I to know you were ten going on forty-five?'

'In my day,' grumbled Sandra Next Door, 'You were glad to get a tangerine and a bag of sweeties.'

'In your day, they used to send small boys up chimneys,' said Jim. 'Actually, that's an idea. We could send Cameron up the chimney and see where it leads.'

Penny eyed the flames currently leaping up said chimney and shook her head.

'Nah. His mum might get a bit annoyed if we return him as charcoal.'

'You're all very funny, I'm sure,' said Cameron. 'Assuming Disco Bob fell down the chimney straight from the roof, why don't we take a look and see how that happened? Clues and such like.'

Jim nodded and said, 'Aye, well, you're going to have to

wait until all the trousers dry out. Seeing Sandra Next Door wandering around the castle in her knickers isn't my idea of Christmas fun.'

Sandra Next Door, whose dignity was currently being preserved by the tablecloth she was sharing with Eileen, eyed Jim's underpants and snapped, 'I didn't imagine spending Christmas Eve with you flashing either, but before we go skulking around the roof, there's something you need to do.'

Jim looked bewildered, so Sandra Next Door clarified. 'Put your wet trousers on, go down to that kitchen and tell the children that Santa's okay. Tell them you had a wee accident on your way down the chimney, but you're fine now.'

Eileen nodded her agreement and asked, 'Do you think you can keep what really happened a secret, Cameron?'

'Who am I going to tell?' Cameron shrugged. 'None of them talk to me.'

'Good,' said Jim, then seeing Penny's slight shake of the head, he added awkwardly, 'Not good that they don't talk to you. I mean, good that you won't tell. Right. Kitchen. That's what I'll do. Go to the kitchen.'

He reached over to feel his trousers and, deciding that moist was fine, he slipped them on and stuffed the slightly soggy pillow back down his top. Not comfortable but provided none of the kids hugged Santa and got a whiff of damp dog, it would do.

Struggling to keep a straight face, he asked, 'Which one of you lovely elves would like to help me empty my sacks?'

Yawning, Penny stretched and said, 'I don't know about you, Rudelf, but I could really hit the sack right now.'

Eileen grinned. 'Yes indeedy, Gandelf. And I'd like to punch Jim in the balls as well.'

'I think you'll find that I'm first in the queue,' said Sandra Next Door.

'Very subtle, ladies,' said Jim, turning to wink at Cameron. 'Women, eh?'

Cameron looked away and winked at Eileen.

'Aw, come on!' Jim complained. 'A bit of male solidarity, pal.'

'Colouring pens and join the dots, *pal*,' said Cameron, a smug smile playing on his lips.

With a smile and a theatrical roll of her eyes, Penny stood to check her tights, which were currently dangling from the antlers of a stag's head above the fireplace. They'll do, she decided, unhooking them and budging Jim off the Santa chair so that she could sit down to stretch the things over her feet.

'Come on then, Santa' she grinned, 'If you're very good. I'll let you put your baubles on my tree later.'

The children were huddled together on long benches either side of the kitchen table, clutching steaming mugs of hot chocolate and helping themselves to marshmallows from three large bowls. An oil-fired range, set into what would once have been a fireplace, belched welcome warmth into the candlelit room and, despite there being nary decoration nor ornament, the scents of hot chocolate and gingerbread combined to infuse the air with the very essence of Christmas.

Anticipating the likelihood of alarm should the newly resurrected figure of Santa suddenly appear, Penny had asked Jim to remain in the big hall while she went ahead to break the news that Santa lived. Jeeze, she thought on the way down, some of these kids are probably going to need counselling after this, poor wee souls.

Mrs Goggins had drawn a curtain over the stairs to keep the heat in the kitchen, and Penny poked her head around the edge, whispering a sharp, 'Psst,' to Mrs Hubbard, who was sitting at the end of the table.

Mrs Hubbard immediately rose, took a torch from the table and slipped behind the curtain. Much to Penny's amusement, she was sporting a very fine hot chocolate moustache.

'Oh dearie,' she said, tears in her eyes, 'I'm so sorry about Jim. Are you okay? What am I saying? Of course you're not okay. Goodness, I remember when I found Elsie on the floor of her pantry. I wasn't okay for a very long time. And I wasn't even sleeping with her! You were sleeping with Jim, weren't you? Because I'd hate to speak ill of the dead by accusing him of fornication, just as he's up there explaining himself to the big man.'

'Mrs H!' hissed Penny. 'You're babbling.'

'Och, you know me when I'm upset or nervous. My tongue never stops. I was the same the day I married my Douglas. The minister asked if I takethed this man as my awful wedded husband, and I said I'd thought long and hard about it. I told him I wasn't very sure about the snoring, and I thought I might be okay with wet towels and underpants on the floor, but if this wedding was to be done that day, he had to get Douglas to make a promise. That's why my Douglas always looks so smart. He took a vow to love, honour, cherish and do his own ironing. I really hate ironing.'

'Have you been on the mulled wine, Mrs Hubbard?' asked Penny.

'A couple of wee glasses,' Mrs Hubbard admitted. 'Maybe three. Certainly no more than five.'

Penny took a deep breath, using the moment to think. Was she doing the right thing by telling Mrs Hubbard that Jim was still alive? What if she and Mrs Goggins were the Santa Killers? No, surely not. Oh lordy, what if Jim had been their intended target? Bugger, she should have thought of this before she even came down here. If Mrs Goggins and Mrs Hubbard were killers, they should never have let them near the children.

Another thought struck Penny. Oh, double bugger, she hadn't even told Jim and Sandra Next Door what she and Eileen had overheard! But there was no choice about sending Mrs Goggins and Mrs Hubbard off with the kids. In the heat of the moment, she'd forgotten about the two older women killing someone. In fact, what with the flaming corpse of Santa landing at her feet and then having to transport Disco

Bob's body to the Ford something something, Mrs G and Mrs H's conversation had completely gone from her mind. But it was alright, she supposed. Mr Black and Mrs Snipples were here to keep an eye on things. And, really, the two women weren't killers. Well, certainly not Mrs Hubbard, although Mrs Goggins was made of pretty stern stuff. Mrs Goggins might have bodies all over the place; hidden down wells and under flagstones like some serial killer, only with an apron and a special rolling pin that made Christmas tree patterns in cookies.

Penny remembered how devastated Mrs Hubbard had been last year, when she thought she'd accidentally poisoned half the island with bad ice cream, and decided that no matter what, there must be a reasonable explanation. She had to trust her friend.

'Listen,' she whispered, 'Jim's not dead. That wasn't him in the fireplace. He's upstairs in his Santa outfit, waiting to deliver the presents, but we didn't want to terrify the children. Could you explain to them that Santa is sorry he fell down the chimney and frightened them, but he's alright now? If they all still want to see him, I'll send him down.'

Mrs Hubbard nodded and handed Penny the torch, then slipped back into the kitchen. Penny waited behind the curtain, listening as Mrs Hubbard explained to the children that Santa's sleigh had hit a bump on the roof, and he'd come tumbling down the chimney by accident. However, what with Santa being magic and all, a glass of milk and a mince pie had made him as good as new. Any children who still wanted to see Santa could come with her, and any who didn't want to see him could stay with Mrs Goggins.

'Good idea, Mrs H,' Penny whispered into the darkness beyond the torchlight. 'I was going to take Jim down but far better to give the children the choice of going to him.'

'I'll put him in the entrance hall,' she declared, when Mrs Hubbard returned to tell her that the children were happy to see Santa. 'I don't want them to see him in the big hall in case it's traumatising. Plus, Eileen and Sandra Next Door are still in their knickers. Long story. I'll explain later.'

She rushed upstairs and ushered Jim into the entrance hall. Apologising to a suit of armour, she pushed it aside and dragged an enormous ornate wooden chair forward, before dashing off to the big hall to borrow some candles.

By the time the children arrived, the baubles on the tree by the front door were twinkling in the candlelight and Santa, with large sacks of presents either side of him, was installed on his throne.

'Ho, ho, ho,' said Santa Jim, smiling warmly behind his white beard. 'I'm sorry if I frightened you. Mrs Claus is always telling me off for going too fast on the sleigh and I shall have to tell her she was right.'

'Where is Mrs Claus?' asked a small girl in pigtails and a green jumpsuit.

Penny recognised her as the child whom Mrs Snipples had taken to the toilet earlier. In fact, come to think of it, where were Mrs Snipples and Mr Black? She hadn't seen them in the kitchen. What was happening in this place? All the adults were slowly disappearing.

'Mrs Claus is playing dress-up with her friend Ernie On The Other Side,' said Santa Jim, and Penny had to stifle a giggle as she recalled their conversation about Mrs Hay earlier.

'Now, when Gandelf says your name, come up and collect your present,' he continued. 'Gandelf, can you pass me the first gift please?'

Penny rummaged in the nearest sack and pulled out a box wrapped in shiny red paper. She read the name on the label and said loudly, 'Maybelle Smith.'

They proceeded through Kade, Kane, Kyle, Inaya, Merlot and Lian, all the way to twins Dingo and Tesla Bottomley, before eventually finishing with a flourish on Scaramouche Patel.

Jim beamed at the boy and asked, 'Can you do the–'

'Fandango? Aye, like I haven't heard that one before,' said the lad, grabbing his present and hurrying back to his friends.

'That's them all, dearies,' said Mrs Hubbard as Mrs Goggins led the crocodile back downstairs.

She folded the sacks neatly and handed them to Penny, saying, 'You don't need to worry about the children. They got a scare, but they seem to be fine. Mrs Snipples and Mr Black said they'd let the parents know.'

'Where *are* Mrs Snipples and Mr Black?' asked Penny. 'And I don't suppose you've seen any of the Deers, have you? Raine, Cara and Hamish have vanished.'

'It's very strange. Mrs Snipples disappeared for a while, too. She only came back just before you came down to tell me Santa was ready, Penny. That wee one she took to the toilet had to find us all by herself. Anyway, she and Mr Black went to see if they could get the minibus moving. Mrs Snipples, I mean, not the wee girl. Mr Black drove most of the children here in the minibus and Mrs Snipples took the rest in her car. They're hoping the bus at least can get through the snow. It's not looking good out there, though.'

'I phoned Randy Mair when we arrived,' said Jim. 'Asked him to come and plough the castle road with his tractor.'

Mrs Hubbard frowned and shook her head, her silver curls glinting in the soft light from the candelabra beside Santa's throne.

'He'll be busy tonight,' she said. 'The official ploughs will keep the main roads clear, but the tractors will be needed for the back roads. I wouldn't expect him any time soon.'

Mrs Hubbard shuffled off, following the tail end of the crocodile downstairs to the kitchen, and Penny turned to Jim.

'We're stuck, then. Not much to do but wait until Randy Mair rocks up on his Massey Fergie.'

'Aye, well, at least I can get rid of this pillow now,' said Jim, pulling the damp bag of feathers from under his top. 'It was making my chest fair itchy. I forgot to take a change of clothes. Do you think Hamish would lend me some?'

'We have to find him first,' muttered Penny. 'I think there's a fleece and a spare pair of joggers in the car from your last great five-a-side match. Let's nip outside and get them. On the way, we can ask Mrs Snipples and Mr Black if they've seen Hamish.'

Although it was dark outside, the latest blizzard had finally exhausted itself and given way to a pale moon which peeped from behind drifting clouds, reflecting off the snow and bathing the castle grounds in an eerie twilight. It seemed that the worst was over, or at least a temporary détente had been called by the gods, to allow the good citizens of Vik to regroup and clear their drives. However, there was no clearing the castle drive. The immediate area around the castle itself, yes, but the long drive up to its splendid gates, well, that was going to take more than a snow shovel and a bag of grit. Already, the tracks from their earlier sojourn had been filled, and Penny and Jim found themselves knee-deep, pushing through the thick, white powder.

They heard the argument before they rounded the corner. Drawing to a halt, they cautiously peered around the edge of the castle wall, unsure as to whether they should announce their presence or wait until Mrs Snipples and Mr Black had finished yelling at each other.

Naturally, being nosy, Penny and Jim stayed put and listened as Mrs Snipples said in a high, hoarse voice, 'Mark, you have to accept that it's over. Now that Joe's gone, I need to move on. Be free. Go on cruises and see the world.'

'For God's sake, Norma, it was fine to have an affair when he was alive, but now that he's gone you want to end it? That makes no sense.'

Behind her, Penny heard Jim snicker and whisper, 'Norma S–'

'Shh!' she told him. 'Just listen.'

Mrs Snipples was firmly telling Mr Black that she'd handed in her notice, and she was leaving the island before Hogmanay.

'Where? How?' asked Mr Black. 'It's not like he left you anything but debts.'

'I'll be grand. Anyway, my finances are no longer your concern.'

Mark threw down his snow shovel and shouted, 'Fine! If that's the way you want it, don't bother speaking to me again.'

He stomped away from Mrs Snipples, towards the back entrance, and she leaned against the minibus, gazing after him with what appeared to be some regret. After a few moments, she sighed and laid down her own shovel to follow her erstwhile lover into the warmth of the kitchen.

'Wow,' breathed Penny. 'It's all going down at Port Vik Primary School. I'm surprised Mrs Hubbard doesn't know about this. She's in there every Friday reading stories to P6 and 7.'

'Never mind the local scandal,' said Jim, rubbing his arms. 'Can we get the clothes and go back inside? It's bloody freezing out here. Maybe we should get away for a winter sunshine break. Join Mrs Snipples on her cruise?'

'Let's focus on getting back to Port Vik for now. Come on. The quicker we get you out of that Santa suit, the quicker we–'

'Get me naked?' suggested Jim with a cheeky grin.

'I was going to say, "Get to the kitchen for some hot chocolate." The thought of being naked right now…brrr.'

Penny shivered and dug in Jim's pocket for her car key.

'You're right,' laughed Jim. 'The thought of borrowing Mrs Snipples' big cardigan is actually turning me on.'

And so it was that, with hot chocolate firmly in their sights and all thoughts of teacher scandal set to one side for the moment, Penny and Jim ploughed through the snow in search of a pair of stinky football joggers.

CHAPTER 8

'Why can't *you* wear them?' asked Eileen. 'I look silly.'

'Because they're too small for me. Surely anything's better than wet tights and elf shoes,' said Penny.

Her car had turned out to be a treasure trove of useful, dry clothing, courtesy of the fact that she'd packed the Christmas presents in the boot in preparation for the big day at Jim's dad's house. As a result, Eileen was now wearing Len's new pyjama bottoms and gardening clogs, and Sandra Next Door had exchanged her damp jeans for what were, according to the packaging, "Multi-pocketed Action Trousers." Jim's dad, Ivor, was a big fan of pockets and Penny had hoped that these would go nicely with the "Multi-Pocketed Rugged Man Gilet" she had bought him for his birthday.

'Anyway, I don't know why you're complaining,' Penny added. 'Look at me!'

She gestured to her own zebra-skin leggings and novelty gorilla slippers.

'Mum dresses like a six-year-old on safari!'

They were once more sitting by the fire in the big hall, ostensibly taking stock of what they knew about Disco Bob's crispy demise, although the conversation had somewhat segued towards the sartorial. It took Cameron, tiny in his oversized coat yet quite possibly the only adult in the room, to bring them back on course.

Counting on his fingers, he said, 'So far, we have Mrs Hubbard and Mrs Goggins in the kitchen, discussing killing someone then bringing him down to be buried, and we have Mrs Snipples and Mr Black, who are no longer having an affair because Mrs Snipples wants to go on a cruise.'

Cameron looked at the others to check he was correct, before continuing, 'Disco Bob is dead. Hamish and Raine haven't been seen since around the time my classmates and I arrived. Cara was seen arguing with a mystery man then she vanished too. Mrs Snipples disappeared before Disco Bob came down the chimney and didn't reappear until just before Jim gave out the Santa presents.'

'Correct,' Penny confirmed. 'I don't think Mrs Snipples would have had time to kill Disco Bob, so she's out. I don't think any of us really believe that Mrs Hubbard is the killer, but I suppose we'll have to keep her and Mrs Goggins on the suspect list for now. Cara, Raine and Hamish are all firm suspects, as is Cara's mystery man. But I think the key to all of this is - why was Disco Bob dressed as Santa, and what was he doing on the roof?'

'Which brings us back to the original plan of going to the roof and finding out,' said Cameron.

'Och, we've only just got dry,' moaned Jim. 'Do we have to go back outside just because *he* says so?'

'Aye, we do,' said Sandra Next Door, 'so put on your big boy pants and suck it up.'

'I saw some wellies when we were in the kitchen earlier. I could go and get them,' Eileen offered.

While she went off to rustle up rubber boots, the others continued their discussion.

'What if Disco Bob was trying to steal the Christmas Star?' Penny asked. 'We haven't even checked to see whether it's missing.'

Sandra Next Door nodded and said, 'I think those security guards...what are they called again?'

'Noel Bowes and Jack Hughes,' said Jim.

'That's right. Noel and Jack. I think they'd be shouting the place down if the diamond had been pinched. Anyway, isn't it all supposed to be super-secure with remote alarms connected to the police?'

'No electricity, no internet, no phones,' Jim pointed out.

'Yes,' said Penny. 'Just people. If we're going to understand any of this, we might have to find out more about the people.'

Any further discussion was forestalled by Eileen, who returned bearing gifts not of gold, frankincense and myrrh, but of posh wellies, coats and warm mince pies.

'Here, Cameron' she said, 'Mrs Goggins even had an old pair of Raine's.'

'A good home should be judged by the number of spare pairs of wellies by the back door,' Penny declared, slipping her foot into a fleece-lined boot which probably cost a few days of her salary.

'Nonsense,' said Sandra Next Door. 'Coasters are a far better measure. They're used every day.'

'Are they?' asked Jim, a note of doubt in his voice. Jim had never been quite sure about the point of coasters.

Sandra Next Door shot him an incredulous look and seemed about to launch into a diatribe on heathens who don't use coasters, when she was interrupted.

Ever the peacekeeper, Eileen said, 'Sorry, Sandra Next Door. I know you have strong views on coasters, not putting feet on the furniture and scrubbing the front doorstep, but would you mind if we get going?'

Muttering darkly under her breath, Sandra Next Door followed the others to the entrance hall, where it became clear that nobody could remember the way to the battlements.

'Oh, for goodness' sake,' she said. 'There must be a map of the castle around here somewhere. They do get tourists!'

'I can't see any,' said Penny. 'Perhaps they put them away when the castle's closed. Where would they keep them? Jim, is there an office for the staff?'

'How would I know that? I'm Hamish's friend, not his housekeeper. It would be like me visiting Sandra Next Door and going for a wee wander round upstairs.'

'You really are a complete idiot sometimes,' said Sandra Next Door. 'You wouldn't get very far.'

Looking slightly hurt at this, Jim protested, 'I could if I wanted to. Like, if you were making a cup of tea and didn't notice.'

'I live in a bungalow,' snapped Sandra Next Door. 'Right, put that wee mouse to work turning the wheels inside your head. Where will we find a map?'

'I dunno,' said Jim. 'Hamish's library?'

'Tally ho and lay on, Macduff. We haven't got all night.'

'We did when you wanted to have a row about coasters. I can't believe you scrub your front step. What's that all about?'

Bickering with Sandra Next Door, Jim led the way to the library on the first floor. In daylight, it was a beautiful, wood-panelled room, the walls lined with bookshelves straining under the weight of hundreds of castle ledgers and carefully curated first editions. In the light from the torch that Penny had purloined from Mrs Hubbard, the room felt cold and spooky, the creaks in the ancient walls only serving to heighten the disturbing sensation of there being something sinister out there in the darkness.

'Can you feel the ghosties?' whispered Eileen, making Penny jump.

'Aye, well, they can bugger off and find someone else to haunt,' said Jim, shining the torch on Hamish's desk. 'Here's hoping it's not locked.'

The desk wasn't locked, and a quick rummage through the papers uncovered several maps of the castle.

'These must be what he sent to the insurance company,'

said Penny, shining her phone torch on a large, detailed drawing. 'Look! This one even includes the secret tunnels.'

'We should take that one,' Cameron told her. 'We might be able to use the tunnels as shortcuts.'

Penny held her torch to her face and smiled.

'Another good idea, young man. You're a natural at this detective stuff. Have you ever thought about taking up codebreaking? It has come in handy for me a few times, and I have a feeling you'd be excellent at it.'

'You know, I can see all the hairs up your nose when you shine your torch under your chin like that,' said Cameron.

Jim gave a short bark of laughter and asked, 'Can you see all her chin hairs as well?'

Before Cameron could reply, Penny batted Jim over the back of the head with the rolled-up map and led the way out of the library towards a narrow, winding staircase at the end of the hallway.

In single file the group climbed, feeling the temperature drop as they rose higher towards the battlements. The only sounds were the scrape of wellington boots on stone and the puffs of breath, quickening with every laborious step until, groaning, Penny pushed open a door and staggered onto the moonlit battlements.

Once there, she stopped dead, oblivious to the muffled cursing as those behind her stumbled into one another.

'What's going on?' asked Sandra Next Door. 'Why have we stopped?'

'There are footprints in the snow,' said Penny. 'Barely visible because they've filled up but look here by the wall, where the snow's not so thick. See?'

Sandra Next Door took the torch from Jim and shone it over Penny's shoulder.

'At least two sets,' she said. 'They've messed up the snow.'

Penny moved forward to take a closer look and her companions crowded in beside her.

'Larger men's boots, I reckon, and the smaller marks could have been made by shoes. Hard to tell if those are a man's or a woman's. You're right, Sandra Next Door. Two people at least. What do you think, folks? Should we search around, or should we back off in case Sergeant Wilson shouts at us for not preserving the evidence?'

'I vote for search,' said Jim. 'Another fall of snow or a strong wind and these will be gone. Take a photo with your phone and, while you're at it, take a shot of these marks on top of the wall. I suspect that's where Disco Bob went over.'

They peered over the wall to the slate roof below. The staircase had brought them out in the area closest to the centre of the castle, and the giant chimney of the big hall was almost within touching distance.

Eileen leaned over the edge of the battlements and looked down.

'A lot of snow has been knocked off this wall,' she said. 'You can see the uneven patch down there. There must have been a struggle. It's weird, though, because if Santa got stuffed in the chimney, he'd begin to shout'

'You girls and boys won't get any toys, if you don't pull me out!' sang Jim.

'His beard was black, with soot on his sack,' sang Penny.

'His nose was tickly too,' laughed Cameron.

Sandra gave a wry smile and joined in.

'When Santa got stuffed down the chimneeeeey.'

Giggling, everyone shouted, 'A-choo, a-choo, a-choo!'

With a spring in their step, the group busied themselves photographing the footprints, wall and roof, and brushing through the snow to find anything they may have missed.

'What's this?' asked Eileen, holding up a small, white, plastic loop. 'I almost missed it.'

'I don't know,' said Cameron, taking it from her. 'It looks familiar, but I can't place it. Do you mind if I hang onto it?'

'No problem,' Eileen shrugged. 'It might be nothing anyway. Do you want these three cigarette butts as well?'

It was with some relief that the group retreated back downstairs to the warmth of the big hall fire to examine their finds.

'I didn't get much,' said Jim, examining the blob in his hand. 'Just this frozen grey and white thing. I thought it might be chewing gum, but it's melting already, and it seems to be more liquid than gum.'

'That's because it's bird poo,' said Penny. 'Anyone find anything more useful than poo?'

'I found three cigarette butts, a crisp packet, a button off what I think might be Santa's suit and a bit of white plastic that I gave to Cameron,' said Eileen.

Sandra Next Door and Cameron shook their heads, so Penny sent Jim down to the kitchen to wash his hands and find some freezer bags for the evidence.

When he returned, they laid their bagged treasures out on the side-table and contemplated them.

'At least we know that Disco Bob was definitely killed up there and pushed down the chimney. By whom, though? And why was he up there in the first place?'

She spread the map out on the floor, weighting the corners down with sausage rolls from the buffet and ignoring Jim's grumbling about the "waste of a good sausage roll."

'Look on the map. Here's where the Christmas Star is being displayed. Second floor. There's no fireplace or chimney. There aren't even any windows. The only way in is through the main door or via the secret passageway, both of which are protected. I know Disco Bob had a reputation for being a thief, but this is quite a sophisticated job for him to pull off on his own. Perhaps he had a partner? Maybe they argued and the partner killed him then hid the body in the chimney?'

Jim slowly nodded. 'It's the only explanation that makes sense.'

'Yet it still doesn't explain why he was up there,' said Sandra Next Door.

'Maybe he just went for a smoke,' Eileen suggested. 'And a bag of crisps.'

'Dressed as Santa?' said Penny, a note of incredulity in her voice. 'The only reason to dress up as Santa would be to pass yourself off as Jim so you could move freely around the castle, provided you weren't spotted by the kids, of course. None of the adults would have challenged him. I didn't.'

'You met him!' Eileen exclaimed. 'Why didn't you tell us?'

'That's not the point. The point is that, dressed as Santa, Disco Bob had the run of the place. Och, stop laughing, Jim. Okay, I kissed Disco Bob. There. Now you know. And I might have…' Penny put her hands over Cameron's ears. '…sexually assaulted him as well.'

Eileen joined Jim, who was lying on the floor, crippled by hoots of laughter, and even Sandra Next Door cracked a genuine smile.

Ignoring the inexplicable behaviour of the supposed adults around him, Cameron leaned forward and picked up one of the bags from the side-table. He turned it over in his hands, staring fixedly at the contents, before looking at Penny and saying, 'I can't explain why Disco Bob was dressed as Santa, why he was killed or who shoved him down the chimney, but I think I know why he was on the roof.'

CHAPTER 9

Gordon sat cross-legged in pink disco boots on the Bields' revolting, red Axminster carpet, tethered to the plug point next to the telly by a metre long charging cable. His entire being was focused on the stopwatch on the phone in his hand.

'Are you nearly there yet?' he asked Fiona.

In response, she lobbed a cushion at his head and told him that if he didn't shut up and let her watch Eastenders on the Bields' big telly, she'd batter him to death with one of Lizzie's vile china cats.

'Honestly, what is the point of breaking into someone's house if you can't take advantage of them having a nicer telly than you?' she huffed.

Gordon paid no attention. The goings on at the Queen Vic were a mere side-show to the Hollywood blockbuster that was running on a loop inside his head. Each minute brought the reality of fatherhood that one step closer and, while his eyes remained glued to the little clock timing Fiona's contractions, vivid scenes of holding a fragile little life in his arms were playing out in his mind.

At the sound of a pained "ooh," his head shot up.

'Is that another one? We're down to eighteen minutes.

Where the bloody hell is the ambulance? It's Christmas Eve. People are supposed to be safely tucked up indoors, not needing emergency care and preventing ambulances getting to folk who are squatting in other people's houses. Have they no consideration?'

'Och, shut up,' Fiona hissed between gritted teeth.

The Bields' sofa was looking the worse for wear from her writhing and squirming. The dusky pink sofa cushions were positioned at awkward angles, and the wet patch on Fiona's dungarees had soaked through onto the one beneath her bottom. At the other end, her wellington boots had left marks on what was probably a very expensive brocade cushion cover.

Unable to ignore the urge to do something, anything other than be a bystander to his wife's discomfort, Gordon declared, 'That's it. I'm phoning Doc Harris. He'll give us an update on the ambulance.'

'They said they'd be here as soon as they could,' said Fiona. 'There's no point in…oooh…oooh…do what you like. Just don't talk to me. Can't talk.'

'Would it help if we sang a song?'

'What? What? Get out and don't come back for at least half an hour.'

'Kumbaya, my Lord, kumbaya.'

'OUT!'

'Alright,' said Gordon, hurt that his best efforts were being spurned. 'I'll be in the kitchen if you need–'

'OUT!'

Gordon hastily unplugged the phone and scuttled from the living room, leaving Fiona to groan through yet another nefarious plot to wipe out the residents of Albert Square. Gosh, she thought, all these murders in one little place. The scriptwriters are so out of touch with real life.

In the kitchen, Gordon had unearthed the kettle from behind a tower of unopened mail and was attempting to make them both a cup of tea, all the while mumbling

Kumbaya under his breath. He went through the cupboards, searching for mugs, only to discover six tea-stained specimens, bearing all the hallmarks of having once housed Easter eggs, dangling from a mug tree under a pile of clean tea towels. Despite Fiona's recent disinfection of the entire house, Gordon had always liked the homeliness of kitchen clutter, yet with the detritus of life covering every available surface, he reckoned the Bields were on the wrong side of homeliness and quite possibly veering towards hoardiness.

He cleared some magazines off a chair and sat down to make his call on the house phone while the kettle boiled. To his relief, Doc Harris answered straight away.

'What time did you phone the ambulance?' the doc asked, his clipped tones signalling that he was under some pressure. 'It's okay. I've got the notes here. You would not believe the night I'm having. There's been a crash on the main road towards the village and I've had to admit Ernie On The Other Side to the hospital. I don't want to think about what he and Mrs Hay were up to, but the Viagra played havoc with his blood pressure.'

'How long do you think the ambulance will take?' asked Gordon.

'It could be hours, which is worrying. Fiona's swollen feet and ankles could be signs of pre-eclampsia. Or it may be nothing, but I'd prefer her in the hospital. However, there's the crash, a suspected heart attack and a stroke ahead of you in the queue. Normally not a problem, but where the main roads have been mostly cleared, the back roads haven't. So even if you weren't in a queue, it's doubtful we could get to you.'

'Is there nothing you can do? We can't have the baby out here on our own. What if something goes wrong?'

The doc thought for a moment then said, 'I'll tell you what. Randy Mair isn't too far from you. I'll get him on the radio and send him over. He can take you both up to the castle in his tractor. It's only a mile away and he was going to clear the road so they could get the kids home anyway. You can stay there until Randy manages to clear a path to the main road, then we'll get you all to the hospital. The power is down out there, but at least Jim has some medical training.'

Gordon's voice rose an octave as he exclaimed, 'On cows!'

Unperturbed, Doc Harris said, 'He started off on people before he became a vet. It's the best I can do. Hang on a sec.'

The line went quiet for a moment then Gordon heard the doc talking in the background. It sounded like he was giving someone instructions. Eventually, there was a rustle and Doc Harris' voice was back on the line.

'Randy says he should be with you in the next half hour. Wrap up warm. It's not going to be a comfortable ride. Only a mile, but it'll feel like ten.'

Fiona was contrite by the time Gordon hesitantly pushed open the living room door.

'Sorry for yelling at you,' she said, gratefully accepting the proffered cup of tea. 'I'm scared. Have you any idea what it's like to know that in a few hours you'll be in the most pain you've ever experienced in your life, and it's inevitable? There's no escaping it? Then at the end of it, you're responsible for this whole other person. Forever!'

'The responsible bit, yes. I can't stop thinking about it. And if I could carry the pain for you, I would. God, what a complete scallydoodle this is.'

Fiona giggled, 'Scallydoodle.'

'Aye, I was going to say scunner, but it's a few levels above scunner. Nae sure there's a word for super-scunner. Listen, you're not going to like this. The ambulance can't get to us, so Randy Mair's coming by to take us up to the castle in his tractor. Jim's there and he's had some medical training.'

Fiona took a moment to absorb this then firmly stated, 'Jim Space is *not* looking at my fur china. Penny has enough trouble with him taking the mickey out of her about chin hair. I don't want a critique of my lady gardening or lack thereof every time we go to the pub, thank you very much.'

'I promise I won't let Jim look down there. I'll make him keep his eyes closed. Hopefully it won't come to that, though. If Randy can get the roads between the castle and the main road cleared, we should be able to get you to hospital.'

'Why can't we just stay here.'

'Fiona. This is me. Do you honestly trust me to help you give birth?'

'Actually, I do. You managed it before with the lambs.'

'There's a big difference, and Jim was there to help with the lambing. We need our friends. The doc's a wee bit worried about your swollen feet as well. If something went wrong, I couldn't cope on my own.'

'Okay, castle it is, then. But he's still not looking at the old fandango. Promise?'

'Promise. Now, come on and we'll get you wrapped up warm for this tractor ride. Do you think Bieldy would mind if we used his duvet?'

With a shrug, Fiona said, 'We've broken his window, trashed his sofa and you've ruined his wife's good disco boots. Why would he mind if we stole his duvet?'

They didn't have as much time as expected to get ready. Within ten minutes, the lights from a large tractor appeared at the top of the farm lane and Randy Mair tooted his horn. Gordon hurriedly finished scribbling the note he'd been writing to explain to Bieldy that he hadn't been burgled, then he bundled Fiona out of the front door.

'Leave the shopping,' he told her. 'Giving Gary and Lizzie the last packet of Jaffa cakes is the least we can do.'

With a note of defiance, Fiona said, 'Oh, I ate them when I was annoyed at you for singing. There's a microwave vegetarian curry there, though. I'm sure they'll be delighted with that. Hang on, I quite fancy a curry.'

Fiona made as if to go back into the house, but Gordon gently linked an arm into hers and guided her in the direction of the tractor, which was now turning in the farmyard.

Close up, the tractor was a beast of a thing, its size made

all the more intimidating by the snow plough attached to the front. Fiona eyed the steps up to the cab doubtfully, wondering how she could possibly heave her bump up there. She didn't have to wait long. Gordon had his hands under her armpits and was trying to boost her up. Her wonky feet slipped on the step and no matter how hard he pushed, Gordon could not get his wife up and into the machine.

Over the sound of the engine, a gruff voice said, 'You get in and pull. I'll push from this end.'

Randy Mair had jumped down from the cab and was putting a hand out to steady Fiona. He was a stocky, bearded man, with a practical nature and a penchant for home-grown tomatoes. In the summer months, Fiona and Gordon kept him well supplied from their own small farm, in exchange for the odd bale of hay for their growing herd of sheep.

'Get yourself into the pillion seat and pull,' Randy instructed. 'Fiona, I'm going to put my hands on your bum. Don't tell Mrs Mair or she'll be asking me to feel her bum as well.'

Between them, Gordon and Randy manhandled Fiona into the cab until she found herself sitting on Gordon's knee. This suited her fine. She didn't think there was room for Gordon to sit on her knee and, anyway, he made for quite a comfy seat. For his part, Gordon wrapped his arms around her and braced for both of them as Randy slowly manoeuvred the tractor back down the lane.

It was a long, bumpy ride. Fiona leaned forward, fascinated by the mounds of snow being cleared in front of them, piled high at the sides of the road so as to almost form a tunnel. Randy was silent, focusing all his attention on the road ahead, and Gordon was desperately clinging on to Fiona, who was uncontrollably bouncing around on his knee and crushing his bladder.

He winced as Fiona landed particularly hard on his stomach, her bottom pushing deep into his groin. For a second, he thought they must have hit a deep snowdrift, but feeling her stiffen, he realised that another contraction was starting. He leaned forward to reassure her just as she threw her head back to moan. And crack! The back of Fiona's head collided with the bridge of Gordon's nose. Instantly, he felt something give and blood began to stream into his mouth. Oblivious, Fiona flailed wildly, groaning in pain. Randy Mair remained silent, his eyes fixed on the road ahead, an oasis of calm despite the turbulence to his left.

With one hand holding onto his nose, trying to stem the bleeding, and the other hand grappling with the duvet wrapped around his bouncing wife, Gordon silently prayed for this nightmare to be over. This was a million miles from how he'd imagined the birthing experience. Even a forceps delivery on the moon with the Clangers for bloody midwives was closer to what he'd imagined than this. He knew that any story anyone ever told him in future would always be trumped by the time Fiona broke his nose in a tractor whilst giving birth. Gordon had this story in his back pocket for every time he went to the pub for at least the next year. Which would probably be zero times, he realised, now that there was going to be a miniature blend of themselves running them ragged.

It was with an enormous sense of relief that they finally reached the castle. Randy switched off the ignition then turned the cab light on, and Gordon realised that anything he had written to assure Bieldy of the swift return of his duvet was now a lie. Unable to fish a handkerchief out of his pocket to mop up the blood, Gordon had resorted to burying his face in Fiona's back. The result was quite alarming, and he hoped that Bieldy had a spare because this duvet was beyond saving.

'Ah dink you broke ma dose,' he told Fiona. He could feel it swelling already and breathing through his mouth was now the only option.

Randy helped Fiona down from the cab then put out a

hand to steady Gordon, wincing as he saw the state of his face.

'Aw, man,' he said.

'Aye,' Gordon replied.

'But you canna…'

'Doh, I cadda.'

'How will you…?'

'I wod't.'

'Nae even…?'

'Sad.'

'Aye.'

'How long…?'

'A wee whilie.'

'A thochtie?'

'A puckle.'

'Och.'

'Ye ken.'

'Aye, I ked.'

'What was that all about?' Fiona asked after Randy had gone.

Gordon was hauling her up the castle steps and couldn't answer until they had stumbled through the front door.

'He was sorry for ba dose, and we agreed I couldn't boan about it coz you're going through butch harder ting. I said I couldn't sing Kubaya for da baby den he said he'd probably be back in a couple of hours. Den he said good luck wid da baby.'

'I have no idea what you were talking about then and I have no idea what you're talking about now,' said Fiona. 'Now, help me to somewhere warm and comfortable please.'

Gordon supported Fiona through to the big hall, where he expected to be greeted by the noise of a party in full flow. He was, however, disconcerted to find the hall empty. By the fireplace, three pairs of trousers hung on the backs of chairs and, above them, two pairs of tights dangled from the antlers of a glassy-eyed stag.

'Okay, this is weird,' he said, settling Fiona onto the sofa. 'Where is everyone?'

Clutching her belly, Fiona grimaced and replied, 'I don't know, but you better find them. The Anglo Saxons are here again, and it doesn't feel like five minutes since their last visit.'

CHAPTER 10

'Well, bugger me with a sprig of holly,' said Jim. 'A drone? That wee bit of plastic comes from a drone?'

Cameron nodded enthusiastically and said, 'I expect that once the snow melts, we'll find more pieces. Judging by this one, it's unlikely that the drone was stable enough to fly very far.'

'Or maybe whoever killed Disco Bob used the drone to smash him over the head,' Eileen suggested.

'I'm not going out to the garage to check this,' said Penny, 'but when we removed his hat earlier, there were no obvious head injuries. Anyway, it doesn't really matter...well, it does to Disco Bob, obviously. We know Bob was killed then put down the chimney. We think he had a partner. Is it possible that he and his partner stole the Christmas Star diamond and were going to fly it out of here using a drone? One of them crashed the drone, they argued and then the partner killed Disco Bob?'

Sandra Next Door slow clapped. 'Good theory, except we don't have any evidence that the diamond has been stolen. But let's assume it has. Who is Disco Bob's partner?'

Jim thought for a moment about the timeline then said,

'Och, it's no use. We need a pen and a big bit of paper to work out who was where and when.'

Penny flipped the map over and Sandra Next Door dug in her handbag, producing an expensive pen. She warned Jim that if he ruined it, she really would shove holly where the sun didn't shine.

'Aye, well, you know how to keep a man on his toes…or is it his knees?' Jim said, removing the pen lid and sketching a grid on the back of the map. 'Last time anyone saw Disco Bob was about the time the kids arrived, so let's call that zero hour. The next time we saw him was just over an hour later when he made his dramatic entrance. We know who was missing from the party.

Jim completed the grid to show the known locations of everyone in the period between Disco Bob's disappearance and reappearance.

'Mrs Hubbard and Mrs Goggins would only have had about twenty minutes, maybe half an hour, between the time Mrs Hubbard left the big hall and when Penny and Eileen heard them talking in the kitchen. Not much time to steal a diamond then kill Disco Bob. Also, neither of them would know a drone if it landed on their heads. Hamish and Raine would have had about an hour to do the dirty deed, but what would be the motive?'

'Exactly,' said Penny. 'All three of them own it…well, technically Raine's the heir. Hamish could take it any time he wants without resorting to plots and violence. Raine's mum is popstar rich, and Hamish isn't doing too badly either, so there's no financial motive.'

'Which only leaves Cara and your mystery man unaccounted for,' said Cameron.

'Both of whom do have a motive, Penny agreed. 'If the mystery man was pressuring Cara into giving him money for some reason, then she might have resorted to stealing the diamond.'

Eileen, who had been quietly listening and trying to make

the pieces fit together in her mind, said, 'The only problem is that Cara and the mystery man would have to plot in advance with Disco Bob, and if they were having this conversation about money after he disappeared, then it doesn't sound like they were in league with him.'

'You're right,' said Penny despondently. 'That's everyone ruled out, then. We're back to square one. But Disco Bob must have sneaked the drone in using the big case for his equipment. How else could it have got here? He has to be connected to it, and there must have been a second person on the battlements.'

Losing patience, Sandra Next Door snapped, 'Much as I love going round in circles, I feel obliged to point out, yet again, that we don't even know if the Christmas Star has been stolen.'

Reluctant as they all were to leave the warmth of the fire for the cold corridors of the castle, everyone agreed that they should settle the question of the whereabouts of Hamish's diamond. Penny flipped the map over and checked the route.

'We won't get past the guards, and we don't want them to know we're worried in case it affects Hamish's insurance, so we should go through the same passage we used when we went with Hamish. It's quite twisty and there are branches going off here and here.' She pointed to two junctions where narrow channels veered off towards other parts of the castle. 'If we go left at the first junction, take the stairs, go right at the next and take the stairs again, we should end up at the diamond room.'

'I hate to be a party pooper,' said Sandra Next Door.

'That's not true,' said Eileen.

'You're right. I love being a party pooper. What about the code for the door? Didn't Hamish say he was going to change it?'

Penny snorted and said, 'This is Hamish we're talking about. He couldn't even remember his wife's birthday. He won't have made it his own birthday because that's too obvious, and if he couldn't remember Cara's, what are the chances he remembers Raine's?'

'So, what other date…ah! You clever girl!' Jim exclaimed.

Penny smiled and tapped the side of her head.

'Gosh, you two are total psychopaths,' said Eileen, her eyes wide with wonder.

'Do you mean psychics or telepaths?' Penny asked.

'Those as well. All the paths.'

'In that case, pop Dad's gardening shoes on, my lovely friend, because we have a path to follow with a lovely, big diamond at the end.'

Penny pushed her own feet into her mother's novelty slippers and shuffled off, map in hand, towards the tapestry in the entrance hall. Grumbling, the others followed, and soon they found themselves once more squeezed single file into the narrow passageway. Just as the door closed behind Eileen and Cameron, who were bringing up the rear, Penny held up a hand and hissed, 'Shh!'.

'What?' asked Sandra Next Door.

Penny listened for a moment then, hearing nothing, shrugged and said, 'I thought I heard a car or something outside. Probably just my imagination.'

Jim was in charge of the torch, alternately shining it to light the way ahead and shining it over Penny's shoulder to check the map. At one stage, he turned to berate Sandra Next Door for bumping into him and accidentally shone the torch in her eyes. This set off a bout of griping and sniping between them that not even Eileen's interventions could resolve.

The warmth of the fire in the big hall soon leached from their bones, leaving everyone shivering. In the torch beam, Penny's breath formed little clouds which quickly dissipated onto the cold stone walls that seemed to press in either side of her. Earlier, when they had travelled this route with Hamish, it had felt like an adventure. Now, navigating in the dark with only a torch to light the way, it was akin to a ghost ride.

Indeed, she could hear Eileen telling Cameron, 'If you're scared, hold my hand.'

'And if you're scared, you can hold my hand,' Cameron retorted.

'Thanks,' said Eileen.

Penny suspected that her friend was now firmly clutching Cameron's hand.

She stopped to check the map again, something in the back of her mind telling her that they should have reached the second flight of stairs by now.

'Are we nearly there yet?' asked Sandra Next Door. 'Jim, if you stand on my foot one more time, I swear I'll–'

'What? What will you do? We're stuck in a fffudging wee tunnel and…ouch! Penny, she nipped my bum!'

'Just be glad you weren't facing the other way because I would happily have nipped your…ouch! Penny, he stamped on my toe!'

'Quit it, both of you. Jim, shine the torch on the map.'

Jim, who had been shining the beam over his shoulder in a vain attempt to blind Sandra Next Door, brought the torch to bear on the map.

Penny whispered, 'There should be no doors between us and where they're keeping the Christmas Star but look over there.'

She took the torch from Jim and shone it into the passageway ahead, where a narrow opening had been cut into the stone wall. Quietly, she moved forwards, the others shuffling behind her, and pressed an ear to the door. Above her, Jim leaned in and did the same. Sandra Next Door and Eileen squeezed in beside them and Cameron crawled into the gap at their feet. Soon, all five were listening intently to the conversation in the room beyond.

'What do you expect me to do?' said Cara. 'I can't move the money until the power comes back on.'

'Which is why we'll both stay here until it does,' said a male voice.

Penny gasped, 'That's the mystery man! The one she was arguing with earlier.'

'Shh,' said Eileen. 'Listen.'

'Somebody's bound to come looking for me eventually,' said Cara.

'They haven't yet. Maybe you're not as important as you think,' the man scoffed.

'We should have gone looking for her and Hamish and Raine,' Jim whispered.

'We were a bit tied up with kids and dead bodies,' hissed Sandra Next Door.

Eileen put a hand to her mouth and breathed, 'Yes, but what if they've all been murdered?'

'It seems unlikely, unless Cara's talking to that man from beyond the grave,' said Cameron.

Penny could almost feel her best friend trembling beside her, so put a calming hand on Eileen's arm and whispered, 'She's alive. But I'd like to know who that man is. There's something about him...familiar...I'm sure I've seen him somewhere before.'

'What...who's that?' said the man sharply.

Penny almost answered that she didn't know but his face definitely rang a bell, when her brain kicked in and she remembered he was talking to Cara.

'Who's what?' asked Cara.

The man snapped, 'A noise. I thought I heard something. There aren't any secret doors in here as well, are there?'

'It's my dressing room. Why would I have a secret door in my dressing room? That would be seriously creepy. Calm down. Look, why don't you untie me, eh? It's not like I can go anywhere. We're all cut off until they plough the road in a few days, and you can't keep me here for that long. People really will come looking.'

'You didn't seem so worried about secret doors when you sneaked me into the castle.'

'Only because you gave me no choice.'

'You better pray the power comes on quickly and you can get me my money, or it will be the last time Hamish sees his daughter. Now, shut up and let me think.'

Beside her, Penny felt Jim tense and move his hand towards the door handle. Silently, she pulled his arm back and gestured with the torch beam to indicate that he should follow her further along the passageway. Cameron, Eileen and Sandra Next Door came behind them and Penny finally stopped when she felt confident that they wouldn't be overheard through the thick walls.

'Why wouldn't you let me go in?' asked Jim.

'Cara's clearly not in danger so long as she can't give him his money. But you were right – we need to check that Hamish and Raine are okay. It sounds like he's planning to do away with one or both of them.'

'Rescue Hamish and Raine then go back for Cara?' asked Jim.

'Something like that,' said Penny. 'This place is too big for us to easily find them. We need help.'

'What are you suggesting?' asked Sandra Next Door. 'We get the kids to run around the place looking for them?'

'No,' Penny sighed. 'There are five of us, two security guards, two teachers, Mrs Goggins and Mrs Hubbard. I'm saying double our numbers. Leave the kids with one of the teachers, split up and start looking.'

'What if the security guards killed Disco Bob? We never thought of that before, did we?' asked Cameron.

'Gosh, you're right,' said Penny. 'But why would they?'

Somewhere in the dark, Cameron thought for a moment then shrugged, saying, 'How should I know? I'm only ten.'

'Aye, well, somebody killed him and, bugger me with a pig in a blanket, we need to rule that somebody in,' said Jim. 'You're right. Maybe they're his accomplices and they killed him. Maybe the plan was to slip him the diamond and get him to fly it out on the drone, all the while they're still standing outside the door, pretending to be guarding it so nobody can point a finger at them.'

'Then why kill him?' asked Penny, handing the torch back to Jim. 'They probably know all the alarm codes, so I suppose it's possible for them to steal the diamond, but if they were relying on Disco Bob to fly it out, killing him doesn't make sense. As the people who know the alarm codes, they'd be the prime suspects for the theft, so without Bob's drone, how would they get it out of the castle? Ooh, my brain hurts. Let's start by figuring out where we are and take it from there.'

She unfurled the map and pondered where they might have lost their way. She hadn't noticed it before, but just before they came to the second set of stairs, there was a small fork in the road where their passage cut left then met up with a second, larger passageway. They should have gone straight on but had somehow taken the cut through and were now in the second passageway behind the first-floor bedrooms.

She pointed at a mark on the map, about halfway along the second passageway.

'If we come out here into the first-floor hallway, the stairs there will either take us to the second floor, just outside the diamond room, or back down to the ground floor where we can recruit some help to find Hamish and Raine.'

'No way,' said Eileen. 'If Noel and Jack stole the diamond and killed Disco Bob, I'm not going anywhere near the diamond room.'

'Fair point. How about you, Cameron and Sandra Next Door go downstairs and organise the search? Jim and I will sneak back to the right passageway and find Hamish's secret door. We'll check on the diamond then catch up with you in the kitchen?'

Everyone agreed that splitting up was the best way to achieve both objectives, so Penny guided her friends to the exit before she and Jim plunged into the chilly darkness to find their way back to the original passage.

'You need to stop arguing with Sandra Next Door,' Penny told him.

'Och, normally I just ignore her when she's all spiky, but she's getting on my nerves today.'

'Yes, she's even more sour than usual. You have to remember, though, that she loves being in control, and at the moment things are far from being under her or anyone else's control.

'Aye, you're right. How about I just fight with you instead?'

'You do remember I'm on a short fuse today?'

'You're a feisty one, true enough. Do we have time for a quick…you know…because your thigh muffins in those leggings…ouch! What is it with women nipping me today?'

They bickered their way back through the cut and up the original passage until they came to the stairs which led to the second floor.

'After you,' said Jim.

'If you shine that torch on my bum all the way up…' Penny growled.

'I promise I won't,' said Jim, giving her a gentle shove in the right direction and promptly shining the torch on her bum.

He really liked her bum. He really liked all of her. Every single inch, from her dark brown bob to the tips of her surprisingly hairy toes. Except he wasn't allowed to mention the toes because the last time he'd made a crack about Penny of the Apes, she'd "accidentally" deleted his fantasy football spreadsheet from his laptop.

Their squabbling continued all the way up the stairs, turning into a series of whispered reproaches as they approached the secret door. It was only Penny's sharp squeal that brought the argument to an end.

'Look,' she gasped. 'Shine the torch on the floor. No, not there. By my feet.'

Jim directed the beam towards the floor in front of her.

The sight was so unexpected that it took them both a moment to understand that this was not a bundle of clothes on the floor.

'Well, bugger you with a soap on a rope,' said Penny.

She sank to her knees and pressed her fingers to the man's neck.

'It's Hamish. He's dead,' she said, anxiety and the tears instantly springing to her eyes causing her voice to catch in her throat.

Jim squatted down and handed her the torch, saying, 'Hold it steady. Do you mind if I double check your pronouncement? Here we go. He's very cold but…aye, you're not quite ready for the grave yet, are you pal? I have a pulse. He's just unconscious.'

He rolled Hamish into the recovery position, noting with some concern the bruising on the man's neck and the blood matting his hair.

'Somebody has either strangled him or hit him on the carotid. It looks like he's bashed his head on the way down and lost some blood.'

'We can't leave him here,' said Penny, 'and we can't carry him back along this passage. We'll have to take him into the diamond room then out the main door.'

'But the security guards…' said Jim.

'There is no choice. I'll get the door, and can you lift him? Or do you need a hand?'

'He's too big to lift in this narrow space. If you hold the door open, I can drag him through backwards. It might make his injuries worse, but so could leaving him here to freeze.'

Penny took the torch from Jim and shone it on the keypad. Mentally crossing her fingers, she pressed 1521, the year the castle was built, and pushed the door. Nothing happened.

'I thought he'd use something he could actually remember!'

'Try Cara's correct birthday,' Jim advised.

Penny tried it. Again, the door didn't budge.

Struck by a sudden thought, Jim said, 'Hmm, were the quincentenary celebrations delayed by the pandemic?'

'I take back everything Sandra Next Door ever said about you, Jim Space,' said Penny, grinning. 'Last try or we're locked out. One, five, two, zero.'

They both breathed a sigh of relief as they heard a soft click. Penny pushed the door and, holding it open with her hip, immediately turned to light the way for Jim, who was already slipping his hands under Hamish's arms.

With some difficulty, Jim dragged Hamish into the room and over to the rug which lay beneath the pedestal where the diamond was displayed. He rolled his friend into the recovery position and covered him with the Santa coat.

'At least he'll be warmer. It would be better if we could get him back downstairs, though. Do you think your mystery man whacked him? He obviously knows about the secret passageways, otherwise how would he have got out of that drawing room and followed Cara upstairs?'

Penny didn't reply. She had moved the torch beam upwards and was now shining it into the glass case atop the pedestal, where only a purple cushion remained.

'It's gone!' she said hoarsely. 'Someone has stolen the Christmas Star!'

However, there was no time for either of them to absorb this shocking discovery because, just as Jim was standing up to take a closer look at the glass case, the main door to the room burst open and a dark figure ran straight at them.

CHAPTER 11

Penny swung the torch around just in time to see the figure bowl into Jim. The man…it had to be a man, despite his weird gait…the man was being pursued by Noel and Jack, who were waving torches and shouting, 'Stop! Thief!'

Exactly who they were expecting to stop the thief was unclear, as when they spotted Jim and Penny they came to a sudden halt and looked at each other, confused.

'Stop! Thieves!' Noel cried.

Had there been time, Penny would have pointed out that if she and Jim were thieves, the only people left to stop anyone were Noel and Jack themselves, therefore yelling about it was pointless. She and Jim were hardly going to stand still and say, 'Oh yeah. We better stop ourselves.' Anyway, Jim currently had his hands full. He had landed on his back with the actual thief on top of him. Both were now rolling around on the rug, their flailing fists coming perilously close to Hamish.

Jim could feel the man's breath on his cheek as he tried to push him off. The man gave a grunt of pain and straightened, sitting astride Jim and pinning his arms to the ground. Bucking his hips wildly in an effort to dislodge his assailant,

Jim twisted his shoulders and managed to free an arm. The man leaned forward, trying to grab Jim's wrist, but he missed, and Jim used the momentum to grab the man's shoulder and pull him forward. One final buck of the hips and the man sailed over Jim's head, hitting the carpet near the back wall.

Stunned, the man staggered to his feet then held up an arm to fend off a punch from Jim, who had sprung up from the floor in an adrenaline-fuelled frenzy and come charging towards him. As the man jumped back, his head bounced off the gilt frame of a large oil painting and he stumbled to the side, once more bringing the fight closer to where Penny stood guarding Hamish. The man swung a fist at Jim, catching him on the ear while, simultaneously, Jim landed a sharp kick on his opponent's knee. Again, they both went down, hitting the carpet with such force that Penny could feel the thud in the floorboards beneath her feet.

Jim quickly rolled onto his knees and grabbed the thief's shin. His punch, aimed between the squirming man's legs, missed and hit his thigh. With surprising strength, the thief lashed out with his uninjured leg, catching Jim in the chest with his foot. Jim winced as he felt something sharp against his skin. Jeeze, what was the man wearing? Did he have on those spy shoes with a concealed knife? The fear that he might have been stabbed swooped through Jim's guts, so he let go of the man, scrambling backwards to check if his chest was bleeding.

The man, meanwhile, rolled over, panting and howling, 'Ooh, dead leg, dead leg.'

Penny squatted down, shining her torch on the thief's face, and for what felt like the fortieth time that evening, she gave a shocked gasp.

'Gordon?'

Jim, full of adrenaline and oblivious to everything but the fight, had discovered that he wasn't bleeding so was getting ready to launch himself at the man.

Just as Noel and Jack moved forward to join in, Penny shouted, 'Get back!'

She flung herself over Gordon to protect him from the three men, screaming at them all to stop. Beside her, Hamish gave a small grunt and began to gently snore.

'Noel, Jack, it's Penny and Jim,' she shouted, turning the torch beam on her own face. 'We met you earlier when we were with Hamish.'

For good measure, she shone the light on Hamish, who snored on, oblivious to the mayhem around him.

Noel and Jack stopped. Jim stopped. Gordon peered out from under Penny's left breast. Everyone looked at the supine figure of Hamish and there was a moment's silence while they all tried to figure out just what was going on.

'You better not have hurt the boss,' Jack growled.

'We didn't,' Penny hurriedly assured him. 'We found him unconscious outside the secret door and brought him in here.'

'What were you two doing sneaking around? Come to steal the diamond? Think you can get pally with the Laird then come in the back door and nick his crown jewels?'

'We didn't steal anything. Look, it's a long story. Somebody killed Disco Bob, the party DJ, then we found some evidence that he and someone else might have been planning to steal the Christmas Star, so we came up here to check if it was okay.'

'You could have come through the main door,' Noel pointed out.

'We couldn't because we thought you might be the killers. Or the thieves. Sorry.'

Penny had the grace to look slightly shamefaced.

'And even if you weren't,' she continued, 'it wouldn't look good for Hamish's insurance if anyone found out there was a plot to steal the diamond. Anyway, you're probably not the thieves, otherwise why chase poor Gordon here.'

From somewhere under her left breast came a muffled voice.

'If I wanded do suffocate do deaf, dis would be a great way do go. Bud Fioda is havig aglo saxods so would like to keep breeding, dank you.'

Penny rolled off him and said, 'Fiona's having what?'

'Da baby,' said Gordon.

'Why didn't you say so before? And why's your nose all wonky?' Penny asked.

'And why are you wearing ladies disco boots?' Jim wanted to know. 'You poked a hole clean through my t-shirt. I thought I was a goner.'

'Crashed in sdow. Lost wellies. Broke indo Bieldy's farm. Dese were odly boods in house. Raddy Mair came in dracdor. Drove here. Fioda head budded me. Left her id big hall to look for you.'

'Who is this man?' Noel asked.

'He's our friend. Part of Losers Club,' said Jim then, seeing their bewildered looks, he added, 'Penny's weight loss group. Why were you chasing him?'

'We were just standing there, minding our own business, when this fat, beardy…sorry, pal, but you are a bit on the beefy side. Have you been skipping the diet classes?'

'Aye. Stuck at home for weeks wid da wife,' Gordon confirmed.

Noel gave a knowing nod and continued, 'Okay, so this, eh, stocky, beardy guy in disco boots with blood down his face comes pelting upstairs and running straight at us, shouting, "Peddy! Peddy! Jib! Jib!" and we think to ourselves, oh aye, who's this weirdo, so we try to grab him. Except he's a slippery bugger for a fat man in heels, and he gets past us and comes crashing in here. Have you ever thought about rugby, Gordon? You've got the talent for it.'

'And the nose for it,' said Jim with a wry smile. 'Let's get you back downstairs to Fiona and I'll reset it for you. Noel, Jack, could you help me carry Hamish down?'

Jack shook his head and said, 'Sorry, no can do, pal. We have to stay here and guard the Christmas Star.'

'Oh, there's no point in that,' Penny told him. 'It's been stolen.'

Even in the dim light, there was no mistaking the genuine shock on the security guards' faces. Jack looked like he might be sick, and Noel seemed about to cry.

'But how…what…when,' Jack stuttered.

'We've been here all the time,' Noel croaked.

'Then someone must have knocked Hamish out and come in the back door,' said Penny. 'The thief has what they want now, so you may as well help us get Hamish downstairs.'

'What if they come back?' Noel protested.

'They're hardly likely to come back,' Penny told him, unable to keep the slightly exasperated note from her voice. Then she relented. 'Alright, Noel, you stay here, and Jack, you come with us. You can rejoin Noel once Hamish is settled.'

This agreed, they made their way downstairs, Jim and Jack carefully carrying Hamish between them, and Penny supporting Gordon, who was tottering on his heels and complaining about his sore leg.

The sofa was already occupied, so they laid Hamish on the rug in front of the fireplace. In the candlelight, Jim could see that he hadn't lost a lot of blood.

He said, 'The only thing we can do is wait for him to come round. Right, Gordon, sit in the Santa chair and I'll reset your nose. Jack, can you run downstairs and ask Mrs Goggins for a plaster, cotton wool and some ice?'

Penny looked up from where she had been sitting on the floor beside the sofa, holding Fiona's hand and rubbing her belly.

'What are we going to do if the baby comes before Randy Mair can get us out of here?' she asked.

'Gordon and I did the lambing this year. We are experienced professionals,' Jim assured her.

'I'm not a ewe!' Fiona exclaimed. 'What if something goes wrong?'

'Then we'll have to cross that bridge when we come to it,'

said Jim. 'I have no experience of delivering human babies, but I have delivered plenty of animals. And I watched the one where Phoebe has triplets in Friends.'

'How very reassuring. I watched three episodes of Call the Midwife last year, so we're a room full of experts.'

Jim wasn't sure if Fiona was being serious or sarcastic so ignored her and said, 'Jack, can you ask Mrs Goggins and Mrs Hubbard if they know anything about midwifery?'

Jack rushed off to the kitchen, leaving Fiona, Gordon, Penny and Jim to quietly contemplate the impending birth. For a few minutes, they sat in companionable silence, watching the flames dance in the fireplace.

Penny was remembering her own experience of having the twins. It had seemed as though the hospital was full of people who all knew better than her; people who delivered clipped reassurances that it would be hours before the babies arrived and that she should go home and rest. Goodness, what a fuss she was making. For once, Alex had set aside his habitual avoidance of confrontation and thrown himself into the role of stroppy parent-to-be. By that stage, he had become quite a well-known actor, so it hadn't been a stretch for him to name-drop outrageously and remonstrate gloriously. Half an hour later, Edith appeared, closely followed by the much smaller Hector.

Penny smiled at the memory and recalled the aftermath. How shocking it had been to have these tiny people living in their house; to go from being two to being four. Sixteen years later, how heart-breaking it had been to go from four to three, she and the twins leaving Alex behind in London and seeking sanctuary with her parents on Vik. With a twinge of sympathy, Penny realised how hard it must have been for Alex to go from four to one, although he should have thought about that before he shagged the au pair.

She glanced at Jim and felt the now familiar sensation of being unable to contain so much love, as though her insides were about to spill over. There was an air of stability and confidence about him; a complete lack of self-consciousness and an utter trust that they were, as he put it, pals for life. It was this unshakeable constancy that she hadn't realised until now was missing from her relationship with Alex. Fiona and Gordon already had that. With those two for parents, this baby was going to be the luckiest child alive.

'And doat look at her faddy,' said Gordon, suddenly remembering his promise of earlier.

'Mrs Hubbard's?' said Jim. 'Why would I–'

He was interrupted by a poke in the ribs from Penny, who was pointing discreetly at a mortified Fiona.

'Ah, right,' said Jim. 'Don't worry. I've seen loads of fannies. I see Penny's all the time, and if you've seen Penny's, you've seen them all. She has a very generic one… ouch! What was that for? I was only trying to reassure the lassie.'

He rubbed the spot where Penny had delivered a particularly sharp poke.

'You're being very unreasonable today,' he grumbled, going to the buffet table to find a clean teaspoon.

Jack arrived back with Mrs Hubbard in tow. They were carrying piles of clean towels as well as the items that Jim had requested.

'Oh, dearie me,' said Mrs Hubbard. 'It's lovely to see you, Fiona, although I hadn't expected things to turn out like this. Don't you worry. We'll get you through it.'

Gratefully, Fiona squeezed Mrs Hubbard's hand and said, 'I knew that if anyone had some midwifery experience it would be you, Mrs H.'

'It certainly is. I've watched all the episodes of One Born Every Minute. Goodness, did you see the one where the baby came out needing–'

'Mrs H!' said Penny, seeing the look of dawning horror on Fiona's face.

'Sorry, dearie,' said Mrs Hubbard. 'I just get carried away sometimes. I'm sure it will all be fine. Would you like me to take a look…erm…down there?'

'What would you be looking for?' Fiona asked.

'Not a clue,' said Mrs Hubbard cheerfully. 'They didn't cover the detail on the telly, but I know that a lot of looking down there goes on, and I thought it might put your mind at rest.'

'What? You taking a gander at the old fandango for absolutely no reason at all? What is it with you people?'

'Okay, when you put it that way, I can see why you might not be too keen on the idea. Anyway, my Douglas is a dab hand at the old fandango. Sometimes he gets his castanets out and…oh, listen to me. I'm off again. Sorry, you know what I'm like. Paula McAndrew from the newsagents is exactly the same. We've both said it. When our tongues start, they just can't stop. And then there's Mrs Mitchell from the dairy. Goodness, I heard that the woman once gave a slide show to her church group and the minister slipped into a coma. They said it was a stroke, but personally…och, there I go again. Chatter, chatter, chatter. How far apart are your pains, dearie?'

'No idea,' said Fiona. 'Gordon hasn't been here to time them and I had a wee snooze while I was waiting for him to get back.'

Everyone looked at Gordon, who was sitting in the Santa Chair with the end of a teaspoon shoved up his nose.

'This is going to hurt,' Jim told him, pressing the teaspoon firmly onto the bone.

Gordon tried not to howl; he really did. Respect for Fiona's condition was uppermost in his mind for at least three seconds. However, the lizard brain kicked in and, tears streaming, he emitted a surprisingly high-pitched wail.

Jim withdrew the teaspoon and shoved a wad of cotton wool up Gordon's nostril, deftly applying the plaster over the bridge of his nose to keep everything in place.

Then a voice began to sing.

'Gordon's whining, Lord, kumbaya.'

'Shuddup,' said Gordon.

Fiona flashed him a wicked grin and repeated, 'Gordon's whining, Lord, kumbaya.'

'Shuddup!' Gordon protested.

But it was too late. Five voices joined in.

'Gordon's whining, Lord, kumbaya. Oh Lord, kumbaya.'

CHAPTER 12

They timed Fiona's Anglo Saxons. Fifteen minutes apart. There was some relief all round at this news. A tiny glimmer of hope, even, that Randy Mair would clear the way to the main road in time for the ambulance to whisk her off to hospital.

'Although at this rate,' Jim declared, 'It's going to be a pretty packed ambulance. Fiona's baby, Gordon's nose and Hamish's head. We're dropping like flies!'

Penny slapped herself on the forehead and said, 'Which reminds me, we need to start searching for Raine. In all the excitement, I completely forgot. Mrs Hubbard, have Sandra Next Door and Eileen organised everyone into search parties yet?'

'Yes, dearie, and I have some good news on that front. Mrs Goggins gave us some walkie talkies that the castle staff normally use.'

With a small flourish, Mrs Hubbard pulled a radio from her pocket and handed it to Fiona.

'That's brilliant!' Penny exclaimed, delighted that things were finally going their way. 'It'll speed up the search. We need to leave Gordon with Fiona and someone with the children, then everyone else can split into pairs. Jack, are you going back upstairs to Noel?'

'I suppose so. I like the excitement down here, but I better go and back him up. He's not good in the dark on his own.'

'We could go down to the kitchen and get you some candles and a radio so you can keep in touch with us.'

'I don't think the candles will help,' said Jack. 'Unless you were planning a séance.'

'No, I mean candles for light. Radios for keeping in touch.'

Jack smiled and said, 'I was joking.'

'I'm not,' Penny told him. 'Keep in touch. There's a thief and a murderer among us, and you need to be on your guard.'

Jim said, 'We all need to be on our guard. Right, one down, two to go. Let's rescue Raine and Cara.'

Leaving Gordon to tend to Fiona, they made their way down to the kitchen, where Sandra Next Door and Eileen hovered by the stairs, anxiously awaiting news of Fiona and the Christmas Star.

'She has a way to go yet,' Penny told them, 'and the Christmas Star is gone. But the good news is that Randy Mair has gone to clear a path down to the main road so that we can get out of here. Have you organised everyone?

Eileen nodded and said, 'Myself and Mrs Hubbard will start searching from the top then work our way down. Sandra Next Door will take the first and second floors with Mrs Goggins, you and Jim take the secret passageways and Mrs Snipples said she'd go with Cameron around the ground floor.'

'Cameron!' exclaimed Jim. 'Shouldn't we leave him behind with the other kids and Mr Black?'

'He's very insistent,' said Sandra Next Door, giving Cameron an approving look. 'I like a young man who knows his own mind. The ground floor is safest, and he'll be with his teacher.'

Reluctantly, Penny agreed, although she privately

wondered if Cameron would do a better job of staying to look after the children than Mr Black. Looking a little dishevelled, the teacher was currently nursing a cup of hot chocolate and telling a group of girls, 'Never fall in love. They just ruthlessly cast you aside and break your heart.'

At the other end of the table, next to Cameron, Mrs Snipples was studiously ignoring him.

'Cameron will be fine with me,' she assured Penny and Jim. 'We're going to have a wonderful adventure, aren't we? Do you think we'll find Santa's reindeer?'

Cameron gazed back at her then disappointedly shook his head, saying, 'I need to have a word with my mother about changing schools.'

Grabbing a radio and an old oil lamp that Mrs Goggins had found in the pantry, Mrs Snipples ushered her reluctant charge towards the stairs.

As they ascended the steps, Penny heard Mrs Snipples say, 'Our school is lovely. I've been there for twenty years and remember every boy and girl. I even taught Raine for a little while, although I doubt she remembers me.'

Beside Penny, Jim let out a short guffaw when Cameron responded, 'You're not a very memorable person and you wear too much beige. Now, shall we get this nonsense over with?'

Still smiling, Jim turned to Eileen, Mrs Hubbard, Mrs Goggins and Sandra Next Door.

'Go with Jack then split up,' he said. 'Whatever you do, stay away from Cara's dressing room. Jack, after we've checked everywhere, I'm commandeering yourself and Noel to help me tackle the mystery man. Is that okay?'

Jack nodded in agreement and was just about to help himself to candles and a radio, when Eileen said, 'Stop. We haven't agreed call signs for the walkie talkies. I mean, how will we know who we are? Obviously, I'm Winnie the Pooh and Penny's Rubber Duck, but what about everyone else?'

Jim rolled his eyes and sighed, 'Alright. Jack, you and Noel can be Angels One and Two, I'll be Charlie.'

He pointed at Mrs Hubbard, Mrs Goggins and Sandra Next Door in turn.

'Badger, Mole, Ratty. Happy?'

'But what about Mrs Snipples and Cameron?' Eileen asked. 'I wish I'd thought of this when they were here.'

'I think we'll figure it out,' said Penny.

'Why do I have to be Ratty?' Sandra Next Door complained. 'I want to be…'

She tried desperately to think of other characters from Wind in the Willows but could only come up with Mr Toad. She definitely didn't want to be Mr Toad.

'Oh, for goodness' sake,' she said, reaching for a radio and a stout candle. 'Let's just get on with it.'

Mrs Hubbard, quite pleased to be Badger, patted her silver curls, tucked her arm into Winnie the Pooh's and followed Angel One upstairs. Ratty and Mole hurried after them, leaving Rubber Duck and Charlie to clear a space on the kitchen table so that they could examine the map more closely.

Penny said, 'We should decide where to start. Look, there's a tunnel that leads from the woods then goes underneath the castle. It comes out in a space behind the kitchen. That must be how they mystery man got in. And if you follow it up these stairs…hmm.'

She ran her finger along the map and stopped at the drawing room.

'There must be a hidden entrance in the drawing room! That's how he got out without us seeing him. I thought he used the dumb waiter, but he couldn't have. Mrs Goggins and Mrs Hubbard were in the kitchen talking about murdering someone, and they would have seen him. We knocked on all the drawing room walls! How did we miss the door?'

'You didn't check behind the fireplace,' said Jim. 'Look. This must have been a priest hole in years gone by, connected to the tunnel so they could sneak people in and out of the castle.'

'It also connects to another passage which goes up to the first floor. He must have used that to follow Cara. But how on earth does he know about all these secret passageways?'

'I'll ask him when I beat seven shades of–'

Jim paused, seeing Penny eyeing the children, a look of alarm on her face.

'–when I beat him in seventh grade piano,' he corrected himself. 'We will play so much piano that our fingers will hurt. Aye, grade seven piano. Big exam. Big, big piano exam. Nobody can do piano exams like me.'

'Alright, Chopin Trump, go and put your wellies on because we're starting at the beginning. The entrance to the tunnel is in the trees behind Hamish's garage.'

Neither of them was keen on the idea of a night-time stroll through the snow, but Jim retrieved their wellies from the big hall and Penny rustled up a couple of fleece jackets from the coat pegs behind the back door. The jackets were scant protection against the freezing temperatures outside, yet they would have to do.

On the way past the minibus, Penny gathered up the snow shovel that Mrs Snipples had laid down earlier.

She said, 'We might have to dig to find the entrance.'

'If we have to dig it out, Raine's not likely to be in there,' Jim retorted.

'For all we know, someone could have knocked her out, like they did Hamish.'

'For furnace's sake,' muttered Jim, picking up the shovel left by Mr Black.

'You can swear now. There are no children here,' Penny reminded him.

'Aye, well, I'm in the fustigating habit of replacing my words now. I sure as shinty wouldn't want to accidentally offend some bar stool.'

'Mrs Hubbard would be very proud of you.'

'Mrs Hubbard can kiss my hairy donkey.'

The snow in the woods undulated, the deep drifts and shallow, icy patches making the uneven ground more treacherous than usual. Penny ignored the series of funks, fudges and fulminations as Jim tripped over tree roots, sank his boots deep into banks and, at one point, caused a small avalanche when he hit his head on a low branch. Shining the torch on the ground ahead of them, she carefully picked her way to the spot where the map had indicated that the tunnel entrance lay.

Only, it didn't lay. It was nowhere to be seen. With a sigh, she put the torch between her teeth and started to dig. Beside her, Jim did the same, and piles of snow soon stood high either side of them.

'This is finicking ridiculous,' said Jim, eventually. 'We could be here all night. Let's just go inside and start in the drawing room like sensible people.'

Penny looked up, the torch still between her teeth, and he shielded his eyes.

'Are you trying to blind me, woman? Is it not enough that you drag me oot in this frogging freezing weather and make me dig stuff? I hate digging stuff. You know I hate digging stuff. Remember when we buried Hector's hamster? I told you then that I hate digging stuff. And that was just a little hole. Though I like little holes. I mean, we could…you know…in the snow next to a castle, all romantic like, eh? No, you're right. Now's not the time. We have to find Raine. Did I mention I don't like digging? Why are you shushing me? And will you get that funnelling light out of my eyes?'

Penny gave him a gentle push to one side, ignoring his protestations that he'd report her to Sergeant Wilson for being a fornicating nuisance, well, not fornicating because that was clearly off the cards…was it? Her eyes were not on him. Rather, they were on what lay behind him. The dark shape that was at odds with the looming silhouettes of the trees around them.

Catching her stillness, Jim turned and followed the beam of the torch.

'Bugger me with a fondant fancy,' he breathed. 'That looks like just the ticket.'

On closer inspection, the shape was a small, hexagonal hut topped with a slate roof. Its sides were open to the elements, with green benches front and back providing a spot for the weary walker to rest and take in the wonders of Mother Nature. On a cold, dark, December night, however, the benches were covered in snow and made for a less inviting, more bottom-chilling, experience.

Penny and Jim made their way around the hut, inspecting the floors and walls for any sign of a hidden entrance. Jim felt along the sides of the roof for buttons or mechanisms which could be pressed, allowing a hatch to swing open. Yet there was nothing. A brief glimmer of hope sprang up when he touched something knobbly, but it turned out to be an old pinecone, one of many that they soon found littered across the floor and in the gutters of the hut.

Penny brushed the snow off one of the benches and sat down, defeated. Slippery ice coated the wooden slats, and she could feel it seeping into her thin leggings as it melted against the warmth of her bottom.

She said, 'I'm so sorry that I've wasted our time. We could have been indoors and warm, instead of this. We might have found something by now.'

Before Jim could reply, his pocket emitted a squawk and Eileen's voice came over the airwaves.

'Winnie the Pooh to Rubber Duck. Come in Rubber Duck.'

Penny plucked the radio from Jim's pocket and held it to her mouth.

'Receiving, Pooh.'

There was a long pause, then Eileen said, 'Is that over? Because you didn't say over. Over.'

'We're not going over–'

'Where are we not going? Over.'

'No, I meant we're not going...we're not doing this all over–'

'What are we not doing? Where are we not going? I'm confused. Over.'

'We've had this argument before. You get silly when I don't say over–'

'Don't say what? Over.'

'Never mind. What do you want? Over.'

'I just wanted to remind you about the radio protocol. I mean, about saying things like over. Over.'

'You told me about this last time we had walkie talkies! You need to get over–'

'I need to get what? Over.'

'You need to get O.V.E.R. yourself. Over.'

'So, are you actually over or are you just randomly saying over over and over again? Over.'

'This is Rubber Duck saying over and out.'

'Pooh out.'

Penny went to put the radio back into Jim's pocket then immediately cursed her numb, frozen fingers as she let it slip to the ground. Fortunately, the snow which had drifted into the hut provided a soft landing, and she quickly bent over to retrieve it, holding onto the bench to prevent herself slipping off its icy surface.

Suddenly, there was a soft click and Penny felt a rumble beneath her feet.

'What the flank!' shouted Jim as the bench began to sink into the ground.

He whipped his feet up onto the slats beside him and Penny did the same, the two of them sitting back-to-back as the bench descended.

'I must have knocked something when I bent down to fetch the radio,' she yelled above the noise of grinding gears.

'At least you found the tunnel. Well done!'

The hut stayed above them, only their section slowly descending into the darkness below. This is definitely not of the priest hole era, Penny thought, shining the torch on the glass covering the sides of the soil shaft in front of them. Some sort of weird Hamish project, she assumed. The man was a devil for anything mechanical.

Eventually, their strange elevator shuddered to a halt, and they stepped off onto packed earth. Penny shone the torch down a long, straight tunnel ahead, wondering what they would do if they found a locked door at the end. She'd left her elf hat and its bobby pins back in the big hall, and the only thing they possessed that might help was the innards of the fancy pen that Jim had forgotten to give back to Sandra Next Door. He would probably pay for that memory lapse later. Heck, if she broke the pen, they would both pay. Penny briefly wondered what revenge Sandra Next Door had planned earlier for Raine but shook off the thought and put one foot in front of the other, trudging down the tunnel with Jim quietly fussbudgeting and fulminating behind her.

Crouched down and shivering as they were, the careful shuffle through the dark tunnel felt like it had taken an age, so it was with some relief that Penny found herself facing a very ordinary door. It was the sort of back door one would find in any house on the island; solid wood with a small window through which one would normally see a welcoming light, but today displayed yet more inky blackness beyond.

Tentatively, Jim pushed the handle then, with a quiet hiss, let out the breath he hadn't been aware he was holding. The door opened and they were hit with a familiar smell. One they hadn't expected and one which worried them greatly.

Penny swung the torch beam around the room, seeking the source of the smell, before it finally landed on a squat shape in the corner, picking out the dark patch beneath its belly where something had leaked onto the flagstones below. For just a moment, she and Jim stood still, frozen in horror as the realisation swept through them.

'Oh, frock,' said Jim, 'This is really bad.'

CHAPTER 13

Eileen, Mrs Hubbard, Mrs Goggins and Sandra Next Door plodded upstairs behind Jack. Never one to let a silence go unfilled, Mrs Hubbard kept up a steady stream of chatter.

'So, there *I* was, wondering how she was paying for the new car and the holiday *and* the conservatory when, purely by chance, mind you, I happened to look in her window, and there *she* was, bold as brass, taking a half-naked selfie and putting it on this website called Only Fans. After I'd put the binoculars away, I asked my Douglas about Only Fans. He said it was something to do with industrial heaters. At least that explains why she had no clothes on, I suppose. What about you, Jack? Has anything interesting happened to you recently, dearie?'

'Just the Christmas Star getting pinched from right under my nose,' said Jack morosely.

'Ooh, I'd forgotten about that. Didn't you notice anything unusual. It's hard to think how anyone could have got in without you noticing?'

'We heard a noise not long after the power went off, but when we opened the door to look, there was nothing there. It was very dark, though and we only have the wee torches the security company gave us with our kit.'

Sandra Next Door asked, 'What sort of noise?'

'My granny has these old sash windows that are a bugger to open. It sounded a bit like them. But there are no windows in the room. We checked to make sure the diamond was okay, and it was still there, so we didn't think any more of it.'

'What about the secret door?' asked Mrs Goggins. 'I told Hamish he should have blocked the thing up like the insurance company asked, but he had to go all James Bond as usual with the keypad. Even had a spy camera fitted…only, I'm not supposed to tell you that.'

'A spy camera!' Eileen exclaimed. 'Why didn't you tell us before? There might be footage of the thief.'

Mrs Goggins shrugged and said, 'It wouldn't have made any difference. The thing probably stopped working when the power went out. The door has a back-up battery and, before you ask, I only know about that because he asked me to pick up a spare when I was in town last week. He had cameras installed all over the castle, and if they're still working, the footage will be stored on the box in the pantry. That's how I found out about the camera in the first place. We had an almighty row about him disrupting my kitchen with his wires. Why he couldn't put the box in the attic like a normal laird, I will never know.'

'I read a book called the Laird's Ladle recently,' Eileen mused. 'It was quite good, but the characters weren't very realistic. Not proper normal people like us.'

Sandra Next Door snapped her fingers in front of Eileen's face.

'Focus! Back to the point. Jack, did you notice anything odd about the door?'

Jack said, 'No, but you can have a look for yourselves if you like.'

It felt like a long way to the second floor. By the time they reached the top of the stairs, only Mrs Goggins was breathing normally. The others hauled their aching legs up that last step and leaned against the banister, trying to get their breath back.

With some grumbling over the prospect of more stairs, Eileen and Mrs Hubbard eventually peeled off to begin searching the floors above, while Sandra Next Door and Mrs Goggins followed Jack to the diamond room, where Noel was patiently awaiting the return of his fellow guard.

He said, 'It's been dead spooky here on my own. I kept hearing noises. Are there ghosts in this castle?'

'Don't be silly, laddie,' said Mrs Goggins tartly. 'As if I'd allow ghosts anywhere near my kitchen. Open the door and follow me. Jack, candles please.'

Jack and Noel knew when to argue and when to follow orders. And Mrs Goggins was definitely not someone to argue with. Even Sandra Next Door, usually so quick to quibble, seemed inclined to do as she was told.

They set candles around the room, the flames casting flickering shadows on the wood panelling. In the centre stood the plinth, atop which was the glass case containing the purple cushion shorn of its glittering bauble. Although the walls were adorned with the unsmiling visages of Hamish's ancestors, gazing sternly down from gilt frames, there was no other furniture to distract from the centrepiece or encourage the gawping masses to linger. This place was as simple as the public rooms got.

Sandra Next Door commented wistfully, 'I can't imagine what it must be like to live here. All these beautiful things. All the history.'

The awe she had felt upon seeing the diamond earlier hadn't left her. There was still a lingering sense of wonder that an ancient rock, compressed over millennia, had been transformed into a striking jewel passed down through kings and queens; that everything in this place spoke of both the permanence and transience of the past, present and future.

She ran a finger along the edge of the wood panelling,

inspected it and muttered, 'Mind you, it could do with a good clean.'

'Feel free to do it,' said Mrs Goggins with just a hint of sarcasm.

Sandra Next Door's face lit up.

'Really? That's the best Christmas present anyone has ever given me.'

Mrs Goggins looked at her afresh, realising that Sandra Next Door might just be the best ally she had ever made.

Her features softened slightly as she gave the woman a curt nod and said, 'I'll expect you in my kitchen on the twenty-seventh at ten sharp. Although I doubt the police will want you cleaning in here.'

They searched the room thoroughly, using the security guards' torches to examine the rug and floorboards. All they found were some suspicious pink sequins. Sandra Next Door slipped a few of the sequins into a freezer bag, leaving the rest for the police to examine later. Other than the door set discreetly into the wood panels, there were no signs of hidden entrances or places that someone could have used to sneak into the room.

She turned to Mrs Goggins and said, 'We better get on with the search for Raine. She's clearly not here and there are no clues as to who stole the Christmas Star. Daft of me, I know, but I'd hoped we could find Raine and the diamond thief. Kill two birds with one stone, if you'll pardon the pun.'

'Very apt, in the circumstances,' said the cook. 'Follow me.'

The remaining rooms on the second floor were laid out sixteenth century style, with large dressers, four poster beds and an enormous dining table dominating the tableaus. Mrs Goggins advised that this was "pure tourist fodder and a nightmare to dust." The rooms were an interconnected warren, taking visitors along a path that eventually crossed the end of the hall and led back through the rooms on the other side. With no locked doors or obstacles barring their way, the search was swift and efficient. In short order, they found themselves at the top of the spiral staircase which snaked up towards the battlements and down towards the first floor.

'The family quarters downstairs are a far more likely bet,' said Mrs Goggins, gesturing for Sandra Next Door to go ahead of her.

One of the best things about living in a castle, Sandra Next Door mused, was the turrets. As a little girl, she had dreamed of having a bedroom in a turret, although now that they were winding their way down the narrow turret staircase, she could see how impractical that would be. For a start, her Geoff would be catching his heels on the uneven stone steps and tripping up all over the place. Yet there was something inescapably romantic about turrets. The dream of standing Rapunzel-like at a window, suspended in a cocoon above a fairy-tale, was perhaps the only sliver of childhood magic that remained embedded in her world-weary heart.

Such gentle reminisces of girlhood whimsy, however, were soon brought to an abrupt end. She let out a sharp gasp as her toe caught something, sending it clattering down the stairs. Hastily skipping down a couple of steps, Sandra Next Door bent to pick up the object and brought the candle closer so that she could examine it. The screen protector now displayed a long crack, and the case looked a little more battered than it had earlier, but there was no mistaking what she now held in her hand; Raine's mobile phone.

'I don't know the lassie well,' she said, 'but I do know that she'd never be parted from her phone.'

Mrs Goggins nodded in agreement.

'Aye, as she keeps reminding us, she's an influencer.'

'Influencer of what? All the other people who swim in the shallow end of the pool? I'll never get these young ones with their Snapbooks and instant telegrams.'

Mrs Goggins enthusiastically joined in, saying, 'Exactly! And what about their journeys? They're always going on journeys. Sometimes I wish the spoilt brat would take a journey down to the kitchen and influence the dishes to get washed.'

She stopped, suddenly recalling that, given their discovery, Raine may no longer be in a position to influence anything.

'Come on,' she said gruffly. 'We'll start at this end of the corridor and work our way down. Third door on the right is her Ladyship's bedroom and dressing room. That's the one we have to avoid. Stay close and stay quiet.'

Mrs Goggins realised that she may have spoken too soon. With a loud squawk, Eileen's voice erupted from her apron pocket, her urgent call for Rubber Duck echoing off the turret walls. The cook fumbled the radio from the folds of neatly ironed cotton and looked at the array of buttons in bewilderment. Sandra Next Door plucked it from her fingers and immediately turned the volume down.

In response to Mrs Goggins' quizzical look, she said, 'I'm very fond of her, but it'll just be nonsense.'

'Aye, she's a new soul, that one,' the older woman sighed. 'Too good for all this malarkey. How did you know which buttons to press?'

'It's not my first time at this rodeo,' said Sandra Next Door, wondering if that was a real expression or just some random Americanism that she'd picked up from Geoff's endless cop shows.

Observing Mrs Goggins' curious look, she clarified, 'Losers Club is a bit more than a weight-loss group. It's also a magnet for trouble. This isn't the first mess we've had to clean up. And if there's one thing I'm good at, it's–'

'Cleaning,' said Mrs Goggins, slipping the walkie talkie back into her pocket.

The first room they came to was Hamish's library where, despite the clutter, there was very little to search. There may have been mysterious hollows lurking in the walls behind the bookcases, but without the map of secret passages, they stood little chance of finding anything.

The rest of the furniture contained few hiding places, offering only dust bunnies and a cache of unpaid bills. Despite the urgency of their search, the grimy disorder grated on Sandra Next Door to the point that it felt as though someone had raked a fingernail down her psyche, leaving in their wake the overwhelming temptation to tidy Hamish's desk. She could already imagine Mrs Goggins caustically telling her that she wouldn't find Raine under an old copy of the Sunday Times. Nevertheless, she subtly nudged a few letters into a neat pile and slipped the newspaper into her handbag. At the very least, Cameron could do the crossword while they waited to be rescued.

The next door opened to reveal, oh manna from heaven, a cleaning cupboard. This took slightly longer to search, mainly because Mrs Goggins had to prise a top of the range Dyson out of Sandra Next Door's grip and smack her fingers to prevent her fondling the neat stack of microfibre cleaning cloths. If Sandra ever went missing, she declared, they would all know where to find her.

'Because this is clearly your happy place,' she said, her voice strained due to the fact that she was dragging the woman bodily backwards into the hallway.

She kicked the door closed, narrowly avoiding trapping her companion's fingers, and it was as if a spell had been broken.

'Well? What are we waiting around here for?' snapped Sandra Next Door, striding purposefully towards the next room, which happened to be Raine's bedroom.

It was exactly as an eight-year-old Sandra Next Door had imagined a princess' bedroom to look. A white four-poster bed, draped in swags of heavy, peach satin, stood against one wall. The wardrobe beside it was so baroquely French that Sandra would not have been surprised to see it morph into Mrs Potts before her very eyes. At the end of the bed, an ornate copper chandelier hung above a peach, velvet couch, its crystals twinkling in the candlelight. To the left, a dressing table supported an elaborately framed, oversized mirror. Sandra Next Door picked up a bottle from the scattering of cosmetics and sniffed it.

'Chanel N°5. Very nice. I wonder if she realises how lucky she is.'

'I can assure you she doesn't,' said Mrs Goggins, bending down to peer under the bed. 'There's about three thousand pounds worth of handbags under here that she's never used. Hamish can never say no where Raine's concerned.'

Having established that Raine wasn't in her room, they checked the remaining rooms in quick succession, ruling out the other bedrooms and a living room, before finally coming to a locked door at the end of the hallway.

Mrs Goggins rattled the handle. Nothing happened.

Sandra Next Door rattled the handle, just in case Mrs Goggins had been insufficiently rattly. Still nothing happened.

'Do you have one of those keys? The ones that open all the doors?' she whispered.

Mrs Goggins gave her a sceptical look.

'A skeleton key? You're not in a weird murder mystery adventure, you know. This is real life.'

'With hidden doors, secret passageways, a dead Santa Claus who implausibly comes down a chimney and a missing diamond,' Sandra Next Door pointed out.

'Glad you see my point,' Mrs Goggins sniffed.

With no means of unlocking the door they each bent over to peer through the keyhole, seeing nothing but darkness. However, Sandra had not spent years living next door to Penny's mother without reaching forensic levels of nosiness. How else was she to curtail the worst of Mary's excesses? There was the garden shed for a start. She just knew that Mary had purloined some road paint and painted it yellow to annoy her. Every time Sandra's security light went on, the thing sparkled like a jaundiced Christmas tree.

Anyway, she reflected, a fine blend of intense curiosity and so many complaints to the local council that they'd installed a Sandra hotline – these very qualities meant that she trusted nothing and was relentless in her pursuit of answers. Innate abilities which made her a natural investigator. A shrewdness which propelled her to go one step further than simply peering through a keyhole. Well, that and the fact that she wanted to get one over on Mrs Goggins.

Preparing to make the Goggster eat humble pie, Sandra Next Door put her ear to the small opening and listened intently.

'What are you doing?' whispered Mrs Goggins.

'Shh!'

'Don't you shush me!'

'I will if I like. Shh! I can hear something.'

Mrs Goggins bent down to listen, her soft, silver hair tickling Sandra Next Door's nostrils. Yet it was no use. Sandra's ear appeared to have formed a vacuum against the keyhole.

Quietly, she hissed, 'What can you hear?'

'It sounds like…a trapped animal.'

Suddenly, the door handle rattled. Sandra Next Door reared up, her head snapping back and narrowly missing a direct hit on Mrs Goggins' temple. The near miss unbalanced both women, sending them to the floor.

'Give me the radio,' Sandra ordered, getting to her feet and pulling on the cook's apron.

Mrs Goggins had no truck with people who invaded her apron. She tried to pull the cloth back towards her, at the same time desperately trying to liberate the radio from her pocket.

Their frantic, wordless scrabble succeeded only in unravelling the apron strings, leaving Sandra Next Door holding a bunch of cloth, with Mrs Goggins suspended from the neck like she was caught in some gastronomically protective noose.

The door handle rattled again and both women scrambled backwards, staring at it in horror. Mrs Goggins freed the apron from around her neck and shoved it into Sandra next Door's hands, all the while shuffling back on her bottom, trying to put as much distance between herself and the door as possible.

Uncharacteristically heedless of the stitching, Sandra Next Door tore the radio from the apron pocket and pressed the button.

'Ratty to anyone. Help!'

Panting with fear and exertion, she waited for a reply. None came.

'Ratty to anyone. SOS on the first floor.'

Still there was no reply.

The handle rattled again and there was a thud on the other side of the door.

Sandra gave a frightened squeal and joined Mrs Goggins by the far wall.

Thud. Thud. Thud.

Louder and louder it became. But the door stayed strong.

Her heart beating hard in her throat, Sandra Next Door clutched Mrs Goggins' arm and said, 'We better pray that door holds because I think we're on our own!'

CHAPTER 14

'So, are you actually over or are you just randomly saying over over and over again? Over.'

'This is Rubber Duck saying over and out.'

'Pooh out.'

Eileen dropped the walkie talkie back in Mrs Hubbard's giant handbag and said, 'I think she's got the message. Good communication is so important.'

They were on the third floor, having agreed that they'd had their fill of stairs for now. The corridor stretched ahead of them, the walls fading into cold darkness. A faint musty smell spoke of rooms long fallen into disuse, and as they walked towards the first room, Eileen's feet stirred motes of dust which floated briefly in the candlelight before falling back to rest in the thick, red carpet. Perhaps months or years would pass before a new pair of feet disturbed their slumber again.

At this level, nooks and crannies abounded. The castle was a Disney-style affair, with turrets added over the centuries as Hamish's lairdly ancestors built up and out, each seeking to leave their mark for the generations to come. The higher one climbed, the more higgledy-piggledy the arrangement of rooms and hallways. In some places, unwary visitors found themselves heading downstairs only to go up again.

'It's alright, dearie,' said Mrs Hubbard. 'This is where the schoolroom and the children's rooms were when Hamish was a boy. A few years of the wee devil playing hide and seek at bedtime, and you soon get to know your way around.'

She led them to a room at the far corner of the building, set her candle on the floor and began to rummage around in the cavernous maw of her handbag.

'Matches, handkerchief, emergency cardigan, ooh two for one pizza coupon, sausages, och I wondered where I'd put the remote control…ah! Here it is.'

With the satisfied smile of a woman who would definitely be watching the Strictly Come Dancing Christmas Special tomorrow, she held up a very large iron key.

'When I knew we were coming up here, I liberated it from the odds and sods drawer in the kitchen. The fourth laird was a miserable old skinflint. Because the jail burnt down, the third laird added this floor to keep prisoners in what was then the top of the castle.

By the time the fourth laird came along, they'd built the new jail in Port Vik, so he turned this floor into the servants' quarters. He didn't bother changing the doors, and that's why all the locks have the same key. He also didn't bother putting any glass in the windows, so not only did the poor beggars have no privacy, half of them froze to death in the winter of 1603. Fortunately, so did he, and the fifth Laird Deer was a much nicer man. He put in glass, although he never got rid of all the window bars.

That's why the family don't use this floor now. Cara says it's too creepy.'

Eileen shivered, unsure whether her goosebumps were the result of the chilly air or the fact that she was standing in the place where the fourth laird had inadvertently slaughtered half his staff. Either way, she thought, I wish I'd said we would search the ground floor.

There was a stale yet slightly cheesy…Eileen could only describe it as a waft…when Mrs Hubbard opened the door. It reminded her of that year they'd gone to Spain for a week and Kenny forgot to pack clean underpants.

He'd worn his swimming trunks in the daytime and his pants in the evening, claiming that as they were only on for a few hours at a time, there was no need to wash them. He'd aired them on the balcony every night and been bitten on the todger by a mosquito. All the way back on the plane, he kept sticking his hand down his shorts for a good scratch. Which wouldn't have been so bad if it wasn't one of those flights where they don't sit families together. The cabin crew had to have a quiet word!

As soon as they got home, Eileen insisted that he go to the doctor, which was fortunate because Doc Harris had shaken his head and said, 'You're growing mushrooms down there,' before prescribing a giant tube of cream for the fungal infection and an antihistamine for what he called "the giant toadstool in the middle."

The toadstool had been out of action for a few weeks, and she'd banished Kenny to the sofa because of the scratching. It was bliss. Best sleep she'd had in years. When they were packing to go to Portugal the following year, she'd briefly considered hiding all his underpants.

Eileen's thoughts were interrupted by Mrs Hubbard, who said, 'You're looking very pensive, dearie. What are you thinking about?'

'How I can get Kenny to sleep on the sofa tonight.'

'Och, you won't have any problems with that. Penny told me his brother's going round with a bottle of whisky. And if you really want to make sure, look in here.'

Mrs Hubbard lifted her candle and moved into the room. There was no Raine, but there was rack upon dusty rack of wine.

'Hamish's father liked a drink,' she explained with a wink. 'The castle doesn't have a cellar, so he stashed his booze in here and told me to help myself. It's cheap old rubbish, though, and most of it tastes like ear wax.'

She picked up a bottle and blew the cobwebs off the label.

'Château Lafite 1787. Eileen, you speak French. What does that mean?'

Eileen thought for a moment, then confidently replied, 'Cat water the feet.'

'You see? Cheap rubbish,' Mrs Hubbard declared. 'Probably tastes like feet too. Och well, waste not, want not. It'll do for our Christmas dinner tomorrow.'

She slipped the bottle into her big handbag and led the way out of the room, locking the door behind them. Eileen was starting to suspect that Mrs Hubbard had her reasons for being so keen to search this floor.

They meandered up a few steps, down a few steps and through narrow passageways between thick, stone walls, checking rooms as they went. Most were empty, although Mrs Hubbard lingered in the old schoolroom for a moment, reminiscing about an exceptionally handsome tutor who had been brought in to polish Hamish's French one summer, before he was packed off to boarding school.

'Pierre was very ooh la la,' said the older woman, batting her eyes as if flirting with the ghost of a memory. 'Not a patch on my Douglas, of course. Pierre ate strange food, like smelly cheese and garlic sausage, whereas my Douglas ate normal things like haggis.'

Laughing, Eileen said, 'Buggre-moi avec les neeps and tatties. Sheep offal cooked in an animal's stomach! I can see why cheese and sausage would put you off a man.'

'You've been spending too much time with Jim,' said Mrs Hubbard sharply. 'You're starting to sound like him.'

'Sorry, Mrs H, sir,' said Eileen, picking up a piece of chalk from the desk and crossing to the blackboard where, with a wicked grin, she scratched the words, "I must not be rude to Mrs H (but I will be rude all the other times)."

Giggling, both women left the schoolroom and continued their search.

Each room was like a walk down memory lane for Mrs

Hubbard, and Eileen was starting to worry that their hunt for Raine had lost some of its urgency.

'Do you think we should hurry up?' she asked. 'There are another three floors to check.'

They were in what had been Hamish's childhood bedroom. It was like a time capsule from the late seventies, with orange geometric patterned wallpaper and a brown carpet. On top of the chest of drawers by the bed were an old Action Man and a View-Master. Forgetting her concerns for a moment, Eileen picked up the red box and held it close to the candle. Protruding from the top was an old cardboard disc with the film arranged in neat squares around the edge. She lifted they toy and looked through the viewer, moving the disc on as she watched images from Doctor Who. Tom Baker did do a lovely scarf.

She put the View-Master back where she'd found it and prised Hamish's old teddy bear from the grip of an emotional Mrs Hubbard.

'Come on,' she said gently, 'There can't be many more rooms to check on this floor.'

Eileen was right, there were only three rooms left to check. The first caused them both some alarm. All seemed normal until they opened the door and were met with a flurry of feathers and wings. Three startled pigeons flapped wildly around the room then made their escape through the open window.

Closing it with a firm thunk, Mrs Hubbard grumbled, 'I lost count of how many legs of tights I stuffed with newspaper to make draught excluders for this place when Hamish was wee. Yet he's just like his father. Always leaving windows open. He says it airs the rooms...but in December? And look at the state of this place! Who's going to clean up all the poo?'

Eileen tugged at the sleeve of Mrs Hubbard's cardigan, trying to urge her towards the next room, but succeeded only in dislodging a handkerchief, three packets of mints, a pair of reading glasses and a word search puzzle book.

'Cordon bleu, Mrs H! What else do you have in there?'

She ran a hand along Mrs Hubbard's bicep and felt a large, soft lump.

Mrs Hubbard pulled her arm away and said, 'That's nothing, dearie.'

'Och, away with you. That's not nothing. What do you have in there?'

'Okay, but you have to promise not to tell anyone.'

'My lips are sealed.'

Mrs Hubbard put her hand down her sleeve and pulled out possibly the most enormous bra that Eileen had ever seen. It was like a two-person tent from Playtex.

Eileen nodded approvingly and said, 'You could get your boobs and your weekly shopping in there. Excellent multitasking.'

'It's not mine,' Mrs Hubbard assured her. 'It belongs to Mrs Goggins. That's why she won't take her apron off. Says it's the only thing keeping her nipples from catching on the tops of her Ugg boots.'

Trying to scrub her mind of that particular image, Eileen asked, 'Why are you...why do you have Mrs Goggins' bra up your sleeve?'

'She called me out of the hall just after Penny went to check on you in the bathroom. She'd gone up to the tablecloth turret–'

'The tablecloth turret?'

'Aye, dearie, the turret where she keeps the tablecloths.'

'What does she keep in the other turrets? Is there a tea towel turret and an apron turret?'

'Don't be silly dearie. What would she need an apron turret for?'

'Fair point. Carry on.'

'The tablecloth turret is one of the highest ones. You can

see the roof from it. Anyway, she'd spotted David Meowie on the roof and…what?'

'Is that David Meowie who was run over by a milk float?'

'No, dearie, you're thinking of David Rowie who was run over by a steamroller.'

'Ah, right. I was wondering what he would be doing on the castle roof. Jim said they buried him in a shallow grave.'

'That sounds like the sort of thing Jim would say. David *Meowie* is Hamish's cat. Mrs Goggins said he was stuck on the roof and asked me to help her get him down. We leaned over the battlements and tried poking him with a broom, but he wouldn't move, so Mrs Goggins had the idea of making a sling. She thought that if we could coax him into the sling, we could lift him back to safety.

'He's a big bugger. One of them giant breeds, so we needed something giant to make the sling. And that's how we ended up standing in the snow, with me wielding a broom with Mrs Goggins' bra on the end of it, and her standing there naked from the waist up, shouting at me to keep my eyes shut and not to look at her jumper potatoes.

'That's when things started to go wrong. I was working blind, trying to coax David Meowie into the bra, when I accidentally hit him over the head with the broom handle. Mrs Goggins got quite hysterical, yelling that I'd killed David Meowie. I opened one eye, and there he was, quite still in the snow.

'At that point, all hell broke loose. We heard the door to the battlements open. I don't think I've ever seen Mrs Goggins move so fast. Actually, I didn't see her because I still had my eyes closed, but you know what I mean. She had me by the hand and dragged me round to the other door faster than you can say "there's a puss loose aboot this hoose." She put her jumper back on, I put her bra down my sleeve, and we went back to the kitchen.

'Poor David Meowie. We didn't mean to kill him. I feel terrible.'

'That explains a lot,' said Eileen.

'What do you mean?'

'Penny and I overheard you and Mrs Goggins talking in the kitchen. We thought you'd murdered Disco Bob!'

'Disco Bob? Why would we murder him? We couldn't even get a cat in a bra, so how on earth were we going to get Disco Bob down a chimney? And that's a sentence I never imagined myself saying!'

Despite all the trials and tribulations of the evening, Mrs Hubbard began to laugh. It started as a gentle snort and progressed quickly to an uncontrollable hoot, before ending in a shuddering, tearful wheeze that left her gasping for breath.

Between pants, she wiped her eyes and said 'Oh my, dearie, can you imagine it. Me and a half-naked Mrs Goggins trying to stuff Bob down a chimney. It's bad enough that we thought we could capture a cat with a bra on a broom!'

Eileen couldn't help herself. She caught Mrs Hubbard's mirth and, a moment later, the two women were clinging onto each other in order to stay upright as they made their way to the second last door.

'We need to get hold of ourselves,' said Eileen, in an attempt to bring them back to the seriousness of the task at hand.

'You're right, dearie,' Mrs Hubbard replied, dragging in deep breaths to steady herself.

They looked at each other, desperately trying to suppress the levity, and for a moment it seemed as though they might be able to regain their self-control. Until, bug-eyed and tight-lipped, Mrs Hubbard made a strangled noise in her throat and set them off again.

'We're terrible people,' said Eileen, once the laughter wore off. 'This is really bad. Anything could have happened to Raine and we're standing here laughing.'

'Has tonight been very stressful?' asked Mrs Hubbard.

'Yes, very.'

'Do you feel a bit better for the laugh?'

'Yes, much better.'

'There you go, dearie. No harm done. Let's see what's behind what feels like door ninety-three.'

Mrs Hubbard put the key in the lock and jiggled it. The door was stiff, the shifting of the building over the centuries having warped the frame, and both women had to push hard, throwing their full weight onto the wood until, with a loud creak, it gave way and they found themselves stumbling into the room, their momentum sending them careening into a wardrobe.

Mrs Hubbard went back to the corridor and retrieved the candles which, along with her warm reminisces, had so far kept the ghosts of Christmases past at bay in this chilly, deserted part of the castle.

The candles were burning low, their flames guttering slightly, but they brought sufficient light for Eileen and Mrs Hubbard to make out the figure lying upon a bare mattress on the bed.

The tiara glinted above Raine's pale face, and her skin was starkly white against the rich red of her party dress. Her eyes were closed, and she didn't stir as Eileen sank to her knees beside her.

'Raine, wake up,' said Eileen, shaking the young woman's shoulder.

There was no response, and Eileen pressed her fingers into Raine's wrist, feeling for a pulse.

Mrs Hubbard was looking on anxiously, and there was a moment where the world seemed to pause, until Eileen gave a tight, satisfied smile and said, 'She has a strong pulse. She's very cold, though.'

Together, the women searched through drawers and cupboards, eventually finding some thin blankets at the bottom of the wardrobe.

'As many layers as possible. It's the best we can do,' said

Mrs Hubbard, taking her emergency cardigan from her bag and gently spreading it over Raine's shoulders.

'We should call it in,' Eileen suggested. 'Jim can help us lift her downstairs.'

Mrs Hubbard dipped once more into the giant handbag and produced the walkie talkie. She stared mutely at the array of buttons and dials for a few seconds then silently handed it over.

Eileen said, 'It's easy. You just do the walkie, like this.' She took a few steps on the spot. 'Then you press the big talkie button, like this.'

However, before she could raise the radio to her lips, it coughed a burst of static and they heard a panicked cry.

'Ratty to anyone. Help!'

…

'Ratty to anyone. SOS on the first floor.'

CHAPTER 15

Resisting the temptation to remind Sandra Next Door that she'd forgotten to say "over," Eileen pressed the talkie button and shouted, 'Receiving. On my way. Over. Not on my way over. Just on my way. Over. Over.'

Telling Mrs Hubbard to stay with Raine, she raced along the hallway in what she hoped was the direction of the stairs. As fast as Len's gardening clogs would allow, she thumped up and down steps, through narrow openings, across rooms and, finally, down the spiral staircase. Aware that the gardening clogs were apt to slip on the smooth stone, she clung to the rope balustrade so tightly that by the time she reached the first floor, the skin on her palms was burning. Ignoring the pain, she made a flippity-floppity awkward dash in the direction of the screams.

Deep in the bowels of the castle, Penny and Jim were pondering their discovery, when the hue and cry crackled forth from Jim's pocket. Without waiting to check whether Penny was following, Jim broke into a run.

The small room they were in had two doors and he instinctively headed for the one on the right. He was met by impenetrable darkness. Recalling that he possessed neither map nor torch, he did the sensible thing; he stopped and waited for Penny to catch up.

She briefly considered telling him that the left-hand door led to the pantry but knew this would only lead to an argument about the time she'd directed him to Banff and they'd ended up in a field outside Portsoy, so she obligingly held up the torch and urged him forward up a flight of steps.

Trapped in the warren of passageways carved into the deep castle walls, they soon found themselves faced with a blank, stone barrier.

Penny said, 'I think we must be behind the drawing room fireplace. Try pushing it.'

Jim pressed hard on the wall, throwing his weight against it in an effort to push it forwards.

'Try sliding it,' Penny suggested.

'Stop back seat driving,' he grunted, although he shifted his hands to push to the right.

When the wall didn't move, Penny carefully shone the torch around the edges and spotted what she was looking for. There, on the upper corner, was a catch. Standing on tiptoe, she used the end of the torch to nudge the catch open and watched in amusement as the wall slid to the right, taking Jim with it.

They were in another small room, this time with stairs leading up. To the left of Penny was a pulley system with a wooden handle, similar to the apparatus she'd seen on the dumb waiter. Only this time, when she turned the handle, the wall behind the apparatus began to turn and the drawing room fireplace swung into view.

'This is amazing,' she said, squatting to step through the gap. 'You see bookcases and false walls swinging open like this in films, but I never thought a whole fireplace could do it. There must be a handle somewhere on the other side so you can open it from the drawing room.'

'Stop being fascinated and get your big bum out of the way,' said Jim, adding, 'Not that I'm looking at your bum.'

He was squatting behind her, trying to resist giving the article in question a friendly wobble.

They didn't linger in the drawing room, instead heading quickly for the grand staircase. Penny found herself jogging to match Jim's lengthy strides. He took the stairs two at a time, while she thundered up the steps behind him, silently thanking the powers above that they were only going to the first floor.

As they rounded the corner into the hallway, Jim collided with Eileen, and the few seconds it took for them to untangle themselves gave Penny a chance to catch her breath. Eesh, she thought, too many Christmas biscuits and not enough exercise. Well, there were always New Years' resolutions for that sort of thing, weren't there?

Then, as if someone had shot a starter pistol, they were off again, racing towards the source of the hullaballoo.

Sandra Next Door and Mrs Goggins were crouched against the wall, clinging to each other and moaning in terror as something on the other side of the door appeared to be trying to batter its way through. Low growls and throaty yowls emanated from the room beyond, each preceded by a thump on the door.

'We thought nobody was coming,' Sandra Next Door wailed. 'Why didn't you reply?'

Eileen protested, 'We did! I said over over and over. And I didn't even tell you off for not saying over! I was so loud it wasn't a walkie talkie so much as an outie shoutie.'

A thought struck Sandra Next Door, and she gave a small, embarrassed cough.

'I, eh, I might have turned the volume down and we didn't hear you.'

Eileen had questions about this, but she put them on hold as the door behind her shuddered under another attack.

'Have you tried going in?' Jim asked, jerking a thumb over his shoulder.

Sandra Next Door looked at him like he'd just asked if he could borrow her vacuum cleaner for a couple of weeks.

'Funnily enough we never thought of that, did we Mrs Goggins? What do you think set the ruddy thing off in the first place?'

'What is it? The ruddy thing?'

'If only they made see-through doors in the eighteenth century. Why didn't they think of that, I wonder?'

Jim eyed her, a little hurt, and said, 'No need to be sarky. I was just asking.'

A thud then another strangled howl came from behind him.

Sensing an argument brewing and having no time to waste on such nonsense, Mrs Goggins said, 'The door's locked, so we couldn't get in.'

'Are you sure it's locked,' Eileen asked. 'Only, one of the doors upstairs was stuck and we had to give it a good bash to get it open.'

'Aye, well, I do like a good bash,' said Jim wryly.

He gave the handle an experimental rattle, succeeding only in setting off the creature again.

'Hold the torch steady and shine it into the room as soon as I get this door open,' he told Penny. 'I want to see what's coming at me.'

Penny stood behind him, directing the torch beam at the door, and the others crowded around her to add candlelight to the proceedings as Jim grasped the handle, put his shoulder to the door and gave it an almighty shove.

The door shifted slightly in its frame and the group unconsciously took a step back. Whatever was in the room had gone ominously silent and Penny found herself holding her breath while Jim put his shoulder once more to the wood.

The second shove was the charm. With a crack, the door gave way and swung inwards, carrying Jim with it. As he stumbled forwards, a large, hairy animal, all teeth and claws, flew past him and launched itself at Mrs Goggins. In a flurry of grey fur and apron strings, she landed with a heavy thump on the carpet, wincing as pain shot through her coccyx. Her pain, however, was quickly superseded by delight.

'David Meowie,' she cooed at the purring creature which had almost flattened her.

For his part, David Meowie arranged himself across her lap, his tail end spilling over onto the carpet. He really is an enormous cat, Eileen thought. What came first, she wondered. The cat or Mrs Goggins' big boobs? Because if the cook was in the habit of catching David Meowie in her bra, maybe her boobs had simply evolved. Was that even possible?

Emerging from the dark room, Jim said, 'Well, bugger me with a bag of Dreamies. You wouldn't have a rat problem with that thing around. Come to think of it, you wouldn't have a small elephant problem.'

'I thought Mrs Hubbard killed him,' said Eileen, giving the cat a tentative prod. 'I can confirm he's not a ghost.'

'I thought she'd killed you too, didn't I, my little Wowie Meowiekins,' said Mrs Goggins, scratching the giant furball under the chin. 'How on earth did you get in there?'

'Some eejit left the window open,' Jim told her.

'Och, that'll be Hamish. I don't know how many times I've told him to stop leaving windows open. We end up with all sorts of wildlife in the bedrooms. That's how he got to know Disco Bob. It was when Bob was going through his burglar phase. He got in through the window of one of the locked rooms and it shut tight behind him. Stupid man was in there for two days before Hamish found him. He killed my aspidistra by using it as an ashtray and I never let him forget it.'

Eileen said, 'There were pigeons in one of the rooms upstairs. They're gone now, but they've made an awful mess.'

Mrs Goggins smiled tightly at Sandra Next Door and said, 'There you are, then. Your first cleaning job.'

Sandra Next Door was about to object, but Penny got there first.

She said, 'Let me get this straight. You and Mrs Hubbard thought she'd killed David Meowie? So did you kill anyone else, or was it just the cat?'

'Just the cat. The poor wee thing was stuck on the roof, half frozen to death, and Mrs Hubbard accidentally hit him over the head with a broom handle while we were trying to rescue him. Then we had to run away because someone else came onto the battlements.'

'Did you see who it was?'

'Erm, no. Like I said, we ran away.'

'Why did you run away?'

'That's between me and Mrs Hubbard,' Mrs Goggins snapped, and the tight, determined look on her face made it clear that she wasn't going to elucidate any further.

'It could have been Disco Bob,' Penny speculated.

'Or his killer,' said Jim.

'Or his partner,' said Eileen.

Penny drew herself up and declared, 'We're not going to solve anything sitting here, and we still have a castle to search.'

'Actually, we don't,' said Eileen. 'Sorry, I forgot to tell you that Mrs H and I found Raine. She's in one of the disused rooms on the third floor, out for the count.'

Leaving Sandra Next Door and Mrs Goggins to transport David Meowie downstairs to the safety of the kitchen, Penny and Jim followed Eileen upstairs. Much to Eileen's surprise, the room in which they'd found Raine was close to the top of the staircase, and she rather suspected that she'd taken the long route when trying to find her way earlier.

Mrs Hubbard was very relieved to see them. She'd unearthed a fresh supply of fat church candles from her handbag and had arranged them on the furniture and shelves around the bed. In the centre of this impromptu altar lay Raine. Her eyes were still closed, but the warmth of the blankets had brought some colour back into her cheeks, and she appeared to be stirring slightly.

Jim quickly checked her over, muttering, 'No apparent wounds. Perhaps she hit her head or something. We won't know until she wakes up.'

He slid his arms under the unconscious woman and lifted her, staggering slightly under the dead weight.

'She may be a skinny wee thing, but she weighs a ton,' he grumbled.

Their small procession made its way slowly down the winding stairs, Penny and Mrs Hubbard in front to guide Jim, and Eileen bringing up the rear because, as she freely admitted, she was a liability in gardening clogs. Manoeuvring Raine without bashing her head on the walls was nigh on impossible, and Jim had quickly realised that a fireman's lift was required. Now, instead of being elegantly draped across his arms, Raine hung limp across his shoulder, her tiara barely clinging on and her red, satin bottom pointing the way. There was no dignity involved, yet it speeded progress, and within a few minutes they had laid Raine next to her father on the hearth rug in the big hall.

Fiona, who was mid-Anglo Saxon, grimaced and said, 'Distract me, please. Gordon's being useless. He doesn't dare sing Kumbaya anymore, but he keeps warbling about "Da first Doel da adgels did say." Apparently, bored is da king of Israel. Tell me what's happening?'

'Well,' said Eileen, with the air of someone about to settle into a long and interesting tale. 'Mrs Hubbard and Mrs Goggins killed a cat, then the cat came back to life, and it wasn't a ghost, then we found Raine, and Mrs Hubbard stole a bottle of wine, and there were pigeons, and I had to write on the blackboard because Mrs Hubbard was getting upset about Pierre eating the garlic sausages. I think that's about it, more or less. Oh yes, and people aren't saying over over the radio. Not over over. I mean over the radio over.'

Fiona looked at Penny, who shook her head and said, 'I'll

flesh out the details later. For now, we have something more urgent to do. We still have to rescue Cara.'

Jim was tending to Raine and checking Gordon's nose, so she took a moment to look around, happy to have almost everybody in one place, safe and sound…ish. Eileen was sitting on the sofa, Fiona's feet on her lap, rubbing the wellies as if to bring relief to the swollen ankles beneath. Jim knelt in front of Gordon, gently lifting the bag of ice from his face to inspect the broken nose. Mrs Hubbard had draped the blankets once more over Raine and was now sitting on the floor beside her, patting the girl's hand in an attempt to coax her back to consciousness. In a weird way, Penny reflected, it was both the best and worst Christmas Eve she'd ever had.

'I wonder how the poor wee thing ended up locked in that room,' Mrs Hubbard murmured.

Jim said, 'Buggered if I know, but we have two out of three now, and I'd like the full set. I'll round up the boys and storm Cara's bedroom. Gordon, I know your face hurts, but do you feel up to taking over guard duty while Jack and Noel help me? They're insisting on staying in their posts.'

Gordon nodded so miserably that, taking pity on him, Penny said, 'I'll keep you company. Mind you, you might want to change out of the disco boots first.'

Feeling slightly guilty, Penny squatted down next to Hamish and untied the laces of his brogues. These would look odd with Gordon's denim dungarees but, she reasoned, not nearly as odd as Lizzie Bield's disco boots.

'Why did you tuck the legs of your dungarees into the tops of the boots?' she asked as she slid the brogues onto Gordon's feet. 'Far more classy to let a hint of disco boot peep out from the bottom.'

'I told him that,' said Fiona. 'He's never had any fashion sense. He has a pair of waterproof trousers at home that would look great with those.'

Eileen said, 'I've got a blouse in the same shade. I could lend you it, if you like.'

Catching the three women sharing a complicit smile, Gordon said, 'Very fuddy. Leab me alode.'

Still smiling, Penny stood up and was turning to Jim to suggest he radio the guards, when movement at the back of the hall caught her eye. For a second, she tensed, her brain firing a warning shot of adrenaline in the face of this new threat, but battle systems were quickly stood down when she recognised the figure of Norma Snipples scurrying into the pool of light by the fireplace.

As Mrs Snipples drew nearer, her stress became evident. Her hands were clutched together, as if in supplication, and there were tears in her eyes. A button was missing from her hideous cardigan and the tendrils of hair which had escaped from her tight bun formed moist spirals on her brow.

Penny gasped, 'What's wrong, Mrs Snipples? Where's Cameron?'

'Oh, God help me,' sobbed the teacher. 'I can't find him anywhere.'

CHAPTER 16

Penny couldn't help herself. Her first reaction was frustration.

'Jeeze, it's like one step forwards and two steps back in this place. When did you last see him?'

'We were in the staff lounge, checking all the cupboards, then when I turned round, he was gone! I've looked everywhere. Gone back over the places we've been and–'

'Why didn't you radio us?' Penny asked impatiently.

Mrs Snipples reached into her cardigan pocket and brought out the walkie talkie, which was now a mangled lump of plastic and wires.

She tearfully explained, 'I dropped it when we were searching the tourist shop.'

Her kind nature reasserting itself, Penny patted the teacher on the shoulder, took a deep breath and announced, 'Okay, it's all hands on deck. We have two objectives, folks; secure Cara and find Cameron.

'Eileen, radio Mrs Goggins and Sandra Next Door. Ask them to come up here immediately. Oh, and tell them bring another radio. Jim and Gordon, we'll stick to the plan and rescue Cara.

'You stay here with Fiona, Eileen. Sorry, but Mrs Goggins

and Mrs Hubbard know their way around the castle, so I need them to pair up with Sandra Next Door and Mrs Snipples to search the ground floor for Cameron.'

Jim, Gordon and Penny departed, leaving the others to bring Sandra Next Door and Mrs Goggins up to speed. Finding herself dashing upstairs once more, Penny mused that whatever happened tonight, they'd be leaving a lot fitter than they'd arrived. Already, her leg muscles were burning, and there was another flight yet to climb.

A couple of minutes later, she stood bent over, hands on knees, panting as she tried to explain to Jack and Noel that they had found Raine, but that Cameron was missing.

'Gordon and I will look after things here while you help Jim rescue Cara,' she wheezed. 'Goodness. Must. Hit. Gym. After. Christmas.'

'That seems a bit extreme,' Jim protested. 'It was really hard to decide whether to get you a new iron or an air fryer, but I think you'll be pleased. I went the extra mile this year.'

Penny stared at him in disbelief.

'If you bought me either of those, you can join the bloody Proclaimers; walk five hundred more miles and don't come back. In fact, start walking now because you're just annoying me.'

Jim took the hint and gestured to the two security guards to follow him.

Turning back for a moment, Jack pressed his radio into Penny's hand and said, 'Take this. We'll use Jim's. Oh, and I don't think he'd be stupid enough to buy you an iron for Christmas. You deserve diamonds.'

He leaned over and kissed her gently on the cheek, slipping his torch into her other hand.

'Stay safe,' he whispered.

'Holy shit,' said Gordon once Jack had gone.

'I know,' Penny breathed. 'I'm as shocked as you are.'

'Aye, I was confidet I could do a bird, but I did't dink I could do a rabbit.'

Penny looked down to find Gordon sitting on the floor, candle in front of him, making shadow puppets on the opposite wall.

She murmured, 'Life sure is full of surprises.'

Jim, Jack and Noel were huddled in the secret passageway behind Cara's dressing room. Jim was delivering a final briefing before they made their entrance.

'Yer man will have heard the noise with the cat earlier,' Jim whispered, 'so he'll be on high alert. Angel One, as soon as we're through the door, you and I will rush him. Angel Two, you get Cara and take her back through the passageway, down to the main entrance. Take her into the big hall and keep her safe while we deal with him.'

'On your mark, Charlie,' Noel whispered. 'Hang on. Which one of us is Angel One?'

'Jack's Angel One. You're Angel Two,' Jim hissed.

'That's not fair. I wanted to be Angel One. How come he gets to do all the interesting stuff and I get stuck with the girl.'

Jim exchanged an exasperated look with Jack and prodded Noel in the chest.

'You're the hero here. We're just the muscle.'

'Why are we even using code names? It's daft. We should just be Noel, Jim and Jack.'

Jim shrugged. 'It seemed more professional-like. We're on a clandestine operation. The SAS don't call themselves Eric, Barry and Norman. They don't say, "Barry, when you're done making the tea, can you pass us the MP5 sub machine gun?" They have code names like Warrior One and Delta Six. "I'm out of bullets, Delta Six. Do you have a spare clip?" You're top soldier in this movie, Angel Two.'

'Aye,' said Jack. 'You love movies, man. Just pretend you're Liam Neeson or Jason Statham.'

Not yet ready to accept his starring role, Noel complained,

'How am I supposed to find my way downstairs? You said it yourself; these secret passages are like a maze.'

'Duh, mate,' said Jack. 'Cara lives here. She'll know the way.'

Jim gave them a thumbs-up and whispered, 'Stay low. Charge hard. Ready? One, two.'

On three, he pushed the door and surged forward, only to feel his forehead meet solid wood. Simultaneously, his breath was expelled in a forceful "oof" as Angel One and Angel Two crashed into him from behind.

'I think we've lost the element of surprise,' he coughed.

Without stopping to take stock of the damage, he felt along the edge of the door, undid the catch and slid it to one side.

Then all three men charged.

Then all three men skidded to a halt.

The room was lit with scented candles, their powerful perfume at odds with the scene beyond.

The mystery man had retreated to the far corner of the room and was holding Cara against him. One hand was wrapped in her long hair, pulling her head backwards, while the other held an old-fashioned pistol to her temple.

'Lying bitch,' he spat. 'Of course there was a hidden door.'

Jim held up a hand, cautioning, 'Whoa, pal. I don't know what you want with Cara, but it can't be worth hurting her.'

'I want my money. As soon as the power's back on, the bitch can transfer it over then I'm gone.'

'And what are we supposed to do in the meantime? How long do you think you can hold her like that, eh? How long do you think it will take to restore the power?'

Despite the cold, the man's cheeks were mottled pink. He was around fifty years old, stocky and would have been handsome, had time and alcohol not thinned his brown hair and pockmarked his skin. He had the nose of a drinker, Jim noticed, and his hand was trembling. Yet despite this, there was something about him that looked…Penny was right…he seemed familiar, but Jim could no more put his finger on it than she could.

'I can keep this up for as long as it takes,' the man sneered.

'You don't look like you can keep much up without a bottle of whisky inside of you,' Jack observed.

'What's your name?' Jim asked.

He'd seen enough action movies to know that you had to keep the baddie talking; make it personal so they see folk as real people and start to feel guilty about hurting them.

The man had clearly watched the same movies because he snapped, 'You don't need to know my name.'

Unwilling to abandon his strategy, Jim said, 'I'm Charlie and this is–'

'We're his angels,' Noel stammered.

He was becoming increasingly nervous. He wasn't trained for hostage negotiations. The security company just handed you a uniform, made you watch a video and told you to run away if anything dangerous happened. He was a big lad, and he could handle himself, but this was outside his training.

'You're Charlie's Angels!' the man scoffed. 'In that case, you can call me Kojak.'

Noel put his hands on his hips and turned to Jim, saying, 'You see? I told you we shouldn't have used daft codenames. From now on, I'm being Liam Statham.'

Then he looked the man dead in the eye and said, 'I don't know who you are. I don't know what you want. If you are looking for ransom, I can tell you I don't have money, but what I do have are a very peculiar set of skills.'

'Particular,' said the man.

'What's that?' asked Noel.

'You have a very particular set of skills.'

'No, I'm fairly sure it's peculiar.'

'He's right, it's definitely particular,' said Jack.

'That's weird. I could have sworn it was peculiar.'

The man said, 'If you think about it, that makes no sense.'

'Aye, no sense at all,' Jim agreed. 'Because the next line is

"Skills I have acquired over a very long career. Skills that make me–'

'–a nightmare for people like you,' said Cara.

With that, she wrenched her head forwards then backwards, butting the man square on the nose at the same time as she stamped hard on his foot. He immediately let go of her hair and put his hand to his nose, waving the gun wildly. He swung around, tears streaming from beneath his clenched eyelids. Blood began to seep through his fingers and trickle down his palm until, dripping from his wrist, it spattered onto the carpet.

Frantic to regain his vision, the man took his hand from his nose and wiped his bloody sleeve across his eyes, smearing the dark crimson liquid across his face. New blood gushed forth, darkening his mouth and chin. Tears left trails of pale skin, like milk-streaked liver, and as he span, wild-eyed and leering, the gun oscillated back and forth, up and down, a dangerous, unpredictable beast in the hand of a desperate man.

Jim, Noel and Jack ducked, scrambling backwards and instinctively spreading out so that if one was hit, the others would still be standing. But Cara had no such reservations. Having wrenched herself from the man's grasp, she turned straight back around and charged at him, kicking upwards at the last second to deliver a direct blow between the legs. She followed this up with an uppercut which caught the man in the throat as he sank to his knees.

His bloody hand was clutching his crotch and he began to retch. He had stopped howling now and his breath was coming in pained gasps between heaves. The hand holding the gun wavered left and then right. Through the pain and the tears, he was still searching for a target.

Cara stumbled away from him towards the dressing room door and, her fingers slick with fear, began to frantically fumble at the key in the lock. The man couldn't see the bitch, but he *could* hear her. He swivelled, bringing his gun hand to bear upon the blurred figure.

'Nooooooo!'

Noel's cry came from an ancient place, the visceral wail of an animal driven to protect its own. He hurled himself forwards, diving in front of Cara.

It really was almost like a movie, Jim reflected later. The slow-motion dive, Noel's arms outstretched, his mouth open and the long, drawn-out wail. He saw the gun buck in the man's hand, the flash in the barrel dissipating into curling smoke. Then everything sped up again.

Noel was staggering backwards, a crimson patch blooming beneath the collar of his white shirt. Cara caught him and they both dropped to the floor.

'Noel!' Cara screamed.

She was pulling at him, trying to sit upright and check his wound.

Noel's eyes were wide with fear.

'Did I rescue the girl?' he croaked.

The man was not done. He brought the gun to bear on them again, but this time Jim and Jack were ready for him. There was no slow motion. This was fast and dirty.

Roaring, Jim threw himself onto the man's back, just as Jack kicked the hand holding the gun. The weapon span into the air and hit Cara's dressing table.

The loud crack came without warning. Still clinging onto the man's back, Jim felt himself unexpectedly sinking as the man crumpled to the ground. Jack's expression was one of frozen horror, and behind him, Cara screamed and screamed and screamed.

Jim rolled off the man and staggered to his feet.

'What the frog was that? Shit, is he…?'

Still on his knees, the man was doubled over with his head on the carpet. His blood-stained face was turned to one side, and his eyes were wide and staring. Had it not been for the neat hole in his temple and the pool of blood forming on the floor, Jim would have attempted to revive him. However, there was no coming back from this. The mystery man was well and truly dead.

For a few moments, everyone stared dumbly at everyone else, unsure of the protocol for a dead man on a dressing room carpet. Then Noel broke the spell with a small, pained whimper as Cara dropped his head onto the floor.

'Oh, gosh, sorry,' said Cara, sliding her arm beneath his shoulders.

Jim and Jack rushed to her side and Jim hurriedly undid Noel's shirt buttons so that he could inspect the wound.

Behind them, the door was pushed open, thudding to a halt when it met Cara's back.

'Are you okay in there?' Penny shouted. Her voice was hoarse, and she sounded as though she was on the verge of tears.

Gordon yelled, 'We heard gudshots. What's habbadig… occuried…goeydon…I cad talk, Peddy, you ask dem.'

'What's happening?' Penny shrieked.

Jim assured her, 'We're okay. Hold on a wee minute. Cara's in front of the door.'

He and Jack gently lifted Noel off Cara's lap and placed him on the day bed. Meanwhile, gripping the handle, Cara levered herself stiffly to her feet and opened the door.

Penny gave her a trembling smile, relieved to see her friend unhurt, then her eyes widened as they took in the bloody figure on the carpet.

'Well, bugger Jim with a faulty nail gun. Is that the mystery man? Is he…? On your carpet?'

'Yes,' said Cara, with a grim smile. 'Even Sandra Next Door won't be able to get that stain out.'

'Are you hurt?' Penny asked.

'Only a few bruises where Noel landed on top of me. I'll be fine. Although I wouldn't mind a brandy somewhere warm. Is it just me, or is it colder than ever in here?'

Cara was shivering. Probably just the adrenaline wearing

off, Penny thought, but she might be in shock. She turned to Gordon and handed him the torch.

'Would you mind taking Cara down to the big hall and getting her a sweet drink? I need a word with Jim.'

Without waiting for a reply, Penny strode over to the day bed and flung herself into Jim's chest.

'Will you stop nearly dying?' she squeaked, her voice tight with tears.

He pulled her in close, wrapping his big, safe arms around her, and kissed the top of her head.

She could feel his warm breath in her hair as he said, 'Och, quine, you'd only get bored of me, and we'd have nothing to talk about. Anyway, the bullet missed my head by a good few inches. It's Angel Two here who got shot.'

Penny wriggled from Jim's arms, her attention wholly diverted to the man on the bed, and said, 'Lordy, Noel. You're not dead, are you?'

'Just dying,' said Noel weakly.

His shirt buttons were undone and the collar askew. She leaned over to look at the wound.

'Oh, Noel. What happened?'

'I saved the girl,' said Noel, his eyelids fluttering closed.

'You did indeed,' Penny smiled.

'Am I the hero?' he whispered.

'You are,' she told him, although she wasn't sure if he had heard.

With a heavy sigh, Penny pulled a blanket over Noel's still form.

CHAPTER 17

'Don't worry, it's only a flesh wound,' laughed Jack. 'The boys down the pub are never going to let him forget fainting over a wee scratch.'

Penny couldn't help but smile along with him.

'Is it really just a wee scratch?' she asked Jim.

'More like a nasty scrape. The bullet grazed his collarbone, hit the metal button on his epaulette and ricocheted into the wall. I'll clean the wound, and it'll hurt like a hurty thing tomorrow morning, but he'll be good as new in a week.'

He leaned over the bed and tried to straighten Noel's shirt, growling, 'Slippery little suckers,' as the buttons escaped his attempts to push them through the holes.

Penny took a step back and regarded Jim and Jack with a mother's eye. Both were pale and jittery, which was little wonder after what they'd just been through.

She said, 'Look at the pair of you. You're shaking. We all need some of Mrs Goggins' hot chocolate. Let's wake Sleeping Beauty and get out of here.'

By the time they reached the bottom of the stairs, Noel had single-handedly saved the day while the others had casually watched from the side-lines.

'Then I saw him point the gun at her. We couldn't have

that, could we? Cara's a lady. Aye, like a proper lady because she's called Lady, not just a lady who's a woman, although she's that as well. A woman, I mean. And I was like, "Hey, not the bonny lady." Lady lady, not Lady lady.'

'Aye, loon, it's a pity the bullet hit your shoulder and nae your tongue,' Jim said wearily, as they trudged into the big hall.

The hall was becoming a little crowded, particularly as a fast asleep Fiona was taking up the entire sofa, so Eileen and Gordon had taken it upon themselves to expand the seating options. Clasping cups of orange juice and mince pies from the buffet, Jim, Jack and Noel sank gratefully onto the grey chaise longue from the drawing room. From her spot on the floor beside Hamish and Raine, Cara suggested that a raid on the staff lounge might produce a few extra chairs.

Penny contemplated her companions, trying to decide who among the uninjured might be up for some heavy lifting. Out of ten people, only four were vaguely fit for purpose: herself, Jim, Jack and Eileen. Goodness, tonight had taken its toll. Two dead, one missing and six incapacitated. Well, five and a half. Cara had got off relatively lightly, on the outside at least.

Jim's thoughts seemed to have been following a similar trail.

He asked, 'Who was the man, Cara?'

'Which man?'

'The dead one on your dressing room floor.'

'Sorry, I really can't talk about it,' Cara sighed.

'Can't or won't?'

'Both. Sometimes they are the same thing. Sometimes it is best to stay quiet, otherwise people get hurt.'

She glanced at Hamish and Raine and reached out a hand to tenderly stroke her husband's beard. In response, he gave a little snort, then settled back into a gentle snore.

'I think he's beginning to wake up,' said Cara quietly. 'I

felt his hand squeeze mine a few minutes ago. I really am sorry that I can't...won't tell you about the man.'

'Three people put their lives on the line for you,' said Jim, bitterness tinging the edge of his voice.

Cara sounded strained when she replied, 'I am so grateful for that.'

'That's all you're going to say? Thanks, now carry on as you were. Nothing to see here. That's just–'

Sensing that stress was about to spill over into anger, Eileen interrupted to say, 'Jack told me you were very brave. You took some lumps out of the man.'

'Two lumps in particular,' Cara responded with a wry smile. 'Thanks to you two dragging me along to the self-defence classes in the church hall.'

She raised her plastic cup of orange juice to toast Eileen and Penny.

'Here's to you both and Sergeant Wilson. I'm not sure that Sergeant Wilson's methods are very orthodox, but she's a good teacher.'

Penny raised her own cup and said, 'Cheers. Has anyone heard from the Cameron search party yet?'

'Doh,' said Gordon. 'Dey've been away for a while. Dudding on da...och, bloody dose...zero on da radio.'

'If we get some chairs from the staff lounge, we might bump into them,' Penny suggested. 'Could someone give me a hand.'

'Aye, okay then,' said Jim, reluctantly dragging himself to his feet. 'You too, Jack. The little woman needs some proper man muscle.'

'The little woman,' Penny scoffed. 'I'll tell you where you can shove your man muscle.'

Jim merely smirked and raised an eyebrow.

'I'll help as well,' said Eileen, gently sliding out from under Fiona's feet.

Cara made as if to stand up, but Penny said, 'Four's plenty. Stay with Hamish and Raine. Gordon, I have no idea how Fiona is sleeping through the Anglo Saxons. Keep an eye on her, eh, and we'll be back in ten.'

The going was a lot faster when they didn't have to carry candles. Cara had given them directions to the staff lounge, and they'd reckoned that three torches between them would be far more conducive to lugging furniture around than setting the place ablaze because someone dropped a candle on a cushion. In fact, given their track record of death and injury so far tonight, Penny reckoned it was a miracle that nobody had accidentally burnt the whole castle to the ground. However, there was time yet.

So caught up in her private musings was she, that Penny almost missed the glow in a room to their right.

She put a hand on Jim's arm and said, 'Someone's in there. Should we check in with them?'

'Aye, may as well.' Jim turned to Eileen and Jack. 'You go on. We'll catch up with you in a minute.'

The source of the glow was an array of candles on the shelves of the gift shop. Mrs Hubbard was behind the counter and Mrs Snipples was running a novelty "Vik Stick" walking cane under the shelves, yelping every time she hit something solid.

Penny quickly told both women what had happened upstairs then asked, 'What about you? No sign of Cameron yet?'

Mrs Snipples sighed and gestured to the small pile on the floor next to her.

'The only things under the shelves are three Kick Vik footballs, a Prick Vik sewing box and a Take the Mick out of Vik joke book.'

'Ah, we're truly blessed to live on an island that rhymes with so many things,' said Jim. 'Now, if you'll excuse me, I'm just going to help myself to some Pick n Viks.'

'Shouldn't that be Vik n mix?' Penny asked.

'Tomato, tomayto. Ooh, look, they've got my favourite. Dolly Vikstures!'

Penny left him to it and turned back to Mrs Snipples.

'Are you okay?' she asked.

'Stressed. I can't bear the thought of having to tell his mum. She's such a lovely woman and so patient with him. We focus a lot of attention on the kids who are struggling to keep up, but it can't be easy having a miniature Einstein either.'

'He'll turn up. He has to be in the castle somewhere. Why do you think he took off?'

'I honestly have no idea. We were in the staff lounge, and he seemed happy enough. He was chattering about his stock market investments while he went through the cupboards. I was in the wee kitchen area, standing on the worktop so I could lift the ceiling hatch, and it was probably a couple of minutes before I noticed that he'd gone quiet. When I went back into the lounge, he was gone. You don't think there are any hidden doors in the staff lounge, do you?'

Penny agreed that this was a good point, so fished the map from her pocket. Juggling both torch and map was never going to work, so she bade Mrs Snipples follow her and spread the document across the shop counter.

Mrs Hubbard was highly interested in the map. She immediately spotted three shortcuts that she hadn't known existed.

'If I'd known about this one, dearie,' she said, pointing to a bedroom on the third floor, 'I'd be Mrs Pierre Dupont right now, instead of Mrs Hubbard.'

'Who's Pierre Dupont?' Penny wanted to know.

'Never you mind,' said Mrs Hubbard.

'None of the secret passageways come near the staff lounge,' Mrs Snipples pointed out. 'Although there are far more of them than I thought.'

'You knew about the secret passageways?' asked Penny.

'I'd heard they existed. I'm sure there's something about them in the new exhibition at the museum.'

'Ah, Vik by Brick or Click Vik?'

'The Brick one. We took the children on a school trip for their project on the history of Vik's buildings.'

'Sounds interesting, but there's nothing here to explain Cameron's disappearance. Have you heard from Mrs Goggins and Sandra Next Door?'

'No. We're finished our half of the ground floor, so I assume that they must be nearly finished theirs.'

'In which case, we'll leave you to it. We only came to borrow some chairs from the staff lounge. Oi, Jim, put the Vik Chick away and let's go.'

Jim obligingly put the toy chicken back on the shelf and followed Penny down the hallway to the staff lounge. They were just in time to meet Jack and Eileen, who were wheeling out two armchairs.

Jack said, 'There's another couple of armchairs and a sofa to come. One more run should do it. Tell you what, Penny, why don't you sit on here and I'll wheel you back to the big hall? A princess on her chariot. I promise, it'll be the ride of your life.'

Penny noticed Jim noticing Jack's lascivious wink and shuffled her feet awkwardly.

'I'll help Jim with the sofa. Better that we have all hands to the pump,' she said, wincing at the exaggerated breeziness she heard in her own voice.

When Jack had gone, Jim asked, 'Is there something going on between you and him?'

'What do you mean by going on?'

'I mean flirting, kissing, sexy shenanigans, that sort of thing.'

'Don't be stupid,' said Penny.

'Oh, I'm stupid, am I? Did he not just call you a princess and wink?'

'He winked. People wink. It happens all the time!'

'Ah, but that wasn't just a wink, was it? It was a wink wink.'

'What are you on about, wink wink? Next time he nudges

me, are you going to have a go at me about about nudge nudge. Because then I'll have the full nudge nudge wink wink set.'

'Oh, he's been nudging you, has he?'

'No, he hasn't. For goodness' sake, Jim, there's nothing going on between me and Jack.'

'Nothing except a bit of nudge, nudge, wink, wink, I'll give you the ride of your life. Has the man laid hands on you? That's what I want to know. Has he laid hands on you?'

'Laid hands. Stop being so daft.'

'Has he laid hands on you? It's a simple enough question.'

'Technically, no.'

'Technically?'

'Okay, he kissed my cheek once and told me I deserve diamonds.'

'So there *have* been shenanigans!'

'There haven't. When would I have time for shenanigans? I've been with you practically all day. Gordon was there when he kissed my cheek; you can ask him about it. What's wrong with you? You're not normally like this?'

Jim blew out a deep breath.

'Just a few things on my mind at the moment. I don't want to talk about it.'

'When you're ready to talk about it, I'm here.'

'Stay away from Jack, though.'

'No, I won't. You're not the boss of me, Jim Space, and you never will be.'

'Fine.'

'Fine.'

'Fine.'

'Fine.'

Penny's mind was reeling. This had come out of nowhere. She'd never seen jealous Jim before, much less controlling Jim. He'd been there when both her ex-husband and Hollywood legend Johnny Munroe had flirted with her. Then there was Jimmy Gupta from the bakers, whose steady supply of sausage rolls always came with a hint that she should give his son another chance. Even Minky Wallace from the café in town had once said that if Penny ever fancied coming over from the dark side, she should let her know. Jim had been present during all these overtures and hadn't been in the least bit bothered. Although, to be fair, he was a little terrified of Minky.

His reaction to Jack was so out of character that she could only imagine that the shooting had affected him more deeply than he was letting on. Or was she making excuses for him? The stone settled in the pit of her stomach. She'd fret about this properly later, but at the moment she was simply in shock that, over the course of a few minutes, she'd gone from feeling secure in the relationship to wondering if she should be in it at all.

There was a distinct coldness between them as they each grabbed an end of the sofa and steered it towards the door. Just as they were about to leave, a thought struck Penny.

She said, 'Wait a minute. There's probably a first aid kit in here. You can use it to clean Noel's shoulder.'

Jim merely grunted an acknowledgement as Penny swept her torch over the cupboards. They were all neatly labelled to indicate the contents; Mugs, coffee and tea, castle maps (they could have done with some of those a few hours ago!), photocopier paper.

On the wall beside the cupboards, something caught her eye, and she moved closer, shining the light onto the large wooden board so that she could see it more clearly.

'Jim, look at this.'

At a pace sufficiently glacial to make plain his reluctance, Jim crossed the room to join her.

She ran the torch over the top of the board, illuminating the words "Staff Roll of Honour."

'It's a list of the senior staff who served in the household over the years.'

'So?'

'Stop sulking and look at the butlers.'

Jim leaned forward to study the names then gasped.

'Bugger me with a ball of stuffing! I hope his middle name was Mungus.'

'I think Cameron saw this. I think that's why he disappeared.'

'It certainly explains a lot.'

'But not everything. We need to revisit our timeline. I'm starting to get an idea of exactly what's gone on.'

CHAPTER 18

Penny spread the map out face down on the table in the staff lounge.

'Here's your timeline,' she said. 'It doesn't give us all the answers, but if you know what we now know, then someone who we discounted earlier probably knows about the secret passageways and, more importantly, they know about something that isn't on the map.'

'That's a lot of knowing. What's the something not on the map?' Jim asked.

Penny flipped the map over and said, 'Think of the layout in three dimensions. Which rooms are above which?'

Jim studied the floorplans and rearranged them in his mind. Penny watched his finger trace through the rooms until it stopped on the diamond room.

He looked at her, realisation dawning, and said, 'You're right. The diamond room is two floors up, directly above the drawing room, which is directly above the kitchen. But what does that mean?'

'Don't think about what the rooms are used for now. Think about what they were used for in the past, perhaps in the days of butlers, cooks and head footmen.'

Jim rubbed his face, thinking hard. Penny was much

better at this stuff than him. His brain was still rattled from the shooting and how close he'd been to that bullet. God, to put her through losing him after everything she'd gone through to keep him. He couldn't bear the thought of leaving her behind forever. Part of him, probably a very, very stupid part of him, was urging him to push her away now because if they kept on down this road, things would become permanent and eventually one of them would lose the other.

The sensible part of him said he was being daft. He'd spent so many years alone and he'd just had a big scare. It was perfectly fine to have a touch of commitment-phobia, but it was dumb to walk away from a relationship in case one of you died. Billions of people happily spent their lives together in the knowledge that this would probably happen.

Hang on there, Jim m'boy. Rewind. There was a wee chink of light in that last part.

He replayed his thoughts. There was the bit about dying and getting out now before it was too late. Then there was the bit about nae being a dunderheid over a pair of cold feet. Feet. Aye, that was it. He'd told himself he'd be dumb to walk away.

In the darkness, Jim slowly smiled.

'Ha! The thing that's not on the map. It's the dumb waiter!'

Penny beamed at him proudly.

'Well done. I knew you'd get there. I think that the person who stole the diamond used the dumb waiter to move around the castle. Remember what we found when we came out of the tunnel? In the room behind the pantry?'

'Aye, the broken generator.'

Penny flipped the map back over again and said, 'Imagine you know about the secret passageways and the dumb waiter. Now, imagine you want to steal a diamond that's protected by a high-tech security system. You know it's going to snow today, and the power will go out like it always does on Vik.

However, you also need the power to stay out so that you don't trip the alarms when you steal the diamond.'

'So, you deliberately wreck the generator,' said Jim.

'Exactly. I bet if we ask Mrs Goggins, she'll have gone down to switch on the generator and found it broken.'

'But why wouldn't she have said so?'

'Remember when she forgot to tell us about the security cameras? And David Meowie? It won't have occurred to her that someone deliberately sabotaged the generator. She's old school. Battle through adversity and all that jazz. She'll have shrugged her shoulders and got on with things.'

'How did you get to be this clever?' Jim asked. 'My brain's still catching up and you've got it all solved.'

'I don't have it all solved. We still don't know who killed Disco Bob. Was he working with our thief? Were they planning to fly the diamond out on the drone?'

'The thief was counting on quite a lot of luck with the power outage, though,' said Jim.

'It didn't have to happen today,' Penny pointed out. 'Visit the diamond on any day when the forecast is for snow, and there's a good chance that the power will go down. The rest of the plan stays the same.'

Jim thought about this for a few seconds then, with a satisfied smile, told her, 'That's the flaw in your theory. If the thief *was* colluding with Disco Bob, he would also have to visit on the same days. Someone would notice.'

'You're right. That does make it less likely that Disco Bob and our thief were in it together, but not impossible.'

Jim looked at the timeline again and pursed his lips.

'It's a very tight window. Maybe twenty minutes. Half an hour at a stretch. They'd have to go through the drawing room fireplace, down the stairs, wreck the generator, back up to the drawing room, haul themselves two floors up in the dumb waiter, steal the diamond...then what? Go back down to the drawing room?'

'Or out the secret door,' Penny suggested. 'The keypad is

on the outside to keep people out, but once you're in the room, the door is easily opened.'

'Jack and Noel heard a noise and checked the room straight away. The diamond was still there, and the secret door was closed. If the thief made the noise, they couldn't have nipped out through the secret door. They'd have locked themselves out.'

'The thief was still in the dumb waiter. I bet it's behind that hideous portrait of Hamish's great, great, great, great aunt Agatha, or whatever she's called. As soon as Jack and Noel were gone, they stole the diamond and made off.'

Jim said, 'Then there's the problem of getting the diamond out of the castle. If they were counting on us being snowed in, then they knew they'd be trapped.'

'Yes, but they'd eventually be freed.'

'Sorry to poop on your party. If the phone mast hadn't gone down, someone would have contacted the police on their mobile. The police would arrive and search everyone.'

'Which would not have made a jot of difference,' Penny parried. 'The thief isn't planning to take the diamond with them. Not today, at any rate.'

'You mean it's hidden somewhere in the castle?'

Penny nodded, her eyes twinkling with barely suppressed glee.

Jim groaned, 'Aw, how are we supposed to find one wee diamond in this giant castle? Look how long it took us to find Raine, and she's quite big!'

'Worry ye not,' said Penny. 'I know exactly where it is, and it will be completely safe for at least the next two days.'

'Oh, you're sexy when you're cryptic,' said Jim, reaching out to gather her into his arms.

Penny flinched and pulled away, and that moment where they'd forgotten the argument was instantly over. The awkward chill once more descended as she folded the map and tucked it back into the one pocket that every woman can rely on; her bra.

. . .

They found the first aid kit under the sink in the tea point. Wordlessly, Penny laid it next to a cushion, and they wheeled the sofa to the big hall, where Sandra Next Door and Mrs Goggins were holding forth about disturbing a nest of rats in the stables.

'I've never been so scared in my life,' said Sandra Next Door, completely forgetting her hysterics over a trapped cat not so long ago. 'Yet Mrs Goggins was totally calm.'

Mrs Goggins gave Sandra a peremptory nod and declared, 'It took me ten minutes to coax her down from the hayloft. I think we can safely say that Cameron's not in the stables. I'll send David Meowie in to clear the rats in the morning and if that doesn't work, I have some rat poison downstairs.'

'It was good thinking to check the stables, Mrs Goggins,' said Eileen.

'You must have been freezing, dearie,' Mrs Hubbard fretted. 'Out in that weather with no bra on. They'd have been like a couple of icicles. Or chesticles, even. That's what Lorna from the Post Office calls hers. She had a few too many sherries at the bingo last week and said she's getting them reduced. The chesticles, not the sherries. Anyway, she made me promise not to tell anyone and I says, "Don't worry, Lorna from the Post Office, I am the soul of discretion." She's off to a private clinic in Aberdeen to get them done in the New Year.'

Mrs Goggins shot Mrs Hubbard a look that suggested the next time they shared a cup of tea, Mrs Hubbard better hide the tin of rat poison.

Any further mention of Mrs Goggins' chesticles was lost in the general shuffling backwards of furniture to make way for the new sofa.

With a quick apology for getting caught up in the rat drama, Eileen and Jack disappeared for a few minutes and returned with more chairs. This gave Penny the opportunity to claim a spot on the sofa next to Sandra Next Door. In other words, as far away from Jim as possible. She also wanted to avoid Eileen, fearing that her friend would pick up on the tension between herself and Jim, and ask questions. The last thing Penny wanted to do right now was explain that Jim was behaving like a total twat, and that assuming they made it out of this clusterfork alive, she might very well have to murder him anyway. Or perhaps maim him. He wasn't worth the jail time for murder. What did one get for a light maiming these days? A couple of years? She could cope with that. Maybe if she bought enough posh chocolate biscuits, she could even bribe Sergeant Wilson to look the other way.

'Still no sign of Cameron?' she asked Sandra Next Door.

'Nothing. Shame, because I was starting to like the wee lad. He has some good qualities.' Sandra began to list them on her fingers. 'A low tolerance for fools, intelligent conversation and he likes order. That's three more than *him* over there.'

'Jim's intelligent,' Penny protested, before adding, 'Mostly. Even though sometimes he can be an absolute fudgewazzock.'

'That sounds like a Sergeant Wilsonism,' Sandra Next Door observed.

'It does, doesn't it. Ever since she joined Losers Club, my brain keeps coming up with weird words that are somehow very appropriate. It's like she infected me.'

'She might love an inventive insult and be a wee bit unorthodox in her methods, but she's good at her job. Cheer up, Penny. When Sergeant Wilson gets here, she'll probably find Cameron in a fartnoodle.'

Penny laughed, appreciating the woman's attempt to jolly her along.

'What now?' asked Sandra Next Door.

Penny slumped back on the sofa and sighed, 'I suppose we wait. Randy Mair will clear the back roads, an ambulance will come for Fiona and the walking dead over there, and the rest of us will limp home.'

'I might have a snooze. It has been one heck of a day, and

just think of the cleaning up there'll be after this. Sheer bliss! Mrs Goggins has invited me over to help on the twenty-seventh, assuming the snow has cleared by then.'

'Maybe we could all help,' Penny suggested. She raised her voice and asked the group, 'Who's up for cleaning the castle on the twenty-seventh?'

There were no immediate takers, quite possibly because everyone had had their fill of the castle for now. Mrs Goggins looked somewhat crestfallen.

Taking pity on her, Mrs Hubbard said, 'I'll do it.'

The floodgates having opened, the offer of help was, with the exception of Fiona and the walking dead, unanimous.

'Thanks,' said Sandra Next Door. 'Sorry, Mrs Goggins. Even I might have bitten off more than I can chew alone. When I originally agreed to come, there wasn't quite so much blood on the carpet.'

She slumped back on the sofa beside Penny and closed her eyes, murmuring, 'Now I'll make a list of everything we will need.'

'I don't know how you can sleep,' said Penny. 'I'm far too keyed up.'

'If you want something to keep you busy, look in my handbag. There's a newspaper in there. Do the puzzles to pass the time until Randy gets here.'

Grateful for the distraction, Penny retrieved the newspaper then rummaged further through the bag, cursing under her breath when she failed to find what she was looking for.

Oh, bums, she thought. She could sit here and solve the clues in her head, or she could ask the one person whom she knew had a pen.

Reluctantly, she called over to Jim, 'Do you still have Sandra Next Door's pen?'

'Why?'

'I'm going to do the crossword.'

'Can I do it with you?'

'No, because you were horrible to me.'

'But we always do crosswords together?'

'You mean you steal my dad's newspaper and shout out the clues for me to answer.'

'Well, if you won't let me do the crossword, I'm not giving you the pen.'

'Fine.'

'Fine.'

'Fine.'

'Fine. But I want the paper when you've finished with it.'

'Never gonna happen.'

Penny leaned back on the sofa again and opened the newspaper, pointedly blocking Jim's view of her. Petty, petty man. It wasn't even his pen! If he thought he was getting one over her, he had another thing coming. Normally she'd share the newspaper so that both of them had something to do. However, what with him being a big hairy gruntweasel, she'd read the whole thing very slowly, even the sports pages, then do the puzzles in her head. He could sit quietly with nothing to do until Randy Mair came back. So there.

She turned the newspaper the right way up and began to read.

Many of the articles were not Penny's cup of tea at all. She secretly liked to read the celebrity gossip before going on Twitter to find out the real story of who was shagging who. She was slightly ashamed of this salacious side to her nature, so tended to only treat herself to a quick surf through the red tops once a month. Otherwise, most of her news came from the Vik Gazette.

This newspaper seemed quite obsessed with serious things, like pensions and house prices. There was a lot of boring stuff about business and stocks, too. Successful sports people and the royal family were lauded, and all the lifestyle tips were for the sort of things one could only find either in London or in some delicious, little off-the-beaten-track farmers market in the Cotswolds.

The celebrity news was confined to articles about "proper"

stars, as opposed to the antics of minor soap actors and Strictly Come Dancing professionals that were Penny's guilty pleasure.

She skimmed through the newspaper, looking for something, anything, vaguely interesting and was just about to give up and brave the sports section when *it* jumped off the page. An actual juicy headline. More than juicy. Positively dripping. Lactating all over the place.

'Oh. My. Giddy. Aunt,' she whispered. 'I get it now. I've been looking at this all wrong.'

She tore off a section of newspaper, rolled it into a ball and lobbed it at Jim's head. It missed, of course, but it hit him in the chest and that was enough to get his attention.

'I need to talk to you,' she mouthed. 'Now.'

Jim regarded her blankly, then shrugged.

'For flip's sake,' she muttered, before levering herself off the sofa, trying not to wake Sandra Next Door.

She strode over to Jim and leaned down as if to kiss him.

'I don't understand,' he whispered. 'Aren't we having an argument.'

'We'll deal with that later,' she murmured. 'I need to talk to you right now. I have some very big news, and I urgently need your help. Meet me in the bathroom.'

CHAPTER 19

As he moved out of the circle of light, Jim heard Cara whisper to Eileen, 'Where's he going?'

'Shagging,' Eileen stated. 'Penny left a couple of minutes ago.'

'I heard that,' said Jim loudly. 'I'm going to the bathroom.'

'Bathroom shagging,' Eileen whispered, nodding sagely.

Hamish had come round but said he could remember nothing of the attack. The last thing he recalled was slipping behind the tapestry in the main hall with the intention of changing the door code.

He was now sitting quietly in an armchair, watching as his wife tended to his daughter. Next to her, Eileen was kneeling beside Fiona. They had been having an argument about cutting Fiona's wellies off to ease the swelling in her ankles. An argument that Fiona had won by declaring, 'I'm the pregnant one, so I win.' The wellies stayed.

Hamish had a splitting headache. Jim had been kind, and Mrs Goggins had supplied some of the strong painkillers which she'd been "saving for a special occasion." What sort of special occasion demanded morphine, Hamish wanted to ask. Although he had been to a few weddings where it would have been welcome. Nevertheless, he was grateful to have awoken to only a concussion and an admonishment from Jim that he must tell him if he had any of the following symptoms. Jim had gone on to reel off a long list of symptoms, all of which Hamish had instantly forgotten. He strongly suspected that further memory loss was one of them. And that lying was not. Hamish knew perfectly well who had attacked him. What he couldn't understand was why.

Penny was waiting for Jim in the bathroom as planned, yet her intentions were far more nefarious than anything Eileen could have dreamed up.

As soon as Jim had closed the door, Penny handed him the newspaper.

'You've chosen a strange setting to do the crossword together,' he commented.

She snatched the paper from him, swatted him across the head and handed it back, saying, 'Page nine.'

She fidgeted impatiently as Jim wrestled the newspaper into submission and found the page. He laid it across the sink and bent to peer at the print, narrowing his eyes against the glare of the torch light on the white paper. Lordy, thought Penny, this is like the time it took a five-year-old Hector two hours to read three pages of Biff and Chip. She didn't think her will to live had ever fully recovered.

She was alerted to the fact that Jim had read the article and made the required mental leap by the familiar phrase, 'Well, bugger me with a chocolate Santa.'

'And you always take the mickey out of me for liking the celebrity gossip,' she crowed.

'I take it all back,' said Jim. 'What do you think it means?'

'You tell me.'

'I asked first.'

'You don't know what it means, do you?'

'Yes.'

'What then?'

'It means that someone here needed money.'

'And?'

'Well, that's pretty much all I know.'

'Look at the photo. Who's that in the background?'

Jim shone his torch on the photograph. It showed a group of people leaving a courthouse.

'Holy fffundamentals! That's our mystery man.'

'Think it through.'

Jim thought it through. He thought and thought and thought it through, until his brain decided that it had had enough of all this thinking through and supplied him with the answer.

He exclaimed, 'I know who he is! Well, not exactly who. I know *what* he is.'

'Shall we go and find out who he is?' Penny asked.

'It's a bit morbid, no?'

'Cara won't tell us, so the only way to find out is to search his body.'

'But Sergeant Wilson will shout at me.'

'She'll understand as long as we solve the crime.'

'She called me a weeping barnacle on the arse of a rotting walrus when I was helping you with the weigh-in at Losers Club last week.'

'You *were* a pound out.'

'Aye, but it didn't warrant being referred to as the twat-badger for the rest of the night.'

'She's a creative trapped in a uniform.'

'It's okay for you. She likes you.'

'I'm not sure that Sergeant Wilson likes anyone,' Penny pointed out. 'But if it helps, you can tell her it was my idea.'

'Okay, and no takesie backsies.'

'What are we? Seven?'

'I'm just future proofing myself against the fact that you're quite annoyed with me at the moment.'

'Alright, no takesie backsies. Now, can we get on with it please?'

. . .

The scented candles in Cara's dressing room had burned down now. Only a few were left, their flames guttering at the bottom of glass jars. The mix of lavender, jasmine and musk masked the rusty stench of blood, but there was yet enough light to make out the dark pool on the carpet and the huddled figure above.

The mystery man lay where he'd fallen, collapsed forward on his knees, his head to one side and his eyes open and glassy. The snarl and tension of earlier had gone, leaving behind them the blank coolness that had tugged at Penny's sense of déjà vu.

She was just about to begin frisking the man's pockets, when Jim bellowed, 'Fingerprints! Fibres! Hair!'

She froze and sighed, 'We know what happened to him and Sergeant Wilson is going to shout at us anyway, so what difference does it make?'

Jim raised his arms, palms up, as if warding her off.

'I'm only trying to minimise the fallout. She usually takes it out on Gordon because he's the most scared of her, but he'll be away having a baby, so there will be nobody there to soften the blow for us.'

Muttering darkly about annoying twatbadgers, Penny strode to Cara's dressing table and began to pull drawers open.

Five minutes later, she shone her torch on herself and said, 'Satisfied?'

Jim's lips twitched, but he managed to contain his mirth as he grunted, 'Aye.'

Penny was in her bra and knickers. Her hands were encased in Cara's tanning gloves, and her hair, too short to pull into a ponytail, was tied by scrunchies into several smaller ponytails across her head, giving her the appearance of having antlers.

'Perfect, *deer*,' said Jim, smirking inwardly at this most

private of jokes. He'd discounted several, far better responses, all involving some variation of being horny, on the grounds that their earlier argument was still simmering under the surface and there was a good chance he'd end this night as a eunuch if he wasn't very, very careful.

Oblivious to the humour, Penny marched over to the dead man and told him, 'You better have something interesting to tell us because I'm bloomin' freezing here.'

She began her search with the man's outer layers but found only a tissue and a set of keys.

She scrutinized the logo on the fob and muttered, 'Don't let me forget to tell Sergeant Wilson that there's an abandoned Kia Picanto somewhere nearby.'

It proved more difficult to get into the man's trouser pockets, so she enlisted the help of Jim to lever him upright. As this involved Jim stripping down to his Rudolf underpants and wearing another pair of Cara's tanning gloves, his good humour dried up.

Due to the cold air, the body was still pliable, and Jim was able to straighten his upper torso enough so that Penny could slide a hand into the man's trouser pockets.

'Bingo,' she said, pulling out a wallet.

Gently, Jim lowered the body back into its original position and shuddered.

'That was grim.'

Indignant, Penny said, 'I can assure you, it felt a lot worse digging into his pockets.'

She glanced down sadly at the dead man and felt a sudden stab of pity for him.

'I'm really sorry we had to do that. You may not have been very nice at the end, but you're somebody's son. There will be people who miss you.'

It seemed almost poetic when, at that very moment, the last of the candles went out.

Penny and Jim hurriedly dressed, glad to feel some warmth seeping into their bones. They agreed to wait until they were downstairs before opening the wallet, yet they weren't keen to share their suspicions with their friends. There was too much uncertainty hanging over the heads of everyone else. There were too many people involved who could not be trusted.

Jim suggested, 'Before we go downstairs, we should raid the bedrooms for blankets and duvets.'

'Why?' asked Penny. 'It's warm enough in the big hall.'

''Because I don't think we should go back to the big hall,' he told her. 'We should sit outside and wait for Randy Mair. Before anyone else notices he's here, we'll ask him to radio the police.'

'That's actually a good idea.'

Penny's tone of surprise did not escape Jim's notice.

'Aye, well, nae a complete twatbadger after all.'

Penny and Jim huddled on the front steps of the castle, a king-size duvet covering them. Any onlooker seeing the light from two torches bobbing beneath the cover would have wondered if they had stumbled upon a couple of children playing in an imaginary fort. However, they could not have been further from the truth. Inside the makeshift shelter, two adults, wearing layers of blankets, were emptying the contents of a dead man's wallet.

'Just a thought,' said Penny. 'We've been gone for ages. Surely someone will miss us.'

'It's okay,' Jim assured her. 'Eileen told everyone we were shagging. They'll all be avoiding the bathroom like the plague.'

Penny stifled a giggle.

She held the driving licence out to Jim and asked, 'Recognise the name?'

'Brendan Daly. He was named in the article. Wasn't he the one who…?'

'Yep.'

Jim held up some small photographs.

'And what about these, eh?'

'Pretty much confirms it. I think I've got the whole thing figured out.'

'Do me a favour,' said Jim. 'Don't be one of those annoying people from the movies who know something important and get themselves killed just before they tell someone.'

Penny laughed, 'Okay, I'll tell you. Start from the point of view that there were two thieves here tonight and neither of them were Disco Bob.'

She laid out her theory to Jim, testing it from all angles to see whether it would stand up to Sergeant Wilson's scrutiny. When she was done, they returned the driving licence, along with the other detritus of life, to the various slots in the wallet.

Penny closed the clasp and ran her fingers over the brown leather, made smooth and soft by years of rubbing against pockets. The wallet was permanently sculpted into a gentle curve, and the thought of it moulding comfortably into the shape of the owner seemed to Penny to be the saddest and most personal thing in the world.

When someone dies, she thought, the items we keep are so often bound up in our own memories. Yet this object that was the very essence of him every day, for years and years, will probably be thrown away. The shape and feel of him gone. Because who, except the shopkeeper, has memories of a man with his wallet?

Jim was doing some important musing of his own. His mind was running the argument over Jack on a loop, with himself as the villain of the piece. God, he'd done some daft things in his life, but this one deserved to take home the trophy. He'd practically gaslit the woman. A weird mix of fear, panic and coming down off the adrenaline had sent his emotional compass spinning wildly, and Jack just happened to be a convenient excuse for the argument he needed to get it out of his system.

She'd probably want to have a big talk now. Jim hated talking. He preferred to keep things simple. Life is far easier if you ignore the fact that you have emotional depths, he decided. He knew he'd get his backside kicked for saying it, but for him, having to sit through big talks about feelings was a bit like if he made her sit through every game of the World Cup. You could pay attention and be supportive for a wee while, but by the end of the first half, your brain's setting up a crowdfunding page for an all expenses paid trip to the coma ward.

He wondered if he could get away with just saying sorry. He'd give it a go.

'I just wanted to say sorry about earlier. I was fifty shades of flapwomble and bang out of order.'

'Why were you fifty shades of flapwomble?' Penny wanted to know.

Bugger, thought Jim, she wants blood. He decided to face the challenge head on.

'Are we going to talk about feelings?' he asked.

'That's generally how it goes.'

'Will you marry me?'

'No. Did you get that one from the twat handbook?'

'Bugger. I thought it was a good distraction technique.'

Jim thought for a moment then asked, 'If I just say that I suddenly got really scared that I'll die and leave you behind, will that do?'

'Are you still scared?'

'A bit, but not enough to be a flapwomble about it.'

'Fine. You're forgiven.'

'Really? You don't want to talk more about feelings?'

'Shut up and quit while you're ahead.'

Penny felt a big, strong arm snake under her blanket and pull her towards its owner. This time she relaxed against Jim's chest and smiled. His tantrum had thrown her, far more than he knew, but she'd let it slide for now. There would be plenty of time to talk about feelings later, once this interminable night was done.

She leaned into Jim and he leaned into her, the two of them forming an arch; that strongest of shapes which depends on equal forces to create a stable condition. Warm and safe in their snug blanket fort, they dozed together.

Penny couldn't say how much time had passed when they were awoken by the low thrum of an engine. Jim cautiously lifted an edge of the duvet and expelled a deep sigh of relief.

Trundling up the drive was a large tractor and behind it, the flashing lights of a police car.

CHAPTER 20

Penny and Jim sat on the steps, the duvet wrapped tightly around them, as they watched Sergeant Wilson exit the police car. She strode confidently towards them…and towards them…and towards them…then past them.

'Hey!' Penny shouted indignantly after her.

'Sorry, I don't give to the homeless,' she shot back over her shoulder, before opening the front door and disappearing into the castle.

Penny and Jim hurriedly untangled themselves from their layers of bed coverings and scrambled up the steps. They caught up with the Sergeant in the entrance hall. She was looking around her, unsure where to go.

'That wasn't very nice,' said Penny. 'You knew exactly who we were.'

The Sergeant stared at them, feigning astonishment.

'If it isn't Twatbadger and Princess Pubeface. What are you doing here?'

Penny's indignation immediately went up a notch.

'It was one chin hair, one time. You pinned me to the ground and yanked it out!'

'It was putting me off my peppermint slice. Only reason I

went to the church coffee morning in the first place was for Mrs Hay's peppermint slice.'

Jim nodded gravely and said, 'Reasonable use of force.'

Penny ignored him and asked, 'How did you know to come here? Did someone get a phone signal and call the police?''

Sergeant Wilson looked bemused by the question.

'What do you mean? I came here for the Weasleys. The ambulance is busy with all the car crashes, and you told me Fred's my...'. Sergeant Wilson clicked her fingers '...what's that thing called? The one where you like someone?'

'Friend?'

'Aye. You told me she's my one of them, so I thought I should do something...'. The Sergeant clicked her fingers again.

'Nice?' Penny suggested

'About their car. The back end of it is sticking out onto the road and causing an obstruction. I need George to come and help me shift it.'

'You do know that Fred and Geo...Fiona and Gordon are having their baby as we speak?'

'Aye, I'm just pulling your chin hair. I came to take them to the hospital. The world needs another ginger.'

'There's a lot more going on than that,' Penny told her. 'Are you here on your own?'

'I left PC Piecey in the car, charging up the radio. He got his baton stuck in an electric fence out at Hillside Farm earlier and he's still a bit bejiggered. It was quite handy, really.'

Constable 'Easy' Piecey had joined Sergeant Wilson in policing the island earlier in the year. Generally as much use as a fart in a space suit, he was, nevertheless, their only option.

Penny suggested, 'You might want to get him in. It's been quite an eventful evening, starting with the murder of Disco Bob.

'And ending with the fatal shooting of Brendan Daly,' Jim added.

'With the theft of the Christmas Star in between,' Penny finished.

'And how many of the deaths were your fault?' Sergeant Wilson asked, her eyes narrowing.

'Just the one,' Jim admitted. 'Not exactly my fault.'

'I'll want a full confession on my desk in the morning. You're always talking about being buggered by something, so the prison showers will be a treat for you.'

Jim's eyes were saucers and his Adam's apple bobbed to the rhythm of his gulps.

'Stop winding him up,' said Penny sharply. 'Come with us.'

She and Jim led Sergeant Wilson to the drawing room, it being the closest place with a modicum of privacy. There was always the bathroom, of course, but anyone coming to check on whether they had finished their toilet tomfoolery might get rather a shock to find they'd been joined by a third party.

Sergeant Wilson took one armchair and Penny sat on Jim's lap in the other. Between them, Penny laid the map and the torch on the coffee table.

Once they were settled, Penny began to talk.

'There were two thieves in the castle today. One failed and the other succeeded...'

She carefully laid out her theory and her plan. Two plans. Then she waited.

Sergeant Wilson took her time, turning the theory over in her mind, looking for flaws and pitfalls, until eventually she sighed and said begrudgingly, 'Makes sense, Pubeface. I suppose I better tell the ambulance to get a shift on because it sounds like my car will be full. I'll get Easy to take a look at that generator. He might have enough charge left in him to get it started.'

'Jim didn't think it could be fixed,' said Penny. 'The fuel has leaked all over the floor.'

'We need some light. I want to see the whites of their eyes when I arrest them. Otherwise, what is the point in being a police person. Easy may be a wee nyaff, but he knows his machinery, and he'll get it going. He's the reason they won't let me have a shiny new police car. Little bugger keeps sneaking out and fixing the old one. He changed the spark plugs last week and I had to ban him from the police chocolate biscuits.'

They returned to the entrance hall and Sergeant Wilson summoned Easy. He was a long, thin man with big ears and skin still young enough to bear the acne scars of his teens, although the spots themselves had long since disappeared. His role in the police station was mainly confined to manning the front desk and getting the biscuits in, with the occasional day release to find a lost relative or round up school truants. Sergeant Wilson claimed to be teaching him all she knew, yet this seemed to involve an astonishing amount of paperwork. He was quite glad to get away from mundane tasks and attacked the challenge of the generator with some gusto and the spare can of petrol from the boot of the police car. Within ten minutes, a low thrum could be heard from below the castle and the lights flickered to life.

'You see! The boy's nae just an ugly face,' Sergeant Wilson declared. Then she purposefully clapped her hands and said, 'Let's go and give them the good news that there's a sneaky fu–'

She paused, spotting Easy emerging from the kitchen stairwell, accompanied by children.

'–furbaby in their midst. Easy! Why do you have small people? Did someone get water on you? You know what it says in the police handbook. Don't put an Easy near sunlight, don't let it get wet and never feed it after midnight. Put them back where you found them and tell them to stay there while their Auntie Sergeant Wilson goes all scorched earth on the grown-ups. Now, off you fu…pop, little people.'

Penny admired her rare moment of discretion. The police

officer's last talk at the primary school had been titled "Don't Mess with Auntie Sergeant Wilson" and featured a video of a teenage tearaway trying to make a run for it. He was being restrained by the back of his underpants, with a gleeful Sergeant Wilson yelling, 'Super-wedgie!'

When Penny, Jim and the police officers entered the big hall, there was a spontaneous round of applause. The group by the fire were greatly cheered by the fact that someone had finally come to their rescue and, just as importantly, had restored power.

'Do you know everyone here?' Penny asked the Sergeant.

'Bimbo Baggins, Face Like She's Sookin' Lemons Through a Cat's Backside, Chief Curtain Twitcher and the Weasleys,' said the police officer, pointing at Eileen, Sandra Next Door, Mrs Hubbard, Fiona and Gordon in turn. 'I know everybody except the two layabouts on the couch.'

'Noel Bowes and Jack Hughes,' said Penny. 'They're the security guards for the diamond.'

'Ah, pity for you two that the dole office is closed until January. Never mind. They're looking for test subjects at the coloscopy clinic in Aberdeen. They might be able to help you find your elbows.'

Jack and Noel crossed their arms, leaned back on the sofa and fixed their gaze on the floor.

'That's the trouble with the youth of today,' said Sergeant Wilson. 'They don't appreciate a good pep talk. Right, listen up everyone because Merkinchops here has something to say.'

Penny positioned herself in front of the fireplace and regarded her audience with some trepidation. Sandra Next Door was sitting next to Jack and Noel. Fiona lay on the other sofa, muttering about hurrying things up because the next Anglo Saxon was on its way. In armchairs either side of her sat Gordon and Eileen. Hamish had claimed the Santa chair next to Mrs Goggins and Mrs Snipples, and Cara remained on the floor by the still figure of Raine. Quite the crowd, thought

Penny, aware that she was about to cause some division. She noticed Jim and Easy quietly move to guard the exits, then took a deep breath and began to talk.

'Tonight has brought a few unwelcome surprises. First, we had the murder of Disco Bob, then we found Hamish injured. The Christmas Star diamond was stolen, and finally, a man was shot dead.

'You're probably wondering what each of these crimes has to do with the other. We did, too, and the whole thing became very confusing until we found out a few simple facts.

'The man who was shot is called Brendan Daly. He was blackmailing Cara. We overheard him threaten that if she didn't pay up, then it would be the last time Hamish saw his daughter.

'Something bothered me about Brendan Daly. He looked familiar. Jim noticed it too, but neither of us could put our finger on it, until I saw a newspaper article about Raine's mother. Some of you might not be aware, but Raine's mum is the Irish popstar, Carly Sweet. Brendan was in the background of the accompanying photo, so there was clearly a connection. Jim and I went upstairs and checked the man's body, and sure enough, he had photographs of Raine in his wallet. You see, I don't think he was threatening to kill Raine. I believe the man was saying that Raine would no longer be Hamish's daughter. He was going to tell Hamish that he, Brendan, was Raine's real father.'

All heads turned towards Hamish and Cara. She was looking up at her husband, tears in her eyes. For his part, Hamish didn't look surprised. He looked...relieved.

'She's right,' said Cara, her voice catching slightly. 'He's been blackmailing me for a while now. I'm so sorry, darling, so sorry. I know how much you love Raine, and I couldn't let you get hurt like that.'

'It's alright,' said Hamish grimly. 'I won't pretend to be happy, but we can talk about it properly later. How did he get into the castle?'

'I sneaked him in through the tunnel.' Cara hung her head in shame. 'I've done it a few times. Part of the deal was that I let him see Raine. Her mother wouldn't let him anywhere near her. I suppose because he wasn't a rich guy who lives in a castle.'

Hamish rubbed his face in consternation and asked, 'You let him see Raine?'

'She didn't see him. I let him use the secret passageways.'

'You took a stranger into our home and let him sneak around!'

'I was scared, confused, stressed, whatever. I made some bad decisions! I did it for the best of reasons, my love.'

Hamish's expression softened and he reached out to his wife. She took his hand, and they exchanged a look that contained unspoken forgiveness and acceptance.

'Raine doesn't know?' he asked quietly.

'No, she doesn't know.'

The rest of the group had been silently following the conversation, rapt. However, Eileen's voice now rang out, incongruous in its barely contained excitement.

'So, did the man Brendan steal the diamond? If he knew the passageways, he could have made Hamish tell him the code, whacked him over the head then made off with the goodies.'

'Unlikely,' said Penny.

'Then...ooh, ooh!' Eileen pointed a finger at Cara and shouted, 'J'accuse!'

Jack looked up with a shocked expression and protested, 'It wasn't me!'

Penny suppressed a small smile and shook her head.

'The truth is,' she lied, 'we don't know who actually stole the diamond, but we do know who tried.'

Hamish looked away as Penny nudged Raine with her toe.

She said, 'Open your eyes, Raine. I know you're faking being unconscious.'

Raine didn't move, so Penny dug her toe hard into the

woman's thigh, saying a silent thank you to Sergeant Wilson who had taught her the pressure points during self-defence classes.

Raine flinched and her eyes open. She looked at the faces around her, feigning astonishment.

'How…how did I get here? What happened?'

'Cut the crap, Turdwomble,' snapped Sergeant Wilson.

Raine struggled to get off the floor, her tight dress hampering her movements. She glanced up at Cara and Hamish, stretching out a hand, but neither stirred to assist her. The group silently watched as she rolled onto her belly, drew up her knees and pushed herself upright.

Clambering to her feet, she said, 'It's not crap. I was knocked out, alright?'

'Your fath…Hamish was knocked out and he can barely stand,' Penny snapped. 'Look at him. Look at what you did.'

Several people gasped, and Mrs Goggins shook her head in disgust.

'You did that? You attacked your own…Hamish? I always said you were a waste of space, but there was no telling his lairdship here. He thought the sun shone out of your bony wee backside.'

'I didn't attack him,' Raine shouted. 'I've been unconscious this whole time. Somebody knocked me out and locked me in a room. You should be feeling sorry for me.'

'If you were unconscious, how did you know you were locked in a room?' Penny said quietly.

Raine's mouth opened and closed, her eyes wildly scanning the hall as though she might find the answer under the Christmas tree or in the fireplace. Then she froze and slowly turned her head towards Penny, the beginnings of a grin spreading across her face.

'Okay. You got me. I wasn't unconscious. But someone did shove me in that room and lock me in. I've been there for hours.'

'So why pretend you were unconscious?' Sandra Next Door asked.

'Duh. Obviously, there's a killer on the loose and it has to be one of you lot. Probably you, Mrs Grinch.'

Sandra Next Door flashed her an evil grin and said, 'On that note, if you ever get your phone back, you'll find that all your social media accounts have been deleted.' She tapped the side of her nose. 'Eileen's Russian pen pal happens to be very good with computers.'

Eileen perked up at this, asking, 'Ooh, was it Ashov? Did you say hello from me?'

Much to Sandra Next Door's satisfaction, Raine had gone a lovely shade of pale grey, exactly the colour that Sandra had been considering for her new kitchen blinds.

'I will get you for this,' the young woman hissed. 'You will wish you were never born.'

Sandra Next Door gazed at her, sphynx-like, and said, 'I'm a very bitter woman with sixty years of vengeance behind me. You pretended to be unconscious because you thought there was a killer on the loose. Which one of us do you think will win?'

'I'm not frightened of you, old lady,' Raine spat. 'Being scared of a murderer is common sense, not cowardice.'

'But you left the party just after it started,' Mrs Snipples pointed out. 'How could you know about the murder if you weren't here when Disco Bob...made his entrance?'

Stymied, Raine didn't reply. She merely looked at Mrs Snipples with disdain and turned to Hamish.

Her eyes wide and tear-filled, she pleaded, 'I didn't attack you, Daddy. Tell them I didn't attack you. I heard you saying that you couldn't remember the attack, but you must know it wasn't me.'

'I can't do that,' said Hamish sadly, 'because I know it was you. I lied about not remembering the attack. I couldn't understand why you would do that to me, but I do now. Carry on, Penny.'

He shifted in his seat so that he was no longer facing this monster that he had loved so deeply. Later, he would torture himself, going over and over the part he had played in her upbringing, teasing out the minutiae and obsessing about it. Yet, at this very moment, all he felt was contempt.

Defeated, Raine glared wordlessly at Penny.

'You've known for some time now that Brendan Daly was your father,' Penny explained. 'The photographs in his wallet weren't only of you. They were of you and him together.

'Brendan didn't have any money. He couldn't support your lifestyle, and if Hamish found out that he wasn't your father then he might not support you either. That's why you decided to steal the diamond.'

'Wrong, wrong, wrong,' Raine stated.

Her eyes were quite manic now and the tiara sat askew atop dishevelled hair, giving her the appearance of a wild drunk. She had torn her dress when trying to stand up, and a flash of white thigh was visible through the frayed seam. Despite everything Raine had done, Penny still felt a little sorry for this confused child. Raine's mother had a lot to answer for.

Perhaps subconsciously picking up on Penny's train of thought, Raine said, 'I didn't need their money. My mum would support me.'

'That was the other part of the newspaper article,' Penny told her. 'Your mum was coming out of the court where she'd just had her bankruptcy hearing. She doesn't have any money left, but you knew that, didn't you?'

The question was rhetorical. It was plain from Raine's expression that she'd known about the state of her mother's financial affairs.

'You saw the newspaper on Hamish's desk,' Penny continued, 'and your real father was running around the castle, trying to blackmail Cara. You thought it was only a matter of time before Hamish found out you weren't his daughter and cut you off.

'The diamond is passed down to each heir on the condition that the heir doesn't sell it. Any attempt to sell it, and it reverts to the Crown. However, that no longer applied to you. You weren't the heir anymore, so you decided to steal it. Fund the influencer lifestyle for a while longer.'

'This is utter nonsense,' said Raine. 'I. Was. Locked. In. A. Room. I couldn't have stolen it. Anyway, I could have taken it any time I wanted, so why wait until now when there's a bloody audience. Dad's remembering things wrong. I didn't attack him.'

Penny shrugged nonchalantly and said, 'Let's talk about the locked room. Mrs Hubbard, you had the key. You opened the door. Did you actually turn the key?'

'I remember jiggling it, dearie. I don't recall turning it, but I can't be sure.'

'The door was very stiff, right? You and Eileen had to use quite a lot of force to get it open?'

'Oh yes, dearie. We had to practically charge at it.'

Penny turned back to Raine and said, 'Nobody shut you in there. You shut yourself in by accident.'

She held up a hand to prevent Raine responding.

'Let me finish, then you can have your say. You were late coming down to the party because you'd been up on the battlements setting up a drone. As soon as you'd shown your face at the party, you intended to use the secret passage to access the diamond room via the hidden door, steal the diamond and fly it out on the drone.

'You live here and would inherit the diamond. There was no reason for Hamish to keep any of the alarm codes or the door code from you. It would be a piece of cake to knock out the security camera, disable the alarms and steal the Christmas Star.

'Only, things didn't quite go to plan. Hamish was in the passageway. He'd changed the door code and when he refused to tell you the new code, you attacked him. Isn't that right, Hamish?'

The laird nodded miserably.

'She was the Scottish under 18s judo champion a few years ago.'

Penny was on a roll. She continued, 'You couldn't steal the diamond, so you went back up to the battlements to get rid of the drone. But someone else was on the battlements. Eileen was right earlier, when she suggested that Disco Bob went up there for a smoke and a packet of crisps. You stumbled across him and either killed him on the spot or tipped him into the chimney and that did the job for you. Maybe he saw the drone and guessed what you were up to, from one thief to another, as it were. I can't be certain, but the piece of broken drone that we found suggests you smashed the thing over his head. I'm sure there will be other bits hidden in the snow and Sergeant Wilson will find your fingerprints and Bob's blood on them.

'You were in a state after attacking your fath...Hamish. You weren't thinking straight. You killed Bob then went back downstairs, intending to go to the party and give yourself an alibi.

'This is the bit where Jim's clever timeline comes in. About the same time as you were coming downstairs, Mrs Goggins was on her way up to tea towel turret. You heard her coming and panicked. You dropped your phone (we found it, by the way), then you ran back upstairs and hid in the room on the third floor. Nobody ever goes there, so there was no chance you'd be found. Unfortunately for you, it also meant that when you shut yourself in, you couldn't get back out. When Eileen and Mrs Hubbard arrived, you had to feign unconsciousness, otherwise how were you going to explain why you'd attacked Hamish. He was going to wake up and remember what happened, and you were going to claim that Brendan Daly made you do it.

'As to your point that you could have taken the diamond any time, you're right. But the best time to do it was when there was a cast of thousands here. The more suspects, the better.'

Raine's expression had taken on that of a trapped animal, desperately looking for a way out.

Clinging to her one lifeline, she cried, 'Brendan did make me do it. He did. He said if I didn't steal the diamond for him, he would kill my dad.'

'You can argue what you like in court, Turdwomble,' said Sergeant Wilson, stepping forward with handcuffs at the ready. 'Raine Deer, I'm arresting you for the murder of Disco Bob and a load of other stuff that I need to look up in my big police book of crimes. You are not obliged to say anything, and it would be handy if you kept your big mouth shut because nobody believes you, I'm very tired and we all want to go home tonight. Blah, blah, blah may be used in evidence.'

She handed Raine over to Easy and turned back to the group.

'We're not finished yet. We still have a diamond to find, and I have an appointment with two dead men. I'm not going to keep you here all night, but I am going to search you before I let you go. The roads are clear and a helicopter full of police is on its way from Aberdeen. I'm sorry, Hamish and Cara. Just when you think that Christmas couldn't get any more ruined, here I am. Assuming none of you have the diamond on your person, be warned, we'll be searching this place from top to bottom.'

Then Sergeant Wilson leaned over and whispered to Penny, 'The game is on, Fuzzy.'

CHAPTER 21

Sergeant Wilson sent Jim to call the children and Mr Black up from the kitchen, then she frisked everyone and checked their belongings. The children, oblivious to the nervousness of the adults, thought this was a marvellous game. Finally free from their imprisonment in the kitchen, they ran around the hall, chattering excitedly.

Everyone above the age of ten felt fraught and exhausted by the time the Sergeant declared, 'You're all clear to fu...go home. Penny, can I have that map of the secret passageways please? You lot have been through the castle like a dose of salts. Are there any other hidey-holes or ways of getting in and out of places?'

'Just the dumb waiter,' said Penny. 'Eileen and I found it when we were looking for Brendan Daly in the drawing room.'

'You can stay here and mark it on the map for the search team.' Sergeant Wilson turned to the group, seemingly surprised to see them still there. 'On you go everyone. Why are you hanging around? I thought you'd be sick of the place by now. Obviously not you, Hamish and Cara. You live here, so you've no choice about being sick of the place. But the rest of you, feel free to Foxtrot Oscar.'

Eileen stayed behind with Mrs Goggins to help Gordon look after Fiona until the ambulance arrived. She was delighted that she'd been right about Disco Bob going up to the roof for a cigarette.

'Why do you think he was dressed as Santa?' she asked Penny.

'Dunno. Maybe he was getting into the spirit of the party.'

'Are you sure he had nothing to do with the theft of the diamond?'

'Positive. He was just in the wrong place at the wrong time. Raine won't get away with this. At the very least, we can hope that the camera outside the secret door will have caught her attacking Hamish. Forensics will corroborate the rest.'

'What about the diamond?' Eileen asked.

'That's a whole different story. I have to go and help Sergeant Wilson just now, but I'll tell you all about it when I get back.'

Penny joined Jim and the police officer, ready to put part two of their plan into action. She was sure that the thief had hidden the diamond in the castle, so Sergeant Wilson had deliberately mentioned the search in order to put pressure on the thief to move it. Of course, no helicopter full of police officers was on its way. If Penny was right, the Christmas Star had never left the diamond room. Also, if Penny was right, the thief would currently be concocting an excuse to separate from the herd, and like a big, sweary lioness, Sergeant Wilson would be waiting to pick the crook off.

They quickly made their way to the diamond room, where Sergeant Wilson delivered her briefing.

She pointed at Penny and said, 'Little Pig, you and Mr Wolf here hide in the room across the hall and only come out when you hear me roar "No, no, no by the hair on my chinny, chin, chin." Och, maybe I should make that shorter. When you hear me shout "hairy chin," you come rushing in.'

Penny rolled her eyes. There was no point in responding to Sergeant Wilson's insults. It only made her worse.

'Where are you going to be?' Jim asked the Sergeant.

In response, Sergeant Wilson donned a pair of disposable gloves and slid the ugly portrait to one side to reveal the dumb waiter.

Gleefully, she said, 'In here!'

Penny breathed a sigh of relief. Inside, on the lower shelf, gleaming in the soft light, lay the Christmas Star. Had she been wrong in her guess as to its whereabouts, Sergeant Wilson would never have let her live it down.

'Shouldn't you leave it there for when the thief tries to retrieve it?' she asked.

Sealing the diamond into an evidence bag, Sergeant Wilson winked and said, 'Never fear, your Auntie Sergeant Wilson is here.'

'That's usually a damn good reason to be very afraid,' Jim muttered.

'Don't ruin my big moment, Dinglebollocks.'

With a triumphant flourish, the police officer produced Raine's tiara from her pocket. The large, central crystal was roughly the same size and shape as the Christmas Star, and Sergeant Wilson proceeded to remove it from its setting.

Penny said, 'You know that probably cost about two months wages, don't you?'

'Such a shame I dropped it and the big shiny thing fell out all on its own,' the Sergeant retorted, placing the crystal in the dumb waiter.

Jim regarded the dumb waiter nervously, then cleared his throat and asked, 'When you said you were going to be in here, did you mean in the dumb waiter? Because I've been lying to you about your weight for weeks, and I'm not sure the thing will take the strain.'

Sergeant Wilson took out her handcuffs and dangled them menacingly in front of his face, her eyes narrowed and her breath whistling in her nose.

'How many pairs of those do you have?' Penny asked, trying to distract the Sergeant before Jim came to any serious harm.

'In total, or just tonight?' the woman growled.

'Never mind. What is the plan here? You're not seriously going in the dumb waiter, are you? You'll mess up the forensics.'

'Of course not. I'll hide behind the door and scare the living sh...am I allowed to swear now the children have gone?'

'There's still one loose about the castle,' Penny reminded her.

'I'll hide behind the door and scare the living shenanigans out of the thief, like any normal person.'

'Thank goodness,' said Penny. 'I thought you were going to insist on getting into the dumb waiter and jumping out at them from there.'

'I was,' said the Sergeant moodily, 'until Fannygolightly said he'd been under-weighing me, then you came along and ruined the fun by being right about forensics.'

Penny sighed. 'It's for your own good. We're your–'

'If you say friends, I'm going to kick you in the nuts.'

'I don't have nuts,'

'Well, that surprises me because you've clearly got plenty of testosterone to spare.'

The Sergeant pointedly rubbed her chin and gave Penny a wink.

Penny merely shrugged and said, 'At the next Losers Club meeting, I'll do your weigh in myself. Get to the very large bottom of this mystery. How heavy is Sergeant Wilson? Does her Inspector know that she buys her trousers online because she can't fit into the police ones anymore?'

'You wouldn't dare.'

'If you're going to spend all night making chin hair jokes, I bloody would dare.'

'Truce?'

'Truce. Should we go to our hiding places now?'

'Aye, you've wasted enough police time already, getting all petty about your beard,' said Sergeant Wilson, switching off the light and taking her place behind the door.

Penny and Jim tiptoed across the hall and into the room opposite, leaving their door slightly ajar. So used to the dark had they become, that it no longer felt unnerving to be hanging out in strange, shadowy places. The only slightly creepy thing about being here, Penny decided, was Jim's breath on the back of her neck. Perhaps it was time to remove the scrunchies and let her hair down. Truth be told, she'd forgotten that she was still wearing them. She must look a fright.

She was just about to discreetly pull the hairbands out, when there was a scuffling sound in the hallway outside. Penny held up a warning hand to Jim, even though he couldn't see it. They waited, their ears becoming attuned to any tiny noise beyond the door. There it was again, a rustle, only this time much closer.

Jim was holding his breath. Penny knew this because the only sensation on the back of her neck now was a prickle of fear. Easy Piecey should have been here, but he was outside in the car, guarding Raine. What if Jim got hurt again? Sergeant Wilson would lose her job and she might lose her Jim, especially if he started twatting out like he did when he almost got shot earlier.

Such anxious thoughts flashed through Penny's mind, but she had no choice other than to plough through the apprehension and catch the thief. She didn't do tension. She was Penny Moon. She did fearless and feisty. Good pep talk, Penny. Yay, go you!

Jim's hand came down on her shoulder and she let out a little scared fart. Fortunately, the noise was muffled by the loud creak of the door handle opposite. Unfortunately, there was no muffling the smell, and Jim began to breathe heavily through his mouth.

The light went on in the diamond room and they heard footsteps on floorboards. The sound disappeared as the thief crossed the rug, then returned for those last couple of metres of floorboard beyond the painting. The low scrape of the portrait being moved was incongruously loud in the silent castle.

There was sudden movement in the light beyond the open door and Sergeant Wilson's voice cried, 'Hairy chin! Hairy chin!'

Before they had the chance to respond, a shot rang out, followed by a thud. For a fraction of a second, they froze, shock rendering them immobile. They had not expected the thief to be armed. After all, Sergeant Wilson had searched everyone, hadn't she?

Their breath coming in short gasps, Penny and Jim raced to the diamond room and pushed on the door. It moved slightly, before hitting an object on the other side. Sergeant Wilson was no longer yelling about hairy chins. Why was she no longer interested in Penny's peri-menopausal pilosity?

Panicking, Jim slammed his body into the door and felt the object on the other side shift. They squeezed through the gap and Penny sank to her knees, ready to administer CPR to the body on the floor.

'I'm okay,' Sergeant Wilson wheezed. 'Stab vest. Hurts like a fothermudger, though. You left the bloody gun with Brendan Daly, didn't you? Stop crying like a wet wipe and go after the thief.'

Penny put a hand to her face, but it came away dry. She looked up at Jim and saw that tears were streaming down his cheeks. Good lord, he'd picked a bad time to get feelings.

Sergeant Wilson chuckled, 'CS gas. I only managed to spray a wee toot, but it stings like chilli pile cream. That'll teach you for lying about my weight.'

Penny could see ropes moving behind the portrait. She grabbed Jim by the hand, yelling, 'Hurry! You take the drawing room. I'll take the kitchen.'

She yanked open the secret passage door. Familiar by now with the twists and turns, they flew down the narrow channel. Jim peeled off at the drawing room fireplace and Penny emerged in the generator room. She flung herself though the pantry door, stumbling into the kitchen just in time to see the cupboard open and the thief scramble out of the dumb waiter.

Desperately, Penny looked around for a weapon. Anything she found would be no match for a gun, but it was better than nothing. The children must have been baking biscuits while they waited for rescue. The kitchen table was covered in flour and cooking equipment. It would have to do. She snatched up a heavy iron tray and a rolling pin, holding them up like a sword and shield. Sweating, her hair a mass of horns and her face red from exertion, Penny knew that she looked like a rabid escapee from the Bake Off tent. But if she was going to die tonight, she'd go down fighting.

'You know what they say,' said Mrs Snipples, aiming the pistol at Penny's head. 'Never bring a rolling pin to a gunfight.'

CHAPTER 22

'You won't get away with this. You can't!' Penny scoffed. 'What are you going to do? Drive back to Port Vik with the kids? Then what? It's a bloody island. You're trapped.'

Mrs Snipples took a step forward, the gun never wavering in her hand.

'That's where you're wrong,' she smiled.

In her other hand, she jangled a set of keys and said, 'Somewhere beyond the tunnel is a car *and* a boat. Thanks to Mr Brendan Daly, I have all I need to get away. The slight detour on the way to the diamond room was certainly worthwhile.'

Penny's attention may have appeared to be fixed on Mrs Snipples, but her eyes were on the dumb waiter behind the woman. It was silently disappearing upwards, out of sight. Help was on its way. All she had to do was keep the woman talking. Which would be easy, she thought, because every criminal she'd ever apprehended seemed unable to keep their big gob shut.

She said, 'What I don't understand is why you stole the diamond.'

Mrs Snipples' face contorted into a sneer.

'Joe bloody Snipples,' she spat. 'The man gave me nothing when he was alive and even less when he died. Just a mountain of debts. But after all those years of living with the mean sod, I'm not going to waste my freedom being a schoolteacher on this godforsaken rock, working to pay off his creditors. Money. I need money for a new life. I deserve it.'

'You deserve a prison cell, and that's where you'll end up. Not quite the new life you were looking for, but at least you'll have Raine for company.'

'Strange as it seems, I have a different vision of my future. Pity that I had to take care of Sergeant Wilson. Pity that I have to kill you and that big lummox of a man of yours. You see, with no witnesses, who's going to believe that poor Mrs Snipples, the lovely teacher in the beige cardigans, stole a diamond. Why, anyone could have been prowling around the secret passageways in the dark.'

Penny returned the woman's sneer, saying, 'That's where you've underestimated me, *Norma*. I've known for quite some time now that it was you. Do you think that Jim and Sergeant Wilson are the only people who I've told?'

'Nonsense, you couldn't have known.'

'What do Hugh Snipples and Alec Snipples and all the other Snipples over the last couple of hundred years have in common?'

Penny watched as comprehension dawned in Mrs Snipples' eyes.

She told the woman, 'No need to answer. It was rhetorical. They were the butlers, housekeepers, footmen and head gardeners of this fine establishment. It's all on the big board in the staff lounge, there for anyone to see. Your Joe didn't leave you nothing when he died. He left you knowledge of all the ways in, out and around the castle. Stories, drawings or even maps handed down from Snipple to Snipple as each rose to prominent positions in the castle staff.

'You planned this well, but you left a lot to chance. At first, we discounted you as a suspect because you couldn't have had time to steal the diamond. You'd just taken that wee girl to the bathroom when the power went out, then we saw you outside with Mr Black not long afterwards. The timeline didn't fit.

'However, Mrs Hubbard said the wee one came back by herself. Being in the bathroom shaved off some time for you, so you upped and left her there. All you had to do was nip across the hall and go through the drawing room fireplace to break the generator, then back up the stairs, pull yourself up a couple of floors in the dumb waiter and Disco Bob's your uncle...well, not literally, but you get my drift.

'The camera outside the secret door will show you walking right past Hamish when you left the diamond room. I bet you didn't even stop to check if he was still alive. I think all of the above will convince a jury that poor Mrs Snipples, in her beige cardigans, is a cold-hearted thief.'

'That's as may be, but I have the diamond and all I need is a head start,' said Mrs Snipples, her finger moving to the trigger.

Penny could see the bottom of the dumb waiter coming into view. She said a silent prayer of thanks to whoever kept the thing oiled and quiet. Only a few more seconds. If she could keep Mrs Snipples focused on her for a tiny bit longer...

Mrs Snipples had other ideas. Penny watched as her finger began to tighten on the trigger. Penny's mind was racing, screaming at her to say something, anything. Prolong this moment and live!

'But you don't have the diamond,' she said quietly.

'What do you mean?' Mrs Snipples snapped.

'I guessed where you hid it, so we replaced it with the crystal from Raine's tiara. Oh, and Sergeant Wilson isn't dead.'

'You fu–'

Mrs Snipples never got to finish that sentence. The gun

went off with a loud crack, as she spasmed then collapsed to the floor.

Sergeant Wilson rolled out of the dumb waiter, taser in hand, beaming delightedly at the writhing woman.

'That's for shooting me. Were you not listening when I told your class that you don't mess with Auntie Sergeant Wilson? This is exactly why education is in such a state these days. What chance do the kids have if not even the teachers are paying attention? I'm going to write to the First Minister about this. My taxes are paying your salary, so I have a right to expect my children to get a decent education.'

'You don't have any children,' groaned Penny through gritted teeth. 'Which is just as well, because you're a bloody liability.'

Sergeant Wilson looked down at Penny, who was now slumped in front of the range cooker, clutching her chest.

'Now's not the time for a nice wee lie down,' she declared.

'You tasered her and she shot me!'

'You better not be hurt. You know how I feel about paperwork. My paperwork takes up far too much of Easy's time when he should be out arresting the hoodlums that *she…*' Sergeant Wilson pointed accusingly at Mrs Snipples. '…that she turns these lovely wee kids into.'

Penny held up the heavy baking tray. It was solid and ancient, and there was a hole through the middle of it. She let it fall to the floor with a clatter then opened her hand to reveal the tightly folded map that she'd stuffed down her bra earlier. Embedded in the folds was a shiny bullet.

She said, 'The tray took the brunt of it, but I'd still have been dead if it wasn't for the map. You're right though. Hurts like a fothermudger.'

Jim, closely followed by Mrs Goggins, suddenly appeared in the kitchen stairwell. Breathing heavily, his eyes wide with panic, he rushed to Penny's side and swept her into his arms, clutching her tightly into his chest.

'What have you done?' he roared at Sergeant Wilson, all

fear of the woman gone. 'If you've hurt Penny, I'll...I'll... Penny, are you okay? Are you okay? Are you okay, Penny?'

'She's been hit by. She's been struck by. A smooth criminal.'

Only the taser wires tethering her to Mrs Snipples prevented Sergeant Wilson from moonwalking around the kitchen.

Penny's muffled voice emerged from somewhere near his armpit. 'I'm fine. Whatever Sergeant Wilson did, I might have been a goner. Are you going to get all weird again and finish us because I got shot?'

Jim had tears in his eyes as he stood up with Penny still in his arms. He gazed down at her beautiful face, framed by scrunchie horns, and whispered, 'No. If anything, quite the opposite. I love you so much, you bloody annoying woman.'

'Are you talking to me?' asked Sergeant Wilson. 'Because that's my Inspector's nickname for me. I don't love you, but you're a good man...for a twatbadger.'

Mrs Goggins was looking around her at the state of the kitchen and muttering about Mr Black having a lot to answer for. She didn't appear to be in the least concerned about the teacher on the floor.

'If I'd known they were going to leave this much mess, I'd have made them stay and clear it up.' She gave Mrs Snipples a disdainful look and turned to Sergeant Wilson. 'Be a good girl and make sure you take the rubbish out when you leave.'

With a grin, Sergeant Wilson snapped a pair of handcuffs onto Mrs Snipples' wrists and hauled her to her feet.

'It will be my pleasure, Mrs Goggins.'

As she escorted Mrs Snipples upstairs, Penny heard her telling the woman, 'Climate friendly policing. That's what it's all about. You get to car-share with Raine.'

'I asked Easy to find out if the Vik Hotel has any rooms,' said Mrs Goggins glumly. 'With this place being a crime scene, we'll have to find somewhere else to stay. Sandra Next

Door will be so disappointed that she's not allowed to come and clean the place on the twenty-seventh.'

'Aye, me too,' Penny lied.

She'd had a vague plan to catch the thief red-handed during the clean-up but realised now that there was never going to be any clean-up. Things had become far too messy for that.

Jim's pained wheeze of, 'Me as well,' made Penny look up sharply.

'Are you okay?' she asked.

'Bugger me with a figgy pudding,' he groaned. 'How many boxes of Christmas biscuits have you eaten?'

He unceremoniously dumped her on the table and stretched his back.

'When we get married, I'm not carrying you over the threshold.'

'Here comes the bride. Forty inches wide. Sitting on the table with a floury white backside,' Eileen sang from the bottom of the stairs.

'Aw, no, I didna mean…'

'No takesie backsies,' Penny and Eileen said in stereo.

Seeing his flushed face, Penny took pity on him.

'You're safe enough. I have no intention of marrying you.'

'Thank God for that,' said Jim, then clocked his beloved's expression. 'I mean, not that I don't want to, but…'

'Shut up and quit while you're ahead,' Penny smiled.

'Och, that's the posh hat back in the cupboard for another year, then,' said Eileen. 'I only came down to tell you that the ambulance is here. Fiona and Gordon are leaving now.'

This news galvanized Penny, Jim and Mrs Goggins into action. There was a scrum as they all attempted to rush upstairs at the same time. Mrs Goggins won the right to go first by dint of both her age and her sharp elbows. They arrived in the entrance hall just in time to see Fiona being stretchered out, Gordon limping after her. Jim caught up with Gordon by the front door.

'Aye.'
'Aye.'
'Aye?'
'No.'
'Aye, well.'
'Well, aye.'
'Pal.'
'Mate.'

Once Gordon had gone, Mrs Goggins bustled off to pack for what she was now optimistically calling her "Christmas holiday" in the Vik Hotel. Hamish and Cara were presumably doing the same because Penny, Jim and Eileen now found themselves alone in the big hall.

'There's just one more mystery to solve,' said Penny. She ambled over to the Christmas tree and called, 'It's safe to come out now. Mrs Snipples has been taken away by the police.'

A small, muffled voice said, 'How did you know I was here?'

'Because you told me you'd found a good reading spot behind the tree.'

Cameron, still in his oversized coat, slowly emerged from behind the branches.

He looked up at Penny, misery etched on his little face, and asked, 'Am I in trouble?'

Gently, Penny took his hand and said, 'No. You did absolutely the right thing. As soon as I saw those names on the board, I knew you must have seen the same thing and figured it out. She was a very bad woman, and it was quick-thinking on your part to hide. Come on, we'll give you a lift home, and I'll tell your mum how brilliant you've been.'

EPILOGUE

Jim's dad, Ivor, had gamely foraged in the attic for the old fold up chairs so that they could accommodate the extra guests. It hadn't seemed right that Hamish, Cara and Mrs Goggins should have their Christmas dinner at the hotel, so everyone had squeezed together to make room for them at the table.

Ivor Space sat next to Eileen's mum, Jeanie, who was deeply embroiled in a heated argument with Mary and Mrs Goggins over whether a parsnip would win in a fight with a carrot. Len had tried to intervene, but Mary had abruptly told him, 'I don't know why you're sticking up for parsnips,' before turning to Cara and saying, 'They give him terrible wind. Honestly, if you ever have another power cut, feed Len a few parsnips, stick him on a whirly thing, and he'll keep the lights running for a week.'

Hamish, Jim and Eileen's husband, Kenny, had broken out a bottle of malt after pudding. Kenny was still sporting a fine Sharpie moustache courtesy of his brother the night before, yet he seemed game for another round. He had let Ricky and Gervais try a few sips of whisky from his glass and, despite screwing up their faces in disgust and spitting the stuff into their lemonade tumblers, the boys were now reeling around, loudly declaring themselves to be drunk. Penny's dog, Timmy, had managed to find a quiet spot from which to ponder the erratic behaviour of these humans and keep an eye on the leftover turkey.

Penny's phone buzzed. She checked the caller ID and gestured to Eileen to follow her as she left the table.

A few minutes later, they returned to the room, happiness positively radiating from their every pore. Penny clinked a spoon against her wine glass to draw everyone's attention.

'As if this day could get any better, we have some good news!'

Smiling, she exchanged a complicit glance with Eileen.

'Fiona and Gordon have had their baby girl!' Eileen announced. 'Gordon is fine. He's resting just now.'

A small cheer went up and glasses were raised to toast the new arrival. The questions were soon flowing. How heavy? What colour hair?

'About sixteen stone and ginger,' said Eileen.

'Not Gordon! The baby!' Jim shouted, roaring with laughter.

'Oh. Seven pounds and ginger. Fiona's going to text a photo.'

'Do they have a name yet?' Cara asked.

'Elsie,' said Penny, feeling an unexpected catch in her throat as she remembered the librarian who had been so much part of Losers Club and whose efforts to get people reading had begun the chain of events that had led them all to be together here today.

'Mrs Hubbard will be so touched,' said Mary, patting her daughter's hand.

'I think a few of us will be touched. The baby's full name is Elsie Araminta Penny Eileen Sandra, or Ellie-Minty for short.'

'I knew Gordon could do it,' said Jim. 'Before he got in the ambulance, he told me he was terrified, but I said he'd be fine.'

'When did he say that?' Penny asked.

'You were there, woman! You never listen.'

Later, once they'd tidied away the dishes, watched the King's speech and taken a call from a joyously tearful Mrs Hubbard, who was missing the Christmas Day Strictly Come Dancing Special so that she could visit the baby, Jim pulled Penny onto his lap and murmured, 'I have an extra Christmas present for you.'

'Does it involve something I can feel stirring under my backside right now?' Penny asked.

'Aye, well, that too,' Jim admitted. 'But there's something here I want you to have.'

He pulled a small velvet box from his pocket and opened it. The glittering cluster of diamonds and rubies took Penny's breath away, yet she couldn't help the niggle of dread in her stomach.

'Don't worry,' Jim hastily assured her. 'I know you don't want to get married. This was my mum's ring. It's special to me, and so are you. It's my commitment to us and I'd be really proud if you'd wear it on your right hand.'

'Oh, Jim,' Penny sighed, as he slipped the ring onto the third finger of her right hand. 'This means so much. Our adventure yesterday has had such a deep impact on you.'

His romantic depths plumbed for the day, Jim scowled at her and said, 'If you're going to make me talk about feelings, I'll take it back.'

She laughed and kissed him tenderly on the cheek.

'It's not about how much time we have together, Jim Space, it's about how we spend it together.'

Jim lowered his head towards Penny's and kissed her deeply on the lips. Coming up for air a minute later, he murmured, 'I think I know how I'd like to spend the next few hours. Your place or mine?'

Quietly, they slipped away from the family and friends who brought so much warmth to their world, for a celebration of their own.

'Where have Penny and Jim gone?' Cara asked.

Eileen stood at the window, watching the brightest star in the sky twinkling above the couple as they made their way down the moonlit path, hand in hand.

'Christmas shagging,' she whispered, raising her glass in a toast to her best friend. 'You finally found your one and only, Rubber Duck.'

AFTERWORD

I hope you enjoyed this book. If so, I would be grateful if you could take a moment to pop a review or a few stars on Amazon.

You can hear more about my books and get access to exclusive material by subscribing to my newsletter via my website, https://theweehairyboys.co.uk . You also can drop me a line using the contact information on the website or treat yourself to a signed copy of one of my books.

Did you know that there's a [Losers Club](#) on Facebook for fans of the Losers Club series? Yes, you really can join Losers Club, although our fellow Losers are far more interested in cake and chocolate biscuits than diet sheets. I think it is best described as a warm, friendly and creatively bonkers place. Please do join us.

Other than this you can find me at:

Facebook [Growing Old Disgracefully](#) (blog)

[Yvonne Vincent - Author](#)

Instagram @yvonnevincentauthor

Threads @yvonnevincentauthor

X (Twitter) @yvonnevauthor

Tik Tok @yvonnevincentauthor

Amazon Yvonne Vincent Author Page

Until the next adventure.

Yvonne

ALSO BY YVONNE VINCENT

Losers Club

The Laird's Ladle

The Angels' Share

Sleighed

The Juniper Key

Beacon Brodie

The Losers Club Collection: Books 1 - 3

The Losers Club Collection: Books 4 - 6

The Big Blue Jobbie

The Big Blue Jobbie #2

Frock In Hell

You can find all of these via my website at https://theweehairyboys.co.uk or on Amazon.